Apologizing to Dogs

JOE COOMER

SCRIBNER

SCRIBNER
1230 Avenue of the Americas
New York, NY 10020

SCRIBNER and design are trademarks of Macmillan Library Reference USA, Inc.,
used under license by Simon & Schuster, the publisher of this work.

DESIGNED BY ERICH HOBBING

Set in Adobe Garamond

Manufactured in the United States of America

1   3   5   7   9   10   8   6   4   2

Library of Congress Cataloging-in-Publication Data

Coomer, Joe.
Apologizing to dogs/Joe Coomer.
p. cm.
I. Title.
PS3553.0574A84   1999
813'.54—dc21   99-26937
CIP

ISBN 0-684-85946-7

Apologizing to Dogs

✻

for my sister,
Sally,
who loves all old things,
including people

ACKNOWLEDGMENTS

Once again, I'd like to thank the employees of the Azle and Burleson Antique Malls, whose efficiency and hard work enable me to pursue my writing. I'd like to thank my wife, who repeatedly allows me to finish the sentence I'm working on before she lays her hand on my shoulder. Elaine Markson represents my work and always calls me by my full name, both of which make me feel special. Marah Stets, my editor at Scribner, made this a better book. To all the antique dealers I've known over the last thirteen years: you're all in here and none of you are. It's been my great pleasure to assemble new people from disparate parts.

. . . this epidemick desire of wandering . . .

SAMUEL JOHNSON

A Journey to the Western Islands

TARRANT COUNTY HISTORIC SITE

The twelve "Shotgun" style houses facing one another on Worth Row are the last of sixty built in 1887 for employees of the Worth Prosthetic Mill. The factory supplied Sears & Roebuck, Montgomery Ward and many other mail order concerns of the period. Sales declined early in this century as Civil War amputees reached old age and passed on. Hopes for a resurgence of business at the onset of World War One were dashed when the Mill and many of the employee houses burned in the aftermath of a tornado in 1917. In the intervening years the neighborhood has become known for its fine antique shops. The houses, each exactly alike, are unusual in that they are constructed entirely of cypress, the same material used by the Mill for its prosthetic limbs.

Marker placed by the Daughters of The Texas Republic May 15, 1955

Worth Row Antiques

Most Shops Open Mon–Sat, 9–5

Shop for fine antiques in an historic neighborhood

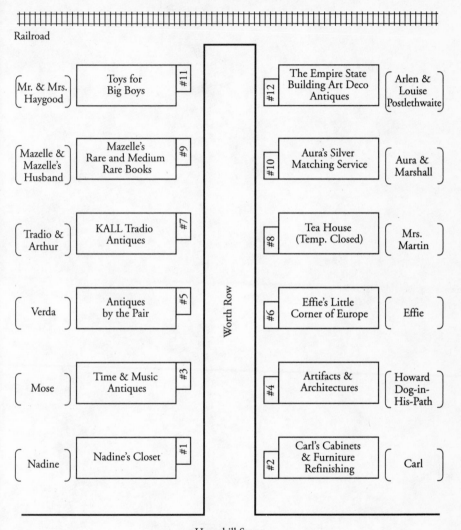

Star-Telegram ad copy

Friday, October 3

8:17 Verda in her tight pants out to get her paper. She has a habit of pulling her dress out of her rear crack when she gets up out of a chair and I noticed she did the same with the pants after she'd bent over to pick up her paper. I was on my front porch watering my pot plants.

The bar was cool that day and he was thirsty and that was all he was thinking about, that and whether or not he'd remembered to tighten down the clamp on the condensation drain of unit number four. If it leaked they'd call. No, that wasn't right. He'd go back first thing in the morning and check on it. He'd spent the day installing six commercial air-conditioning units at a new business on Hulen Street. His elbows rested on the bar and his two front teeth sat on his lower lip like a washer and dryer, the washer having wobbled away on spin cycle leaving a gap between his teeth large enough to see a pink wad of lint which was his tongue. After each gulp of beer, he poked the lint back with the wing bone of a chicken. He'd sucked on a chicken bone for as long as he could remember, so long that some people called him Bone rather than Marshall. He didn't mind. He'd tried and failed to give up the bone, but the bone was stronger than he was. It wasn't such a bad habit. Chicken wings were cheap. His teeth were as white as a dog's. But he knew that the bone frightened women. They stared and then winced and acted as if the bone were in their own mouths. So he avoided people, installed air-conditioning units, heat pumps, ran the ductwork, and took all the solace and flavor he could from his bone. There had been this way of life since he'd graduated from high school seventeen years earlier. He'd scored eighteen points in his final game at Northside High. He was a six-foot-eight, 160-pound second-string center, and when the other boy broke his ankle at the beginning of the second half, Marshall bit through his own bone and went in. He could recall each of the nine baskets but never brought this up in conversation. Lots of people thought he was called Bone for his slender build, then they'd see the bone. The bone he sucked on that evening was relatively fresh. He could still taste the marrow leaching through the epiphysis.

The first thing he noticed that had anything to do with Aura was her drink. Down at the far end of the bar was a short, squat glass containing an aquamarine liquid protected by a little umbrella. It looked as if someone had slit open a blue freezer pack and drained it into a glass. Behind the drink, in shadow, something caught the light. It flashed again and once more. Something like a nickel spinning in midair. For a moment he forgot the bone and it tumbled between his two front teeth, slipped off his lower lip and bounced on the bar. He put it back in his mouth as carefully as he might reinsert a false eye. A hand came out of the shadows and took the cool drink, withdrew. It gave him a chill. The hand was all palm; its fingers hardly protruded from the thick, pumpkin-rind flesh. Marshall put his own hands beneath the bar and clasped them. That flash again. He almost recognized it. He rolled his bone across his teeth and touched the brim of his cap. He had the oddest sensation. He felt as if someone's ankle was on the verge of snapping. He picked up his beer and moved around the bar in three strides, his long legs always carrying him to places and events sooner than his eyes could interpret them.

"Have a seat with us," she said, and she reached out to pat the stool next to her but her arm was too short. In the half-light of the bar she resembled a malted milk ball, round and dark. Her skin was unusually tan for a fat woman. Her cleavage merged with the cleft in her chin. She wore a light cotton T-shirt dress with the distorted face of Felix the Cat suckling her breasts.

"Please sit down, Mr. Lennox," she said.

"Oh no, my name's Marshall. I install Lennox air conditioners." He sat down and his knees hammered the bar.

"Someday, perhaps," Aura said, "I'll be able to call you Marshall without feeling like I'm Festus Haggen on *Gunsmoke*."

He was unsure for a moment but then realized she was comparing him to Matt Dillon, a character he respected.

"Hello," Marshall said.

She rolled a mint across her tongue. That same flash.

"Right now," Aura said, "we're at a loss for words." The mint clacked against her teeth and this was when Marshall saw that the mint was no mint but a sliced white ring of ham bone. The translucent puck of marrow it once contained was still a glistening slick on her porcelain teeth.

"It's very hot, don't you think?" she asked.

"I could keep you cool," Marshall said, "I install air conditioners," and he moved the shaft of chicken bone between his molars where he could lock it down.

"We hope you don't find anything more than you need here," Aura whispered.

He sniffed her bony breath.

"We should include ourselves," she said.

Marshall took her fingertips in his, afraid that she might melt in his hands. He felt an immense heat radiating from her body. But he knew that only a face as sharp as his own could reach her recessed lips. He bent lower, falling into the shadow of her tan, and touched her mouth, first with his chicken bone, then with his teeth and finally with his lips. She gave in to him with the same rubber refusal and release of a refrigerator door. It seemed the whole world was swallowed. The circle of pork slid over the shaft of bone, and Marshall, for the first time in his life, felt included, contained.

8:29 I forgot to mention yesterday that Mose washed his car yesterday but <u>intentionally</u> left his license plate <u>dirty.</u>

8:34 Aura and Marshall's car parked so I cannot see them load and unload it, unless I am in my backyard.

8:42 White Plymouth—license 458-HCJ—still in front of Nadine's. <u>Two days now.</u> Bumper sticker on car—Reagan/Bush '84 and Lucky Me, I Twirl a Baton.

8:44 Tradio and his man friend sitting on their porch like a couple of VULCHERS, waiting to see what else they can get from Effie.

Mose switched off the vacuum cleaner, bent down and gave the roller a good rap with the pair of pliers he always kept in his back pocket. A small screw he'd lost a week earlier from an antique radio dropped out. He must have kicked it from the shop into the bedroom. Mose sold and repaired antique radios, fans, telephones, clocks, almost anything electrical, but his true passion was his search for the idea or invention that would make him rich. He picked up the screw, finished vacuuming in that corner, then backed up to appreciate a clean carpet. The many tracks of the vacuum were plainly visible. How about designing a rug with the pattern of the vacuum cleaner tracks molded into the pile? Your carpet would always look freshly vacuumed. He'd approach his next-door neighbor, Nadine, with this idea.

❦

8:47 Mr. Haygood walking to the store. He was <u>laughing</u> as he passed my house and couldn't help but look my way even though he tried not to.

❦

"What a fine idea, Mose. But your carpet would still be dirty, wouldn't it, even if it looked clean?"

"Well, yes, I suppose, but that's sort of the idea, the beauty of it, Nadine, honey."

"But, Mose, it's not honorable, it's not chivalrous, an invention that's, after all, a deceit."

Mose put his hands in his pockets. There was a washer, a wire tie and a penny there. "I didn't think about it that way, Nadine."

"I'm so sorry, Mose. You'll come up with something, sweetie. Now, Mose, have you ever considered the pure fact that if the first vowel in your name were simply another, your name would be Muse, rather than Mose? Why didn't your mother think of that? She had nine months to think of that, and I've only been thinking about it for a little while and came up with it."

"I don't know, Nadine."

"I love vowels. I wish there were more of them. Isn't it sad that W and Y are only sometimes vowels? And people just pass over vowels when they speak, without giving them their due consideration, without any remorse at all. I think there should be a polite law stating that all vowels should be at least three syllables long, don't you?"

"You speak so beautifully, Nadine," Mose said.

"My momma taught me, Mose."

"She was a good woman."

"I can't bear to think of her now, Mose. It just breaks my heart to think how beautiful she was, like a butterfly that's died on the grille of an automobile."

"Don't think about her, Nadine."

"Can I call you 'Muse,' Mose? Will you give me the pleasure of doing so?"

"But, Nadine, I've been living with 'Mose' for seventy-eight years now and I wouldn't know to come if you called me anything else."

"All right. Mose it will remain. And a fine respectable name it is too."

"Nadine?"

"Yes, Mose?"

"What about edible rubber bands to hold thick sandwiches together? Have you ever accidentally bitten into one of those frilly toothpicks?"

"I want you to do something for me, Mose, honey. I want you to carry this petition to everyone on the avenue for me."

"Which avenue?"

"Our avenue."

"Worth Row?"

"It's a way of speaking, Mose. I want everyone on the Row to mow their lawns Friday evenings so they'll look their best Saturday when most of our customers arrive."

"OK, Nadine. Do I take the petition to the houses that aren't antique shops?"

"Them too."

"What about Mrs. Martin's house?"

"Of course you can skip her house, Mose. The bank owns it now and I've already written them to ask why they don't think it's in their best interest to maintain their property."

"Mr. Haygood won't give me a good reception."

"Mr. Haygood is a businessman, Mose. He'll see the advantage we'll gain. We're all in this together. We've got to be proud of the Row ourselves before our customers will come back home."

"Mr. Haygood says he might take a booth at that new antique mall."

"That's just traitorous. How can he even consider it, Mose? A complete lack of atmosphere, of neighborhood, of history. How can a customer build trust with a dealer who throws his merchandise in a booth in a warehouse and lets some anonymous clerk sell it?"

"I do like to watch over my things," Mose said.

"Exactly. Now, you go on. I want signatures in ink, not promises. Pick up everyone's contribution toward this month's *Star-Telegram* ad too. One hundred and twelve-fifty each, no excuses."

"OK, Nadine."

⋙⋘

8:51 Mose coming back from Nadine's with a clipboard in his hands. Something to do with me, I'll warrant. I don't know yet who told a lie on me. More infernal hammering down at that carpenter's shop. I think he builds coffins.

⋙⋘

Mose knocked three times but Verda didn't answer her door because she was dying on the cypress floor of her shop, dying among a hundred broken figurines: shattered Hummels, shards of Heubachs, limbless piano babies, dancers without feet, dogs without tails, a New Martinsville squirrel who now chewed on the nose of a bisque colonial soldier rather than a crystal acorn. In her fall, Verda swept a shelf clean of chalk salt and pepper shakers, tipped over a small showcase of Occupied Japan, swooned into the cabinet of figurines and finally dropped into the graveyard of her showroom herself, clutching her chest and a single Stangl bird she'd caught in midair with her free hand. She groaned a bit when she realized the jagged edges of a dozen knickknacks had punctured her body, then she tried to remember Jesus' name, then she passed out. Across the room a porcelain nodder in the form of a French gleaner bowed, "oui," every time Mose knocked.

⟫⟪

9:02 Mazelle's husband mowing their front yard. As I turned around my Open sign on the porch, Tradio and his man friend acted as if I wasn't even alive. I <u>am</u> alive.

9:08 Weather—fair and mild.

9:10 Mr. Postlethwaite watering his flowers.

9:11 Mose, still with his big important clipboard, is now talking to Mazelle's husband in his front yard. I distinctly saw them look toward <u>my house</u> as they talked. I am sure I heard Mazelle's breath when I picked up my phone yesterday after one ring and nobody spoke back. I said then, my line is tapped and you will be caught so stay right there, and someone said OK. Mazelle probably.

9:16 Car came up street, real fast, turned around at the dead end and left without stopping at <u>anyone's</u> shop.

9:18 That Big Indian has his wash on the line. Sure doesn't try to keep his underwear a secret. Stains and all.

9:22 I was standing at my window. I was not looking at him but could not keep from seeing him (Tradio's man friend) when he jumped up on his car hood and waved his arms and looked at me. I wished I had my camera ready.

9:25 Mrs. Haygood keeps busy peeping out to see every move I make.

9:26 Aura seems to have a customer. It's sure no one I know. She probably won't send her down to my shop, knowing I have better things.

Mazelle ran the shop, and Mazelle's husband, retired now, took care of the yard and garden. He signed Nadine's petition because he mowed almost every day anyway. The Saint Augustine had to be contained. It was almost his only occupation now, after forty years of driving a truck for three different-meatpacking firms. He'd carried eight million pounds of steaks, chops, hamburger and chili to the restaurants of Fort Worth during his career. He knew which restaurants bought certified Angus and which gristle and sinew. Not once had he stolen as much as a single hamburger patty, even though there were times when he borrowed a few pounds, when his kids were hungry. Four children, the youngest now getting her master's degree at the University of Texas. Her mother had made her into a librarian. Books, books. All those years carrying beef and now there'd been another ten years carrying boxes of books. His wife sold books, and he moved them from the car to the house, from one room to another. He never worked the cash register and rarely answered any customer's question. He'd been allotted the heavy things in life. Four children. Good kids but burdensome. Never a real vacation, never a good car, never steak. He and Mazelle lived in their kitchen, the back room in their three-room home. Where most of their neighbors had a kitchen table and hutch, they had a three-quarter bed and a nightstand. Books lived in the two front rooms.

He finished and pushed the mower back to the shed behind the house. There were more books here, but a corner was his, filled with gardening tools, a box of gimme caps from restaurants and his collection. It was hard for him to understand Mazelle's obsession with books, or the passionate collecting of china monkeys, old clocks and swizzle sticks that his street relied upon to survive. He felt some pride in his collection of four children, all different, all unique. They visited often and kept the phone ringing. But here in his corner of the shed was another collection. Mazelle's husband had saved every object that had given him a flat tire since he began driving: every nail, tack, mesquite thorn, rabbit bone, every screw and rivet. He had mounted them on a board, embedding each specimen in a drop of rubber cement: a collection of happenstance, the infrequent moments when a round object was impaled by a sharp one and everything came to a halt. It was a collection he could never add to at his own whim. Each piece arrived at sixty miles an hour with the urgency and thrill of possible accident or death. He once ran over a belt buckle that impaled his front tire, forcing him to run off the highway. His truck rolled and twelve pig carcasses broke free through the rear door. If his flat tires were ordained by God, Mazelle's husband thought, He had very little to do, but you never could tell what made some people happy. It gave him a cold shiver, like the rise and peak of music, when a mechanic pulled the shiny ground-off intruder from the clutching hot rubber of the tire with his needle-nose pliers. Eighty-five flat tires in fifty years of driving: he could remember where and when he picked up each one of them, just as if they were his children.

His mood changed abruptly when he saw Mrs. Haygood (her first name was Dorothy, but Mr. Haygood insisted Mazelle's husband call her Mrs. Haygood) in the garden. The houses of Worth Row were built on small lots. Only twelve feet separated them. In order to make room for a productive garden, Mrs. Haygood and Mazelle's husband had taken down the fence between their houses. They'd been neighbors for thirty-four years now and had produced thirty-three successful gardens. Mazelle and Mr. Haygood had participated initially, but for the past thirty seasons Mazelle's husband and Mrs. Haygood alone worked the vegetables and the decorative border of flowers. By careful planning and hard work they were able to provide food for not only their families but most of the neighbors. The soil was remarkably fertile, and they'd added much loam and fertilizer to sustain the productivity. The garden was, in fact, their greatest joy.

Mazelle's husband picked up a cucumber, cradled it in his hands like an infant. "Look here, Mrs. Haygood," he said.

She stepped across a row of beans, their second planting of the year, and parted two okra plants to squat by his side. "Why, it was no bigger than a mouse two days ago." She put her hand on the dark green nubbly skin, felt its warmth and suppleness. She let her wrist rest on his. He looked down in the dirt at Mrs. Haygood's bare feet. Soil oozed between her brown paper bag toes. But then, something. He took one hand off the cucumber and reached under her cotton dress. Mrs. Haygood closed her eyes. Mazelle's husband bent lower, squinted. A marble? Between Mrs. Haygood's feet. No, it was an eye, looking up her skirt.

"Move back, Mrs. Haygood."

"What?"

"There's something in the dirt."

Mazelle's husband brushed back a clod, then dug his finger into the soil and flipped out the glass eye.

"Look at that," he said.

"It's horrible," Mrs. Haygood whispered.

"The corner is cracked. A blue eye. Do you suppose someone lost it? It's concave on the backside. I always thought they'd be round. Gosh, Mrs. Haygood, if we could only see the things this eye has seen."

"It hasn't seen anything," Mrs. Haygood said flatly.

"I'm going to clean it up and show it to Mazelle."

"I'll finish watering."

Mazelle's husband carried the glass eye into the kitchen and rinsed it off. Then he held it in his open palm and walked into the bookstore. "Look what I found in the garden."

Mazelle looked down into his palm, at the blue eye there, the discolored white with its bloodshot crackling. She lost her balance but caught herself on a bookcase. "Why are you showing it to me?"

"I don't know. I just found it," Mazelle's husband explained.

"Well, get it away. I don't know why you'd want to show a thing like that to me." And she rolled away, pushed herself along the shelving on a wheeled ladder.

Mazelle's husband looked into the eye himself and in the darkened pupil saw his own reflection. Then he twisted the eye in his fingertips to make the reflection spin, but it remained steadfastly detached. So he wagged his head and found the result he was looking for.

9:35 Mrs. Haygood and Mazelle's husband at it again in their garden. Shameless. I know so well their lifestyle that I can trace every move they make.

9:40 From my back window I can see that one of Marshall and Aura's fence panels they put up to hide their movements from me has blown down.

9:42 I took a picture of Tradio and his man friend on their front porch.

9:44 Aura's customer left. She had on blue jeans and a tacky shirt. Looked like someone I sure would not care to even know.

9:49 Verda hasn't been out all morning since she got her newspaper. Guess her pants are too tight.

9:51 That Big Indian is sweeping off his porch and sidewalk. Finally, it being almost 10 AM, he has turned around his Open sign.

9:59 Mose, with his big important clipboard, was going to skip my house, but I made him come up onto my property. What is Nadine up to now, I politely asked. Nothing, he said. (It's always nothing.) She just wants everybody to mow their front yard on Friday so the street looks good Saturday morning. I made him let me look at the clipboard and of all things he was for once telling the truth. I said, Is there some reason you don't want me to be included? I asked him this straight out. Oh, no, Effie, he says, like saying my name will make me fall in love with him. I was coming up to your house, he says. I just didn't want to step on your grass. I was waiting to turn till I got to your walk. I took the pen from his hand and signed before he had a chance to squeak another lie. Just because I have the best piece of property on the row, and just because I sell better quality things is no reason for Nadine to try to keep secrets from me, I said, and then I said, And you can tell her I said so. He started to whimper and said, She's not trying to keep you out of things, Effie. I'm supposed to collect your part of this month's *Star-Telegram* bill too. I wasn't trying to skip over your place. I said, You skipped over Mrs. Martin's place. I saw you, I said. He couldn't deny this and responded, But no one lives there, Effie. I told him then that I think the bank ought to pay a share of the ad cost. But they don't run an antique shop, he whined. He makes me sick. It's our businesses that keep up the value on their property, I explained to him, like you'd have to to an idiot. Mose trembled because I stamped my foot. Big coward. Then he said, Can I have your part of the ad money now, Effie? I thought he was going to cry. I'll pay when the bank pays its share, I told him once and for all. If Nadine doesn't get your payment she'll take your shop off the ad next month, he said. I write it down here so if I'm found dead the police will know why. As soon as Mose left, I called the police and told them to please be sure and watch my house tonight. This was certainly no "hallucination" on my part. I write it down here just as it happened.

10:14 The Postlethwaites off in their car to the mall wearing their jogging suits. I don't know how she keeps her sneakers so white and would not ask her for all the Wedgwood in China. They hardly ever open their shop anymore. I've stopped sending my good customers their way.

The Postlethwaites, Louise and Arlen, own and operate The Empire State Building Art Deco Antiques, but lately they've found themselves spending more time at Ridgmar and Hulen Malls than they do at their store. They've become addicted to the developing machines in the windows of the one-hour photo processing shops. Hour after hour they sit and watch other families' snapshots roll out of the machines: birthdays, weddings, vacations, office parties, pictures of cars, cats, homes, babies. Even though they're both in their early seventies, the variety of these other lives, the vastness of the world, holds them transfixed. They can't help but point and smile. They watch a dozen rolls peel out of the machine, have lunch in the mall food court, then they're back for another couple of dozen rolls. They never know where they'll travel, who they'll see, what family they'll become part of, however momentarily. The only drawback is the photographs spin out of the developing machines upside down. Some things have to be reinterpreted: a frown is really a smile, grass isn't often the color of the sky.

10:16 Tradio and his man friend have gone back inside. I still think the bullet hole in my front window came from his front porch. The police said the tragic story wasn't right coming from that angle. All I know is it would be right between my eyes if it had come on through the window curtains. The police said I was lucky it was only a bb bullet.

10:19 Just now Tradio, or his man friend, peeked out their blinds at my house. It made a perfect eye shape in the blinds when they peeked. Big secret agents. I should ask for the underwear I gave him that Christmas back.

10:21 Mr. Haygood went to the store and got lots of something. Nadine sure took it all in. I happened to just look out in time to see them. Nadine keeps Mr. Haygood advised on everything I do and adds some to it.

10:24 The empty house next door is an open invitation to vagrants. One is lying on the front yard right now, big as life.

✖

He was hoping the mail would come before he had to leave for work. It gave him the sweetest pleasure of his life to walk out to his streetside box, in Effie's full view, open his mail as he slowly walked back up his sidewalk, then let out a whoop at a letter's contents, clutch his face, twirl once or twice and then bolt back indoors screaming. It didn't matter if the letter was a dun, junk mail or the winning lottery notification. It was the thought of Effie's wide eyes behind the blinds, her mind performing somersaults of explanation, her constricting throat, her inability to grasp. But the mail hadn't come in time. He'd have to wait till later that evening to perform.

He told Arthur to get in the truck and then he gathered up the postcards he'd received from the Cleburne area the past week. He put on his KALL TRADIO cap, snugged it down the way a fighter pilot would and jumped in the truck. Arthur wasn't there. He looked in his rearview mirror at Effie's house. She was on her front porch, watering her flowers for the fifth time that morning. He leaned on the horn. Why was it that a fifty-year-old man couldn't just get in a truck when you told him to? He leaned on the horn again.

"All right, all right," Arthur yelled. He'd changed his shirt and put on his cowboy hat. "You embarrass the pee right out of me."

"What took you so long?"

"I just cleaned up a bit, Tradio. You know, people don't like people showing up at their places looking like slobs," Arthur said.

"Well, you look real nice."

"Thank you."

"You look like a French whore."

"You're just saying that."

"No, Arthur, no. You look real good."

"At least I try, Tradio. Now, don't look at her when we back out of the driveway."

"What?"

"Just don't look at her. You know it makes you mad."

"You were the one jumping up and down on your car and waving your arms at her."

"Well, I thought it might shame her, always peeping at us."

"She doesn't understand the word, Arthur. I can't help it. I've got to look."

"Don't!"

"Goddamn it, there she is. On the side of the house, pretending to rearrange her rosebush."

"I told you not to look. It just gives her the satisfaction. You play right into her hands."

"We're moving. I can't stand it anymore."

"You've been saying that for two years."

"It's like her eyes bore right through a person."

"I feel sorry for her," Arthur said. "You know Michael never visits her. How would you feel?"

"Let's not talk about her anymore."

"All right, all right. Did you notice I arranged your postcards in the order that we'll come to them?"

"That's good, Arthur."

"Tradio, I always call you by your nickname. I know you like it. Why don't you ever call me Pie Bird?"

"Arthur, you're a fifty-year-old man."

"I know that."

"Don't pout, Pie Bird."

"It takes so little to make me happy."

"I know."

10:25 Tradio and his man friend left for work. As they were leaving they both looked <u>directly</u> at my house. While I was rearranging my roses That Big Indian snuck up on me and forced himself to say hello, being extra courteous and overly polite. I know he wants something that I won't offer. He started to tell me how beautiful Oklahoma is again, so to stop him I told him flat out that I've never been there and I'm not going back. After that I was standing out in my front yard, minding my own business.

Mr. Haygood bought, sold and traded toys, despite the sign in his shop window: UNRULY CHILDREN WILL BE EATEN. He specialized in cast iron, pressed steel and tin wind-up transportation toys from the first half of the century, the golden age. His shelves were lined with Bing, Marklin, Ives, Arcade and Marx rarities, many in their original boxes, toys that were rarely, if ever, played with.

Mrs. Haygood leaned against the doorpost of the front room of their home, the showroom, and sighed.

"You know what's wrong with you, Mrs. Haygood? You've got opticum rectitus, a growth connecting the optic nerve to the rectum, producing a continual shitty outlook," Mr. Haygood said. He was oiling a gear on a blue tin tank.

"I just wanted to tell you, Mose came by with a petition and I signed it."

"Why did you do that?" He slammed the tiny oil can down on the glass counter.

"You don't even know what it was about yet," she said.

"I don't need to know."

"Nadine just wants everybody to mow their lawns on Fridays so the street will look good for the weekend traffic. She's just trying to get us all to pull together."

"Well, she can just include us out. She's always trying to control the whole block. I live on my land. I'll mow when I please. Don't you ever sign anything like that again."

"You don't mow. I mow. It's nothing to you."

"This is my house and my business and it pertains to me. Now move out of my way. I've got to squirt my loser."

Mrs. Haygood stepped aside, her arms folded over her breasts, and let Mr. Haygood pass. Before he reached the bathroom door, he turned back to her, his dark penis already in his hand, and yelled, "What won't you do, woman?" Then he turned and slammed the door.

Mrs. Haygood walked slowly across the shop and wiped up the two drops of oil that had fallen on the counter. This was a trespass, because she wasn't allowed in the shop when Mr. Haygood wasn't there. But she already knew Mr. Haygood's secret.

She'd discovered it years and years ago: the trapdoor beneath his stool, the steep staircase to the tunnel below, the small dark chamber beneath her garden.

❧

10:39 I was sitting on my front porch when two customers, kids, walked up. The girl sure had a big black bag, so I followed them into my shop to keep a close eye on them, as they were most suspicious. I knew they were not the buying type, so I did not say, Welcome to Effie's Little Corner of Europe, like I do to customers who are dressed well. They looked at everything in the shop, with a special eye on my showcase items. When the little girl placed a comb box on the counter, I said, Someone's switched this price tag. She sure looked shocked that I would know my merchandise so well. I didn't switch it, she said. It was right here on the counter. You saw me pick it up. I said, I'm not saying you did it, sweetie, but the price should be five dollars higher on this item. It's tortoise shell. Then the boy (he had a hole in the knee of his jeans, hair over his ears, probably from Texas Christian University, but not dressed as nice as most of those kids) picked up the comb box, looked at the tag and said, It's OK, honey, I'll pay the extra five dollars. Then the little girl said, No you won't and then they stalked right out of the shop without so much as a Thanks for letting us look around. It's disgusting how many people think an antique shop is a museum for their pleasure. How many times have I heard, Oh my mother had one of those, or If I'd known it was worth that much I wouldn't have thrown it away. I've got those kids' descriptions if they come back. Verda hasn't even turned around her Open sign today. That comb box is easily worth five dollars more than I had on it.

❧

The life of Howard Dog-in-His-Path left a long, sinuous yellow trail, like that of a water hose left lying in the grass too long. He stood on his own shadow as if it were a raw chicken neck. His nervous energy seemed out of place on a big man. People shied from him. He scratched his forehead and everyone around him ducked. Dogs cowered when he changed direction. When he was a boy, even his family was afraid to get too close because he might take his billfold from his pocket suddenly or decide to comb his hair. Every morning the nervousness would flare up in him again, minnows darting through his veins. The only way to control the flow of energy was to use it up, moving quickly, lifting heavy things, eating. For the most part he tore down entire houses, wielding a wrecking bar like a scalpel. He'd tear every board singly free from the condemned house, remove the nails and sell the stacks of lumber to restaurant jobbers, decorators and craftspeople. The salable architecturals, the oak commodes, the stained glass windows, newel posts and brass doorknobs, he brought back to Worth Row and sold as antiques. His front yard was full of claw-foot bathtubs and pedestal sinks, sections of cast-iron fencing, an occasional chimney pot. When customers came they made their choices quickly, paid and left. Howard would load the heavy tubs into the backs of their trucks single-handedly, as their back tires were peeling away.

He could move toward a woman only at night, when he was completely exhausted. But then they wanted to dance. "I've carried too many bathtubs today," he told them. Words, feelings, hurts, and there wasn't enough beer in Texas to make a man his size drunk. So he'd go home and sleep, and the energy would rise in him during the night, the fluttering of hands, the feet that started and skittered as if the earth were hot, the eyes like wasps trapped in bottles.

But this morning, when he woke, Howard Dog-in-His-Path was merely anxious, only nostalgic, just old. He felt smaller than he had the day before. The trail he'd left behind had been too narrow, too treacherous, for anyone else to follow. And the load of his wet clothes from the washer seemed unfairly heavy.

⇻⇇

10:55 Mrs. Haygood was sitting on her front porch but went inside when I walked out on my front porch, as if there wasn't enough room in all the outdoors for both of us. That's what guilt does to a person—makes them afraid of other people.

10:57 Strong marijuana odor from That Big Indian's. I think one of his bathtubs is creeping over my property line.

10:59 The liar and gossip Verda must be gone but I didn't see her daughter pick her up. Her other daughter sure does not ever come, not in three or four weeks.

11:02 Mose and Nadine sitting on her porch together real close as if they are reading something of utmost importance, believe you me. It's shameful how he goggles at her as he is almost eighty and she is somewhere below sixty. (I do not keep track of other people's birthdays like some.)

11:06 Mr. Haygood came out and got his newspaper in front yard and stood and gazed in all directions as if he were lost, but not in my direction where I was watering my pot plants. I yelled over at him, You're at home you Big Idiot, and so then he looked at me and frowned.

11:10 My phone rang once and there was no one on the line. I am quite sure someone is trying to catch me away from my shop so they can rob me.

⇻⇇

File Copy
Internal Memo
10-3-86
Bank of Fort Worth
To: Jack Besso, Senior Vice-President
From: Steven Giles
Subject: 8 Worth Row

Jack, we've been trying to sell this property for more than two years now with absolutely no prospects. The old house is just a rat's nest. The back door has been kicked in. The last time I was there two stray dogs were living under the porch. Can we look into demolishing the place to reduce our taxes and liability insurance? Or simply donate the whole mess to Habitat for Humanity or something else we can write off? The neighborhood is on the verge of collapse and I'm afraid a gas line is going to give way, or some kids will get in there and get hurt, or somebody will be bitten by one of the dogs, etc., etc. This is one we should take the loss on.

Response: Steve, lets run over and take a look this afternoon. My folks furnished their house shopping on that street when I was a kid.

Jack

11:15 The mail has come and I thanked the new postman to shut the door completely on my box as he has the habit of not closing it the whole way. The cabinet maker got a letter he seemed quite concerned about. When he went out to his mailbox, Nadine went out to hers and waved at him. It looks as though she didn't have on any hose. I walked across the street to make sure the postman had closed Verda's and Tradio's mailboxes. She had a water bill and a handwritten letter from Weatherford. Probably from her friend who almost bought my opal bracelet. Tradio had five or six postcards—people wanting to sell things on his show. One of the items was a set of Dresden china. I took this card as I know Tradio and his man friend don't deal in better things.

The stray dog that lived under the porch of number eight had no knowledge of being stray. He loved to pee. He loved saving a little for the next spot. He knew there was a tire in the backyard that held water for weeks after a rain. He had special knowledge that the Earth would float away like a balloon if he did not hold it down by walking or lying on it. And so he tried to avoid jumping whenever possible, because previous experiments resulted in the ground slamming up into his body from below. He had no name, referred to himself as Himself, the thing not separate from each thought, but he was troubled whenever he heard the word "GO," as if it were part of him, perhaps his foot. Was there a greater joy than digging, a muzzle frosted with fresh dirt? On a full stomach, no. Every morning, Himself ate an appetizer from the tiny bowls of Dideebiteya and Yeseedid across the street. Their water was lapped up in a few slurps. The sawdust house always provided. There was garbage at the end of each driveway every Monday and Thursday. Most of the year there were insects. He'd been alive for two years now but it seemed like always. He had lived under the porch for most of this time. There were more once. Others. For the first year of his life the hole in the lattice got smaller every day, but lately it's stayed the same size. Himself weighed what he weighed, heard what he heard, ate what he ate, peed when he peed, shat when he couldn't see a human, and was hungry now, now, now, now, pain was pain, sleep under the porch was not fear. The people on Himself's street moved more slowly than humans on other streets. The old woman next door threw rocks at his house when she knew he was there. Now was the time to go to the sawdust house for something to eat, but hurry, because soon it would be water everywhere except under the porch. Himself not feeling pride because he knew it would rain hours before the humans would realize this. Himself just knew.

11:25 That Big Indian is just wandering around in his yard. Rare and strange that he would do so on a Friday. I think he is on drugs.

Dogs came out of Carl's cabinet shop coated with sawdust. That was why Nadine wouldn't go in. But Carl was stubborn. He wouldn't tell; he'd only show. She asked him once if he was really satisfied with a life of so much dust, so many empty cabinets with sharp corners. This was a year and a half ago. He sat on her front porch and told her that sawdust, other than freshly ripped oak, was sweet smelling. But he didn't dare reveal to her the curved milling he was already devoted to. His project was only in its beginning stages at that time anyway. She loved her street and the old houses so. But Carl anticipated the end and so he'd begun to take action. Even before he began he understood he was building for Nadine.

When he bought the old house on Worth Row it was because he could live in the back room and have ample space to build cabinets in the two front rooms. Nadine was angry with him at first because he wasn't an antique dealer, but she'd forgiven him when he built her a custom showcase and added a line to the bottom of his sign saying he'd refinish and repair old furniture. He never did so, always quoting a ridiculous fee, but the sign kept

Nadine agreeable. And he was fond of an agreeable Nadine. Every day he looked out his front window to see what she was wearing, always something old, something with layers of sheer fabric, something flowing. He longed for her the way he longed for the grain of lumber, to join and merge with it.

A week after moving in, when he was pulling up the linoleum in the front room so he could bolt his shaper to the floor, he discovered the cypress. The more linoleum he pulled up the more cypress he found, clear of knots and checks, dry and sound, practically impervious to rot. He crawled up into the attic and saw that the roof had been sheathed with boards averaging fourteen inches wide and an incredible twenty-six feet long, lumber from first-growth timber. It was then that he saw the opportunity of his life. He'd paid almost nothing for the old house. He began to dismantle it from the inside out. First the walls, then the floor and ceilings, leaving a skeletal framework of poles to support the exterior walls and roof. Over a weekend, when Nadine was ill, he reroofed the entire house, taking up the long cypress and replacing it with thin plywood and cheap asphalt shingles. With the flooring gone there was no need for joists and piers, so those came out too. The house was now an empty shell with a dirt floor, save two small corners where he left flooring for his toilet, tub, stove, refrigerator and sink. As the months progressed and he required more cypress, he removed the clapboards from the house, took up the cypress sheathing, and then simply stapled the thin clapboards back to the bare studs.

Through this entire process Carl kept his blinds closed. He slept on a couch that was pushed up against the wall between his radial arm saw and drill press. The hangar that was once his house gave him more than enough room, thirty-six feet long by sixteen feet wide, with twenty feet of height at the peak, to build, on weekends and evenings, between cabinet jobs, the hull of a thirty-two-foot sloop from the scavenged cypress. There wasn't a sharp corner aboard, only curves to match Nadine's; in every line he saw the swell of her hip, or the rise of her breast, or the suggestion of himself and her together. What the world, other than the dogs he fed, saw of his boat were the ripe bags of sawdust he carried to the street corner twice a week.

11:29 As I was sitting on the toilet I could see out the bathroom window and saw Mazelle sneak out her front door and cross over to Mr. Haygood's shop. There was <u>nothing</u> in her hands. I need some more medicine. That doctor hasn't studied me correctly. I had a bad episode and had to flush twice before I got off the toilet because the smell was so bad. Then I had to go back in there because I had forgotten to pee.

11:33 Light gray small car in front of Postlethwaite's. Cannot read its license. I am quite concerned about car bombs, as two blew up in Israel just last week.

"I don't know what to do, Mose. Look at that street. Potholes everywhere, all the way down to the old bricks. I've written letter after letter to the city. Wouldn't it be fine if they took up all that old gray asphalt and we had a brick street like the old days?" Nadine whispered.

"They were bumpy," Mose said.

"And look at these houses. Nobody bothers to paint anymore, much less make improvements. Number eight down there like an empty skull. Does no one have the sense of disintegration that I do? I'm telling you it's the South all over again. Aura only cares about becoming pregnant. Mr. Haygood taking a booth down at that antique mall. Carl doesn't really care at all about fine old things. The Postlethwaites are hardly ever open. If it wasn't for you and me and Verda and Mazelle, I don't know what the avenue would be like."

"At least we've got Effie and Howard scaring all the customers over to our side of the street."

"Oh, Mose, I wish there were a number that began with the letter *P*, don't you? I do."

"Nadine, what do you think about applying all this new Velcro technology to other uses, maybe Velcro dentures or Velcro hearing aids or Velcro toupees and such as that?"

"Wouldn't Velcro hearing aids be awfully loud, Mose, when you tore them out? Wouldn't that hurt?"

"I suppose so."

"And how would you attach the Velcro backing to your ear or the roof of your mouth?"

"I don't know. That's what I'd have to invent, some kind of organic Velcro-to-human-skin glue."

"You'll come up with something, dear. You better go on back to your shop now. I've got to go over and collect from that crazy bitch across the street. I swear I'll slap some sense into her some day."

"Be careful, Nadine, honey."

"I miss Momma, Mose. We never had these problems when Momma was with us. Those days are gone."

"She was a beautiful woman," Mose said, and started counting his fingers.

"Tell me how I look in this dress, Mose."

"Beautiful, Nadine."

"It's from the thirties. It's a summer dress, really, but it's such a nice day I decided I could risk it."

"It matches your hat and gloves."

"Would you look at the sawdust Carl leaves when he comes visiting. That man is made of sawdust. I wish he didn't work so hard."

"He's sweet on you, Nadine."

"Oh, I know, Mose, but what can I do about it."

"You know, I kissed your momma once, Nadine."

"I never knew that, Mose."

"She was sitting right where you are and I bent down and kissed her full on the lips."

"I don't believe it."

"Yes, I did."

"What did she do?"

"Told me to never do it again."

"Oh, I'm sorry, Mose."

"I wanted to invent something to make her love me, but I couldn't think of it. I wasn't smart enough."

"Daddy was her only love, Mose. I wish you could have known him. We had him for such a short time."

"But he died so early, and there your momma was, pretty for all those years."

"How old was she when you kissed her?"

"Sixty-three."

"Maybe you waited too long, Mose."

"Oh, Nadine, don't give me that thought now."

"It probably wasn't the case, Mose. Momma was too good for most people."

"She was, Nadine. I felt honored to be rejected by her."

"Nobody could reject a person like Momma could."

"Bless her heart."

"Bless her heart."

❦

11:35 A truck attempted to deliver something to Tradio but was not successful as he is not at home. BSQ-36L Bumper sticker— How's my driving? with a phone number I can't read. These truck drivers are always fishing for compliments. They are professionals. They should drive well.

11:39 They all continue to look at my house.

11:42 Called my lawyer but his secretary said he was unavailable so I left a message for him to call me as I had an urgent message about my cases. I don't think I told him about Tradio teaching me how to dance, telling me how nice I looked.

From the moment Aura and Marshall met she never used the word *I* again, only *we,* only *us,* never *me.* If it was time to eat she told Marshall, "We're not hungry, but let's eat." Marshall always assumed he was included, and even Aura thought that this was the case, her intention. They were trying to make a baby and out of their two extremes hoped to create a beauty. Marshall was skinny, Aura was fat; Marshall had an overbite, Aura an underbite; Marshall had a place for everything, Aura let everything find its place; Marshall tended to suck out a soup stain on his shirt, Aura never spilled a drop. Their child, they reasoned, had an opportunity to meet in the middle, to be perfect. Their child would find no need to suck on a thumb, much less a bone.

But as yet she saw no signs of pregnancy. Aura had gained thirty-five pounds since the wedding, despite the twice daily lovemaking sessions, despite the three hours she spent every afternoon in her bikini tanning in the backyard. She was always hot but never broke a sweat. She wore her weight well, becoming rounder, firmer, like a balloon filled to capacity. She noticed she wasn't one of these fat people whose skin rolled and tucked and swayed. Occasionally, backed up to a mirror, she'd slap her buttocks to see if they'd shake, but there was only a resounding clap left hanging in the air. She did not jiggle, or swoon, no wave moved from cheek to cheek. Her breasts were like great stone pillars at the entrance to an estate. Her stomach was brown and solid as a bean pot. Her entire body was without crease or fold, save the place she reserved for Marshall.

Marshall had taken out Aura's two window units and installed fifteen tons of air-conditioning in their 576-square-foot house, enough to keep the temperature down in the mid-forties where Aura liked it.

"You shouldn't lay out so much, Aura," Marshall told her. "You don't sweat, so all that sunshine is bottled up inside of you. You're like a greenhouse."

"We don't mind," Aura said.

Marshall, who lived in Texas because he was cold-natured, wanted to live inside Aura's body. Every evening he'd come home, put on his down parka that hung on a hook outside the back door, then he'd brace himself and step inside the house where Aura was waiting in a negligee, her nipples like andirons beneath the cool silk. Even in the cold, Marshall found his penis beginning to count the teeth on his zipper.

"Do you always greet your customers like this?" Marshall would ask.

"Only when they're in your pattern, and made of the purest silver."

Aura's business was the matching of sterling and silver plate flatware. Her shop was filled with thousands of odd forks and knives and spoons, creamers without sugars, peppers without salts, olive forks without homes. Her specialty was completing sets. She'd heard all the sad stories of spoons lost in gardens, forks entangled in disposals, the splitting up of a twelve-piece service among six spiteful daughters (This last almost too much to bear). Odd corners of the shop smelled of silver polish and felt and coconut tanning oil. At forty-five degrees these odors jelled and re-formed, giving customers the sense they'd entered a ball-bearing factory that had been closed for a dozen years. Aura moved along behind her showcases with bare inches to spare. A magnifying glass was attached to a cord around her neck but always rested on her breasts, the cord slack and unneeded till she bent over. As a customer described a pattern a great-aunt once owned, or unwrapped the last surviving spoon, Aura would hold out her polishing cloth in commiseration. "There, there," she'd say. "We'll make a family."

Aura and Marshall made love on their full-size bed, Aura balled up against the headboard, Marshall's knees banging uncomfortably against the foot. His long, lanky body was pliable enough to mold to her solid curves, a vine grasping a melon. Their cries were often heard the length of Worth Row. Aura cartwheeled a continuous *weeeeeee,* and Marshall burbled only consonants, boots falling down stairs. The ribs of Marshall's chest raked over Aura's nipples making a ticking music like scuttling bugs. Finally Aura would wheeze, "That's as far as we can go," and Marshall would cease trying to climb inside of her and he'd add more warmth to her vast and accumulated warmth. "That's us replacing ourselves," Aura would say.

They have been married a year now, and Aura's become pregnant, although she doesn't yet realize it because not once in her life has she had a recognizable period. She's nine months pregnant. She's been eating for two.

11:45 "Fraud—deceit, trickery, cheating" and that's just what the dictionary says.

11:47 There was a bone in that leftover fish Verda brought me yesterday. I just had it for lunch. I know she would like to see me vanish.

The first thought Verda had when she awakened was that heaven looked just like her antique shop. She had always hoped it would. The second thought Verda had was that her pants had risen up uncomfortably. When she tried to move her arm to pull her pants down she realized she hadn't died yet, that she was still dying. There was great pain in her chest, and she felt as if big dogs were lounging across her body. She tried to lie very still.

The broken arms and heads of her figurines were strewn across the wood floor at her eye level. She was sad for a moment but then recalled she was dying. She had never really wanted to sell them anyway. Nadine and Nadine's momma had always told her she was a collector at heart, not a dealer. Well, she hated to let precious things go. But the shop was a way to support her habit. She could sell her duplicates; she made good buys. People never suspected a dealer of being addicted.

Her daughters would get her things now. Orene would probably take her inheritance to the dump. But Alma wouldn't. Alma appreciated figurines. Alma knew that it was the mantelpieces that held society together. It occurred to Verda that it would be Alma who'd find her rigid and fouled body among the knickknacks. She felt Jesus telling her to let go of these earthly thoughts. The end of the world had finally come. She could be humble now. There had always been a little part of her that thought things would always carry on, but now she knew she would not survive her life. Still, it seemed ineffably sad somehow, that the world would go on without her: her collection dispersed, her dogs fed by other hands.

Where were the dogs? She opened her mouth to call but nothing came forth. Where were her sweet babies? Not once had they ever broken a figurine. The crashing and break of glass must have frightened them. They're under the bed, they are, her two Pekingese, Dideebiteya and Yeseedid, little male and female figurines brought to life. Who would take care of them? Again her heart faltered, her arm shot out against the pain, and again Verda fainted.

⊷⊶

11:50 Mrs. Haygood working in her garden again. Still in a <u>dress</u>.

11:52 That Big Indian is trying out all of his bathtubs. There must be twenty in his front yard and he's getting in and lying down in every one of them. Why hasn't he gone to work I'll ask and expect no answer.

11:57 Knowing Aura's habits so well I feel sure she is talking on the phone to people I do not know.

"Why don't people think of roses as being waterproof? Some people are born to have servants and I just think I'm one of them. But I don't carry a grudge. I swear if the wind blows one more gust I'll explode and let it carry me away."

11:58 Nadine on her front porch, sweeping the steps, having her daily conversation with her broom. No doubt it is about me.

Mazelle began to buy books because she liked reading them, but as the years and decades turned she understood that they were merely objects to be bought and sold. Books were too small to contain lives, always promised more and realized less. Her own life was an example. What book approached its audacity, its scale, its hidden grandeur, its intricacy, its depths of emotion, its level of sin? None, and none ever would. Searching for a life in a book was like looking for a house in a keyhole. She'd stopped reading and taken up the tending of her children. Books were only valuable to people who hadn't yet come to her understanding and only then when they hadn't been read. So people sold the books they'd finished cheaply and paid dearly for those they hadn't. Mazelle had placed herself in the middle. She looked at her profession as that of a dealer to addicts. She knew her customers would return. Only those readers whose lives became larger than fiction could break the habit. It was true sales had turned down over the past couple of years. Mr. Haygood had advised her to take a booth out at the new antique mall. He said he'd counted seventy-five customers in the mall over a two-hour span: more than the Row saw in a week now. But she recognized the early effect of the computer. While some of her customers bought books as antiques, for their fine bindings or color plates, and while some were collectors of first editions, most were simply looking for something to read, a diversion. She thought many of these last were now finding their diversion on a monitor, a million books in the same binding. But even if sales were down, so were her needs. Her last child was in college. The house was paid off. Her husband had a little pension. There was Social Security and there was the security of her four children. Most of them wouldn't allow her to starve. Strangely enough, they all liked to read. The simple proximity to her books as they grew up addicted them before their lives became full. Her children were in fact her best customers. Their experience, their lives, were so small. It tickled Mazelle when her kids told their friends, "Oh, Mom never reads." Then to see the looks on their faces, as if they'd been told she didn't eat. "Too busy," she'd say, affecting shyness, because it would have been ridiculous to tell the truth, to say, "My life is too full." It would have been immodest.

When Mazelle's husband lifted the eye toward her, the blue eye clinched in the dirty socket of fingernails, she thought for a moment that he was accusing her, that he was trying to make her life small again, that he was forcing her to return to reading. She'd snapped back, unwisely. She'd seen then that he knew nothing; it was just another moment to him, a trifle. All the eyes she'd discovered in the garden were at a deeper level. Odd and troubling, that one had worked its way to the surface. She thought about it lying in the garden, staring into the sun blankly.

➤✦

12:02 I went outside to check the bars on my windows but the sun shined in my eyes. Besides, That Big Indian is asleep in one of his bathtubs. I would like to know what race he is, colorwise.

➤✦

Not wanting to miss the roll of film a young woman had just dropped off, they ordered their lunches to go, an Arby's sandwich for Louise and a slice of pepperoni pizza for Arlen, and then they hurried back to the low bench, part of a plant retaining wall, in front of the photo developer. Breaking for lunch was always anxiety ridden because they occasionally returned to their seats to find them taken, and then they had to stand in the aisle, in front of the developer, till their bench was again available. Today they were lucky. The bench was only three feet from the glass of the shop window, and the developer only a few inches inside. There was no glare on the glass when they sat on their bench, as there was when they had to stand.

As they sat down, arranging their food, Arlen nudged Louise and said, "It's about to start." It was more exciting to them than any movie because there had never been a preview or review to spoil their anticipation. The courier who dropped off the film was their only clue to the contents. Usually the courier was the photographer. They knew this because he or she was rarely in the photos. Arlen smiled and waved at Janice, the girl running the developer. She waved back. Often, they talked about what an interesting job she had. Her hands were in the short white gloves of a magician.

"Think of the things Janice sees," Arlen told Louise.

"I like her in her white smock," Louise said. "She looks so professional. That green one doesn't do anything for her."

Snapshots began to roll out of the machine. Louise and Arlen held their food in midair momentarily. They forgot to chew. The entire roll seemed to have been taken at a John Deere tractor dealership. There were thirty-six pictures of big farm tractors at different angles.

"Tractors," Louise said.

"I can't think where that dealership is," Arlen mused.

"She sure didn't look like the type who'd be taking pictures of tractors. They were very colorful but she didn't seem the tractor type."

"You never know," Arlen said.

"You never know."

There was a five-minute intermission while the technician blew dust from the prints and checked their quality. Arlen and Louise finished eating.

"That was good," Arlen said.

"You've got a pepper in your teeth," Louise whispered.

"Where?" Arlen bared his incisors like an angry dachshund.

"Right there." Louise pointed, leaving the end of her index finger three inches from Arlen's mouth.

Arlen put his fingernail between his two front teeth. "Here?"

"No. Over one."

"Here?"

"Yes."

"Would you stop whispering? Did I get it?"

"No."

"Now?"

"It's still there."

"Now?"

"You pushed it farther in."

"Well, I'll be goddamned."

"You'll have to wait till we get home. Get your finger out of your mouth."

"I can't go on like this. People will see me."

"OK, OK. Let me pull a thread." Louise turned up the hem of her sweatshirt, found a loose thread, tugged another inch free, then broke it off and handed it to Arlen. "Now, use this to floss."

"How did you think of that?" Arlen asked.

"I've figured out lots of things," Louise answered.

"Did I get it?" He bared his teeth at her again.

"It's out of the crevice but now it's on the front of your tooth."

Arlen touched his tooth with his fingertip and the pepper flake came away. "There," he said and smiled.

Louise rubbed his back. "There."

"It's like it never happened," Arlen said.

"Of course it happened," Louise said.

"I didn't say it didn't happen," Arlen explained. "I said, 'It's like it never happened.' "

"Stop talking about it. Let it go. Why do you insist on these distinctions? You and Margaret are just the same. There's nothing you won't divide, make more of by making less of."

"Why bring Margaret into it?"

"She's your daughter."

"She's your daughter too."

"There you go again. Why can't I say she's your daughter and you just accept that? Not say another word?"

"Let's not start, Louise, please."

"All right. I'm sorry."

"I'm sorry too."

"All right."

"Look. Those pictures were taken outside Will Rogers Coliseum. It's an Oriental family. Three kids."

"I'll bet they're on vacation."

"But look at the cars in the background. That roll of film must be fifteen years old," Arlen said.

"That banner right there says '1972.' "

"Why do you think they took so long to have it developed?"

"Some people don't take many pictures. How long has it been since we had a roll of film developed?"

"I can't remember when."

"It was before Margaret stopped seeing us," Louise said.

"You're probably right."

"We should take some pictures someday and have them developed."

"What of?" Arlen asked.

"I don't know."

"I know. We should take pictures of each other."

"That's what we'll do," Louise said.

12:05 Street deserted except for That Big Indian sleeping in his bathtub. Knowing their habits so well I can say most are eating lunch. Verda's daughter made hamburgers for her on Mother's Day—some big celebration.

12:07 Through that panel that's blown down I can see Aura laying out on her chaise lounge in the sun like a dead buffalo. I have never seen her so fat. If there is a glimpse of the sun she is out in it. Disgusting to be out there where I can see.

12:13 Mose mowing his front yard. He has on his hat so he can peek out under the brim.

12:15 Mazelle shook out her rug on her front porch and sure looked my way. I don't like her hair the way it is now, all pure white and tucked in in back like she's smarter than everyone else on the block.

⋙⋘

Tradio runs his call-in radio show five times a week from five different local country stations. People call in with items to sell, trade or give away. Those afraid to hear their voice on the radio send in a postcard. The wages Tradio earns as a disc jockey are negligible, but the postcards make him a decent living. With the postcard as an invitation and icebreaker he calls on homes and farms and offers to buy not only the item these timid people wanted to sell but anything else they might have in the barn or attic. Standing in their living room, he might say, "Did you know this old buffet might be worth a hundred dollars to me? I might give a hundred dollars for it." He might say this almost as an aside. Rarely does anyone take offense. He's a radio celebrity. He wears his cap and gives away free bumper stickers. After two or three hours of picking he stops in at the radio station—Cleburne, Weatherford, Mineral Wells, Stephenville or Jacksboro—and takes thirty minutes of calls.

"Are you there, Caller?"

"I'm here."

"What have you got to buy, sell or trade?"

"I've got a pair of VW running boards new in the box that I'll take twenty-five dollars for and my number is 555-5458."

"All right. Thank you. That's a pair of VW running boards new in the box. The number is 555-5458?"

"That's right. And I won't take no less."

"OK, if anybody needs a pair of VW running boards new in the box, the number, now write it down, is 555-5458."

"Hello, Caller, you're on Tradio."

"Hello, I've got a new pair of loafers for sale. I guess my feet were swollen when I bought them. But I'm afraid I don't have the box they came in. My granddaughter wanted the box to make an eclipse viewer."

"That's all right, Caller. Your phone number?"

"555-2943."

"If you need a new pair of loafers, folks, the number is 555-2943. I guess we didn't get the size. Now folks, things don't have to be new in the box. You can call in your used items, your old items, your duplicate items, anything, as long as it's not puppies. We don't advertise puppies for sale on Tradio. Let me repeat the rules if you've just tuned in. We accept items for sale, giveaway, for trade or items wanted. Please, no more than three items per caller. OK, you're on the air, Caller."

"Hello, I've got a pair of embroidered pillow cases for three dollars, a quilt in the flying geese pattern for thirty-five, a set of flannel sheets for five and a red down comforter for—"

"I'm sorry to interrupt you, Caller, but that's four items."

"But it's all bedding."

"Yes, but it's four separate items and we only allow three so that everybody will get a chance to call in."

"All right. My number is 555-8891 and that comforter is twenty dollars."

"OK, now, she slipped that last one in but let's all agree on three items only. Next caller."

"I need the guy who always has VCRs to call me. My number is 555-3933 and I'm at home right now."

"Next caller."

"I still need a storm door. 555-1819."

"Next caller."

"Is a living room suite one item or five items?"

"Well, it depends on how you want to sell it."

"I want five hundred dollars for it."

"Then it's one item."

"Or a hundred dollars for each piece."

"That would make it five items and so I won't accept your number, Caller. Next caller."

"I've got a four-hundred-gallon bait tank and I need to get

shed of it. My phone number is 555-5468, and call after six and before eight at night."

"Next caller."

"I want to sell a hospital bed used only one month. 555-9423."

"Next caller."

"I have twelve yards of topsoil with very few rocks and a pair of parakeets. 555-1118."

"Next caller."

"I have a pair of aluminum crutches that I don't need anymore and would like to donate them to any needy person. My number is 555-1344. These crutches are adjustable."

"Next caller. That's you. You're on Tradio."

"I just wanted to remind all your listeners that Jesus Christ is free for the asking. And that's all I wanted to say."

"Thank you, Caller. That's important. Sometimes we forget what money can't buy. Next caller."

"I have a 1963 Buick Riviera with something over a hundred thousand miles but she's a good runner and I'm asking twelve hundred fifty. There's a little rust in one door panel but I think that could be fixed. My number is 555-8765."

"Are you a dealer, Caller, or an independent? Caller? Well, he hung up. Next caller."

"Hello. I'd like to trade birdhouses for any useful item and my number is 555-5921."

"Thank you, Caller. Tradio listeners, do you have something you'd like to sell or give away but you simply don't have the time to call? Send a postcard to Tradio, 7 Worth Row, Fort Worth, Texas 76197 and include your name, address and phone number. I'll read your postcard on the air."

It was Arthur who'd convinced Tradio not to allow the exploitation of puppies over the airwaves.

❦

12:18 I have written a note to my lawyer explaining how my son broke into my house and took many valuable items after my husband died on March 3rd, 1969, including his gold Odd Fellows ring and army medals. How I never see him if it isn't for a handout. How he still cannot get over the pure fact that his father left everything to me and that's why I am to be committed in his eyes for my "agitated depression."

12:22 Watered my pot plants and saw everything I wanted to.

He'd had about enough of Mrs. Haygood as he could stand for one day. It was time now to give her an hour or two away from the house. Mr. Haygood, two inches shorter than he was twenty years ago, his ears leaning away from his skull, his fingernails thick, his feet low on air, hasn't had an orgasm in almost a week.

"Mrs. Haygood, I want you to take this money out to Payless Cashways and have them cut me some boards. Here's the sizes I need. Get somebody who can use a tape measure to cut them and I don't want any knots. And get a receipt."

"Can I go later? I was just going to work in the garden."

"No, you can go now. I need those boards."

"But you'll be upset. They'll cut them wrong. I won't know how to tell them. Can't you go?"

"If I could go, I wouldn't have told you, would I?" He took the key to the car off his ring and handed it to her.

"You won't lock me out?"

"Why should I lock you out, woman?"

"I've come back before and the doors were locked."

"It is only because I can't leave the shop open while I am in the can for extended periods. You know how long my movements are."

Mrs. Haygood thought of saying, "I'm just tired of it," but she didn't. She wanted to say, "Aren't you tired of it?" but she didn't. She took the car key, the list, the twenty-dollar bill.

Mazelle's husband was just coming into the garden as Mrs. Haygood backed out of her driveway. She rolled down her window. "I'm sorry, I can't help just now. Errand to run," she explained.

"Not to worry," he said. "I'm just going to spray the tomatoes and weed a bit. It's such a nice day."

"Leave some for me." She was in tears as she pulled away, thinking that he would be finished before she returned, another day's gardening done, the winter only weeks away. It just made her furious, that this late in her life another day was lost.

The boy at Payless was unusually quick and accurate with the saw. "Be careful with your hands," she warned him. He'd cut Mr. Haygood's boards before and knew what he wanted for his display boxes. Mrs. Haygood realized he was all too efficient and so stopped at Wal-Mart on the way home. She couldn't spend any of Mr. Haygood's money. That's why he wanted the receipt: to make sure he got all his change. But she had six dollars of her own in her wallet: three she'd made up from coins found in washing machines at the Laundromat, two left from a gift certificate to Bell's Nursery that Mazelle's husband had given her for her birthday, and the last was a dollar she felt guilty about because another old lady, a cashier at Albertson's, gave her too much change when she paid for her groceries. Mrs. Haygood noticed the extra dollar moments before she gave it to Mr. Haygood, spiriting it away into her dress pocket. Now she stood in the cosmetics department at Wal-Mart, making up the ten minutes the efficient boy had saved. Everything was so expensive. She watched two teenage girls trying on makeup. They not only used the testers and samples but broke the seals on new lipsticks. Mrs. Haygood realized she could save her six dollars. She put on a light base, and Buff Naked lipstick by L'Oréal, then Maybelline Great Lash mascara and finally a squirt of Obsession. One of the girls showed her how a new eyeliner pencil worked.

"You want to highlight your good features and de-emphasize your negatives," she said.

"Oh," Mrs. Haygood said.

"You've got beautiful eyes," the girl said.

"I never think of people looking in my eyes, because I'm always so busy looking out of them," Mrs. Haygood said. "I feel a little guilty about using all this makeup."

"Oh, it's not animal tested," the other girl said.

"I mean, it's not our makeup," Mrs. Haygood whispered.

"Gosh, we come here before every date," they said.

12:25 Mrs. Haygood is off on her weekly errand. Their car makes a terrible noise and why they won't fix it is beyond me. If I had a car I would fix it. Mazelle's husband is spraying chemical and looking my way at the end of every row like I'm a vegetable. He'll be leaving in a few minutes.

12:28 That dog is back next door, lying in the tall grass big as life. I have called the pound three times and there he still sits. I am afraid to step out in my yard when he is there owing to the danger of mange and other outrageous diseases. I don't know what race of dog he is, but he is certainly not a pure breed, as Verda is always claiming for her two mutts.

12:31 Hammer, hammer, knock, knock. As I was sweeping my front porch I could certainly hear that carpenter. It sounds as if he is banging on the walls of my house. That kind of industrial activity shouldn't be allowed in a retail neighborhood. I will call the city hall about it.

12:33 Mose is coming toward my house. I think he's combed his hair for me.

⇥✦⇤

Mose wore khaki pants, a khaki shirt, a brown leather belt and black work shoes. Blades of grass made a derelict picket fence around his heels. His skin was varnished with sweat. He crept up on Howard Dog-in-His-Path in the bathtub as if the old man were a snake coiled in a basket. The tub was full of freshly fallen leaves, and Howard lay among them as if he'd fallen there too.

"Howard?" Mose said softly.

Howard's eyes opened independently of one another, moments apart, shades raised by someone moving slowly from window to window through a dark house.

"You been smoking, Howard? You all right?"

"I'm OK."

"I just wanted to tell you I've about got your radio fixed. I'm waiting on a tube from Milwaukee. It just had the one bad tube."

"Could you teach me how to fix a radio?" Howard asked.

"I guess I could. Why?"

"I've never fixed anything."

Mose wiped his brow. "You all right, Howard? You want me to call somebody?"

"Nobody to call. Take a tub, old man. We're both old men, aren't we. You're hot. Take this tub beside me. The porcelain is cool."

"If I get in that tub, I may not be able to get out of it," Mose said.

"Please," Howard said, closing his eyes.

It was such a strange word, oozing out of Howard's mouth. "All right, all right." Mose eased over the side of the claw-foot tub. There were chips in the porcelain where the faucets once were, and an old red ring ran around the tub as precisely as if it had been put there with a compass. Mose's body was below the ring, his head above. He immersed himself in leaves. "Hey, this is all right," he said.

Howard's shoulders rose above the rim of the tub and his arm trailed over the side, allowing his great knuckles to rest on the earth. "I try to tell the people, nothing like an old tub. Deeper, better angle of lean. I woke up tired, Mose."

"I wake up tired every morning," Mose said. Extra water collected in his eye and he had to blink it away.

"This was my first time. What's it like, being able to fix things?"

Mose squinted. It was as if he'd been asked what it was like to brush his teeth. He'd never thought of himself as having any special ability. He answered, "I always wanted to invent something."

"What?"

"Anything. Something people needed. Something that would replace something else."

"What do you think the guy who invents things wants?" Howard asked.

"I don't know. Seems to me he'd have everything."

"No. I wish I could fix things, and you can, but it doesn't seem to mean much to you."

"Now you're depressing me," Mose said.

"Maybe an inventor wants to be an artist."

"What does an artist want?"

"I think he'd want to be loved," Howard said.

"Well, then, what does someone who's loved want?"

"He doesn't want to be replaced." Howard clinched the rim of his tub with both hands as if someone were trying to pull him out of it. "But I'm making this all up as I go along."

"Do you think it's possible to jump over all the in-between steps?"

"What, and be replaced?"

"No, no, stop at being the loved one."

"I've heard of people doing it," Howard said. "But perhaps they're liars."

"What happens to you when you can't stop there, when you get replaced?"

"I think you tear things down. Do you know what my first job was, Mose? There's no way you could."

"So the trick is to stop the wheel at being loved," Mose said. "I'm just trying to understand you here. How do you do that? I don't think I was ever given a chance to choose."

"Maybe you have to die," Howard said.

"What did you say?"

"If you die while you're being loved, they can't replace you. You're dead. Oh, they could replace you, but you wouldn't know or care."

"No, before that. I heard the dying part."

"I was going to tell you about my first job. I was a grave robber. I plundered the graves of my people."

Mose turned his head slowly and peeked over the rim of his tub at Howard. Looking into the old Indian's eyes was like looking out a window at night: he saw only reflections embedded in darkness. It occurred to him then how much the old bathtubs resembled coffins, and the rows of toilet tanks, marble headstones.

"I thought I might get us some iced tea," Mose said.

"I'll wait here." And just as Howard had opened his eyes, he closed them, each on a different sash cord.

12:38 There goes Mazelle's husband, pulling his little wire cart. Probably to the grocery. He acts as if he has nothing to hide.

12:40 They all think I don't know but I still can see quite well as I so well know their living habits and their friends are very limited and I know them well. I readied myself for Mose's visit but he did not come and finally I looked out and he was in the bathtub next to That Big Indian who had most likely intercepted him to gossip about me, thinking as he does that I owe him my commission but I deserved the twenty percent I kept when I sold that pedestal sink three years ago to that customer who had no one to give her money to but me and perhaps the sink would have even been stolen but it wasn't, Thanks to Me, and he never did even thank me, so I haven't and will not ever provide my services again. A shop should be attended to but he does not do this. Many times I have to apologize to my customers for the appearance of his shop and yard.

12:48 Mose is carrying two glasses of iced tea across the street to That Big Indian! I have never seen such odd behavior between meals. A regular picnic. The tumblers look to be Fenton hobnail blue opalescent. Surely Mose doesn't know their value. I sure never saw them the times I was in his house. Probably a gift from his sister, Novis, who does not hide her feelings about me.

12:51 A customer is knocking on Mazelle's door, but she won't let him in. He put his face right up next to the glass. I can see her "back in a minute" sign is up. It is this kind of thing that causes lost customers on the Row, dealers not paying proper attention to their open hours.

→✦←

From the moment Carl met Nadine, he had no past. There was only the present and a possible future. The skills necessary to build a wooden sloop seemed to appear in his hands suddenly and without effort, a gift he couldn't remember receiving. He awoke each morning with an earnestness and sense of purpose that no school had instilled, that no life experience had prepared him for. Obstacles turned into sawdust, stray dogs ate from his hands, mail found his mailbox. He'd received a letter this morning from a boat hauler out of Houston quoting a price he could afford to carry his little ship down I-35 to Corpus Christi. From there only a narrow sandbar would separate him from the open sea. Carl had never been to sea or piloted a sailboat, but his vision of Nadine provided complete confidence in his capabilities. He called the hauler and set up a time and date that gave him now a full week to make final preparations. The hull, deck and interior were complete, his mast and spars awaited him on the dock in Corpus Christi. He'd already slept three nights in his mainsail. When the truck arrived he'd simply knock the porch and front wall away from his house. The cradle supporting the boat was designed so it could be cut away every four feet, allowing the trailer to back in under the hull. They'd be away.

Carl was living aboard his boat already. His clothes were stowed in the port lockers, his tools beneath the port bunk. He'd reserved the starboard lockers for Nadine. He reached his new quarters by a sturdy cypress ladder that leaned against the gunwale. Over the past few months, as the work on his boat required less of his time, Carl often found himself lying on the forward deck, taking his ease beneath a plywood sky. Knots reminded him of dark moons; the run of grain, windswept clouds. The plywood was so thin that gusts rolling across the roof made it ripple. The house would be worthless, of course, once it was no longer a boat shed. So he'd sold his corner lot to Texaco. They were going to build a small station and convenient store. He knew that Nadine would probably want to keep her house. She'd grown up there. And they'd need a place to return to occasionally, anyway. Perhaps a couple of weeks every year, like a vacation from the boat. He wondered if Nadine would even recognize him after he'd dived into the ocean for the first time. He'd come to the surface and there would be no sawdust on his face.

In the week remaining, all that was left to do was mount the name board (*Nadine*), fit the bowsprit, cut in the eyes, then sell off his woodworking equipment and what remained of his furniture and appliances. And then he had to tell Nadine. He was trying to decide if he should tell her before or after he cut the front of his house away with a chain saw. He began to sharpen a chisel, but then a dog barked at his back door.

12:53 Nadine has a customer who drives a Cadillac—PSW-410. First time I have seen this customer. The doctor at the state hospital drove a similar car, getting rich off of Medicare, paid for by <u>my</u> taxes. This is the very same who told me I was no longer in control and had to be protected and that He was now in charge. I begged him to make one phone call, and told him my son was only after my things and house. My arm was severely wrenched by the uncaring man who came in the ambulance, and he did say rude statements to me. It took my lawyer only two hours to secure my release as he threatened to sue not only my son but the doctor and I have not spoken to my son or he me since that date, October 8, three years ago.

1:00 My show is about to come on so I hope no customers interrupt.

"To be good at fixing things you almost have to be glad when they break," Mose said. He held the glass of iced tea toward Howard, whose hand slid out of his sleeve like a pocket door. "You look forward to searching for what's wrong or missing."

"I've always been able to eat a piece of watermelon," Howard replied. "But no more. It upsets my stomach."

"Me, I can't eat olives. What do you think of that tea?" Mose eased back down into his bathtub.

"It's good. I can say that at the end of a long life: this tea is good."

"It won't water down on you either," Mose said. "It will be good to the last drop. The ice cubes are made of iced tea too."

Howard put two fingers in his glass and pulled out a cube. "I'll be goddamned. Did you think of that?"

"Little invention of mine."

"You could do Coca-Cola and coffee ice cubes."

"I've done them all. But as Nadine pointed out, anybody can make them. You can't patent them. There's no profit in an iced tea ice cube except pleasure."

"Still, Mose, it was a good idea."

"Well, some day. I'm working on a rain alarm right now. Say you open your windows for the breeze, then you take a nap. It starts to rain. I've got an electric doorbell wired to a switch in the window."

"How does the switch know it's raining?" Howard asked.

"That was my big problem. I had the two contacts with voltage between them. I needed something between them that would melt when the rain started. It was sort of a similar problem that Edison had with his lightbulb. You know he tried hundreds of materials before he came up with a filament that worked. I tried a Tums, an Alka-Seltzer, a piece of toilet paper, even a suppository, but what finally worked was a thin slice of Bayer aspirin. First drop or two of rain dissolves the aspirin, the contacts come together, the bell wakes you up, you shut your window."

"You'll sell a million of those," Howard sighed.

"I don't know. People don't open their windows as much as they used to. And the percentage of those who take naps after opening their windows must be pretty small, and nobody likes an electric bell. I've got one hooked up to every window in my house but it hardly ever rains here. I haven't been able to test it."

"Rain is a good thing. I know I can say that too. Bells ought to go off when it rains." Howard drank off the last of his tea and set the glass down gently on the brittle grass.

"Now," Mose said, "you wait a few minutes, let those ice cubes melt, and you've got another mouthful of tea to drink. Or you can suck on the cubes."

"Not a customer in sight," Howard said. He pulled his arms over into the tub and crossed them at his belt.

"No."

"It seems to me now that things are not what they should have been."

"We've had our day, that's right," Mose said. "Antiques are big business now. Everybody's out on the interstate in big warehouses, importing containers from England and Holland. It's breaking poor Nadine's heart. Thank God, her momma never saw it."

"There was a woman," Howard said.

"Few like her," Mose said. "Nadine will always live in her shadow."

"She should step out," Howard sighed. "The old woman certainly did."

Mose felt the hair on the back of his neck percolate. He'd made tea for this man. "You robbed graves," he said.

"I did."

"Indian graves? Your people's graves?"

"Yes. I began as a boy, working with Henry Grubbs, whose Indian name was Henry Spotted-Horse, and even though he was old then and could speak Indian, I didn't learn it. None of us kids learned then. At first he just had me picking up arrowheads off the ground. We'd walk along creeks till he noticed the signs of an encampment or village. These signs may have been nothing more than a few flint flakes or sandstone burned pink in a hearth fire. He had a mule named Sweetlips hitched to a single-shovel plow that he'd tear the ground open with, then we'd look for artifacts: arrowheads, axes, drills, manos and metates. He sold them to souvenir shops. We worked our way off the reservation into Arkansas and East Texas. The Caddo people buried their dead in mounds. These were easy to find. They had a crude pottery. We sold some of this to museums. We left their bones, what was left of them, exposed to the air. I thought nothing of this. But the real money was in New Mexico and Arizona. Henry didn't want to leave East Texas. He didn't like the desert. He said it was bad for his skin and spirit. So I went alone, learned how to find the Anasazi kivas, the ruins of the pueblos. I can't tell you how many shovels I wore out. The things I found were beautiful and I sold them for a great profit. Perhaps not as great as rain alarms, but I made good money for an Indian. Those people could make pottery. They carved tiny fetishes, animal figurines. South of Santa Fe, I found the blade of a Spanish lance in a chief's grave. In another grave, I found a knife of obsidian. I once sold a single Black on White bowl for two hundred dollars, and that was in 1934. A new Ford cost five hundred dollars then."

"I know that," Mose said. "I'm as old as you. I know what things used to cost."

"I opened a cave east of Pueblo Bonito and gathered up half a dozen baskets, dumping the husks of grain that was still in them into the wind. That grain was probably eight hundred years old. Someone had been saving it for eight hundred years. I am the man who found three prayer sticks, feathers still tied to them with hide, in a stone vessel beneath a stone slab, beneath a skeleton that measured six feet, four inches long. No one knows this but me. He must have been a powerful man. I sold the prayer sticks to a collector in Albuquerque. The Indians would drive the sticks into the ground, the feather would blow in the breeze, broadcasting a spell or prayer. They are very rare. Turquoise beads beyond counting, I found. An atlatl point buried in the skull of a buffalo. Hohokam lip plugs. Hair ornaments with human hair still tousled between the pins. Skulls with decorated teeth. A bone flute that I almost missed until I saw the skeleton had too many ulnas. I took a stone charm in the shape of a bird from a child's disarticulated fingers. Perhaps it was a toy. Most likely it was her medicine. Maybe it warded off evil."

"It didn't keep you away," Mose said.

"I know."

1:15 Why doesn't Natasha leave Dirk? Anyone can see through his lies. He is leaving Santa Barbara to have an affair with that murderous Lacey. But it is possible he is going underground as a special detective to discover her evil publishing empire. Still he doesn't have to keep everything such a secret from Natasha, who only cares for his safety and well being. When will she tell him she's carrying his child?

Nadine's first customer of the day was looking for silk shawls. She drove a Cadillac but that didn't mean anything anymore. Nadine understood this when the woman put her hand to her nose as she stepped inside the shop. A person with manners never revealed their discomfort. Nadine had made every attempt to mask the odor of her old clothes with candles and potpourri. Hers was a pleasant, clean shop.

"May I help you?"

"Do you have any old silk shawls?"

Why did people step into an antique shop and ask if you had anything old? "All of my things are vintage," Nadine answered. She led the woman to a basket of scarves and shawls. "Here's a nice paisley. It still carries its tag from Leonard Brothers in downtown Fort Worth. It's hard to believe they've finally closed their doors. I loved to shop there when I was a girl."

"Can these be cleaned?"

"Yes."

"Is this the best you can do?" The woman held the price tag up to Nadine's face as if she might not be able to see very far.

"I could let you have ten percent off," Nadine said, but saying it made her feel empty inside, as if she'd just thrown up. Her mother had never given discounts, saying bargaining showed contempt for the merchandise, on both the dealer's and the customer's parts.

"Do you have anything else?"

"Shawls?"

"Silk."

"Yes. I have a few silk dresses and of course many men's ties."

"Well, I'm going to have to come back later when I have more time. Thank you." She left.

Nadine watched her walk down the cracked sidewalk, get in her car and pull away. The paisley shawl was clinched in Nadine's fist, and she brought it up to her nose and inhaled deeply. Dust. She stepped out on her porch, folding the shawl as she went, and then wrapped it around her shoulders. The sky was that pale blue of October, shot with southern light. The moon in this chambray field looked like a silver earring someone had lost long ago. If I can get through today, I'll be in tomorrow, Nadine thought. A few leaves skittered up her porch steps, twirled and fell in a heap in the corner. Her momma would have been after them with a broom, dancing with those leaves. I should have lived in her age, she thought. I was born after my time. Fashion has no mystery, no allure, anymore. She looked at the old car parked at her curb and thought about looking in the window to see if she could see an address or phone number of the owner. It had been there for two days now. The car was the color of a dead mouse she'd found in one of her hat boxes, gray, dull. One of the car's tires was beginning to go flat. She wished for a moment that she knew a secret, and thought, Nadine, you are as desperate as the wind. It was then she realized that the car in front of her shop wasn't just broken down. It had been abandoned.

How did it feel? To walk away from something that was worthless, to leave it on someone else's stoop? Her own mother had passed away out in the front yard, staggering off the sidewalk and falling in the Saint Augustine, her head lolling over the concrete curb. She may have lain there for ten minutes before Nadine saw her and screamed. Mose came running then, and Mazelle's husband, who'd been mowing his yard, and together they carried the body up on the porch, but she was already gone. Poor Mose had cried like a child, sitting on his legs like a child. That was ten years ago.

But all her mother had been interested in was trade. When she was alive, Worth Row was thronged with customers all week long. They'd hired a boy on Saturdays to direct parking. Old Mrs. Martin was alive then too, serving tea and soup and sandwiches in the front room of number eight. People would walk up one side of the street, have lunch, and then shop the other side. Tradio set up iron beds in his front yard. Mose played his old radios over a loudspeaker. The Postlethwaites always dressed so well; you never saw either one of them in a jogging suit. Mr. and Mrs. Killebrew had a fine upholstery and chair caning shop where Carl now was. They'd both been in a nursing home for eight years. She was on one floor and Mr. Killebrew on another. They didn't even know each other anymore, but the nurses still sat them together at lunch. It had been Nadine's mother who kept everyone involved, kept the entire street running smoothly. She walked door to door, cajoling, threatening, laughing, making the Row successful by the power of her own will. She made Verda lower her prices, called Mr. Haygood an ass to his face after he'd frightened a newsboy, welcomed Aura to the street with open arms even though most of her business was mail order, didn't allow a single muscle to twitch when Howard bounced around her like an earthquake, and somehow managed to get the city of Fort Worth to put a stoplight at the foot of Worth Row so everybody who stopped there could read her sign at length. Mose loved her, Mr. Haygood was afraid of her,

Mazelle broke her own rule and loaned her books. A flake of paint didn't fall from any house on the street that she didn't nag about or fix herself. The only thing that ever came close to overwhelming her was the ice storm of '57, when the Row lost ten out of twelve of its great oak trees. Overburdened with ice, branches cracked and fell to the street with the report of cannon fire. The Row seemed nude, the sun too bright. Nadine's mother walked through the fallen branches, the shards of ice, until Nadine begged her to come in out of the cold. It had taken those oaks seventy years to grow and she knew she'd never see their likes again on the Row.

Nadine looked out from her porch, up the sidewalk toward Mazelle's. She could still tell where each of the oaks had been by the heaving in the cracked sidewalk. The two trees that survived the ice storm died of disease in the seventies, and they'd all been replaced with a hodgepodge of bushes, gum trees and cotton-woods, Saint Augustine grass. An avenue of shade had been lost.

She looked across the street. Mose and Howard were lying in bathtubs. Mose waved to her, but it wasn't a wave of invitation. They looked like a couple of old drunks down at the stockyards.

Her mother was a lady. Nadine wished she'd lived in her age, died when she died. There was a time when you could count on someone in a Cadillac. They always bought some little thing. Something bit her shin. She reached down and rubbed. There's so much stubble on these legs, she thought, I'll have to avoid my silk dresses, not to mention proximity to Mose's Velcro inventions. She wished she had some secret, something from the past that would be revealed in the future, something that intentionally skipped over the present moment, something worth saving.

❧❦

1:20 Knowing her habits so well I can tell every time when Caroline is hiding something from Roberto. She always looks away, taps her tooth with her long finger nail. No doubt she is thinking of her past life as a prostitute and whether Roberto will discover her former occupation and her breast implants.

Aura became cold. It happened every day near noon after spending all morning inside. She realized that if she didn't get out into the sunshine within moments she'd slip into a lassitude that might end in frostbite. She'd been so warm an instant earlier. Only by lying out, with as much of her body bared to the sun as legally allowed in Fort Worth, could she rid herself of the shivers. It annoyed her at times, that her own body was such a complete secret to her. Her bladder rarely gave her more than a few moments to respond. When she farted, it was a complete surprise, as if it were someone else in the room. It took her hours to warm up in the sun and hours to cool back down in front of one of Marshall's vents. Early in her life she'd been accused of leprosy, but the doctors said no. Hers was a case of reserved nerves. Sensations simply took their time. Her senses only showed up at the theater of her mind bare seconds before the curtain rose. Her body moved as she willed it, but did so without urgency, and often would lose all momentum, rolling back across its path as if she were a marble in a shallow bowl.

Aura locked the shop door and turned the Open sign in the window around to Shut. She tried to wrap her arms around her torso but they wouldn't bend at the elbows. She felt as hard as an automobile tire. The stove burner was still on. She'd been frying a slice of a frozen ham bone when the chill struck her. On her way out the back door, she plucked the ring of bone and marrow from the hot grease and with a great effort of will bent her arm and dropped the sizzling disc onto her outstretched tongue. Then she was out the door, stripping down to her floral bikini on her way to the lounge chair, where she luxuriated in a sun-embracing sprawl. She didn't feel the sun's warmth yet, but she believed in its arrival in the same way she'd known for all those years that Marshall would find her. She rolled the top of each bra cup and the waist of her panties down a quarter inch more, revealing pale strips of flesh that reminded her of the untrimmed fat on a steak at Winn-Dixie. She knew Effie watched her do this. A panel had blown off the fence, allowing her to see. Aura thought about getting up and moving her lounge but then she'd have to rearrange her bikini again. She wasn't sure, but she might be beginning to feel unsettled. There was no way of knowing, of course, until the moment arrived, so she tried to let her anxiety subside. The bone helped. She popped the circle of hot marrow out of the bone ring with the dull nub of her tongue, and then flattened it against her palate, rupturing the cells so she could rinse the rest of her mouth with their sweet liquid centers.

The sun was lower in the southern sky than it had been the day before. The moon was just coming into view. Aura was fond of them both, with their ability to share, to coexist. Fall was her favorite time of the year, when summer and winter mixed in equal parts and made perfect days. She slept without knowing she'd fallen asleep.

And she dreamed of miscegenation, cross-pollination, of a repaired serving fork she'd once seen whose tines were Paul Revere and whose handle was Chantilly, and of a married Queen Anne highboy that experts credited to the work of a single unknown genius, and of hybrid corn. When she woke the sun and moon had traded places. Upon her, like an eagle descending on a trout, was the realization that she must pee and defecate and puke within moments and as she tumbled toward her back door, digging into her side for the downturned hem of her panties, all she could think was bad marrow, bad marrow.

❧❦

1:30 What next? Armando cannot break the cycle of addiction. I worry so about him, and often wonder where he will end up. Wal-Mart has Velveeta on special through Saturday, two boxes for $1.99, and all I have to do is mention my show and their commercial.

⇥⇤

The gates of heaven fluttered pink like the wings of flamingos, but then were slippery and wet, like the tongues of her dogs. Yeseedid licked Verda's flaccid eyelids open, then tasted the film of tears on her eyeballs. Behind Yeseedid, Dideebiteya was trying to do ditto to her wagging heinie. "Bad dog!" Verda snapped, even though doing so stabbed her heart. "I'm sorry, Jesus," she whispered. "Please don't hurt me anymore."

Where was that damned Effie? she wondered. Over here bothering me half a dozen times a day any other time. I took her that leftover fish from Luby's too and not a word of thanks. Verda passed a small dollop of gas. That was a blessing. Bowels in order and there's a good voyage. She sighed. All this time gone by, minutes beyond counting, and still the world hadn't ended. She wondered if meddling with Effie was keeping her out of heaven. She was a tale bearer if there ever was one. A tale bearer revealeth secrets: but she that is of a faithful spirit concealeth the matter. That was Proverbs. Verda had tried to keep secrets from Effie for half her life. She'd failed on almost every occasion, but hoped that holding out as long as humanly possible would count for something. She had tried. Effie was relentless and told secrets on other people as if she had an infinite supply, plucking them off backyard clotheslines like underwear. She shouldn't have meddled with her, but where was she now?

Verda reached out tentatively and dragged her dogs across the floor to her breast. "There, there, babies. It's all right." Dideebiteya tried to tug at the single long hair on Verda's chin.

Verda moved her leg a bit and tucked her head closer to her dogs. At her abdomen was the baby jar of glass eyes. Her dogs had gathered them from the backyard as they appeared over the years, protruding from the paths they wore along the base of the fence. Verda had washed each eye with Visine when the dogs deposited them at her feet. Some were cracked and broken, some over-glazed, some fired at too high heat, some simply had skewed pupils. The lid of the jar had fallen open. Gingerly, Verda took her right arm off Yeseedid and tilted the jar over, then swept it across the floor. The individual eyes scattered before her, and to a one they came to rest looking at her. The eyes of God, Verda thought. Perhaps she could read them, like bones or cards. I have loved things too much. I have loved gossip too much. I have lusted after figurines. She wondered what some future archaeologist would think of her if she were buried with all her broken figurines. That they were slaves to serve her needs in the afterlife? Another sacrilegious thought. The pain returned to her chest. She bore through it this time. Perhaps she'd loved God too secretly. But she'd only done so because she'd thought it was an unrequited love. She knew these thoughts were like leaves dropping from a dead tree one at a time. When they were all gone there'd be only the gray trunk of her body left. She looked up at her front door, then at the phone on her counter. Which was closer?

❧❦

1:35 Mose is still talking with That Big Indian. I assume they are discussing me and my situation. There is no love lost between me and That Big Indian and while I have never caught him look-ing in my windows, I am sure he does, hoping to see something he hasn't paid for. Whenever he folds his wash on his patio table he does so <u>facing my house</u>.

❧❦

Over the years Mazelle's husband had turned back once or twice before he reached the corner, having forgotten his shopping list or his wallet, but once beyond he was safely away for at least an hour. Mazelle watched him pull his wire cart down the street, slap his back pocket in front of the cabinet shop and then turn the corner. She locked the door to her shop and placed a Will Return in Ten Minutes sign in the window. The cardboard sign was tattered and water stained, but she was in love with it because it always promised her ten more minutes. It promised her she'd never be late. It had been so much more convenient when he worked five days a week.

The phone had rung once and not again and this had caught her unprepared. She'd had to make up an errand for her husband, but he liked errands, especially since he'd retired. He oiled the wheels on that wire cart as if it were some sort of hot rod. When he left he always kissed her with extruded lips that seemed to be a model of an ancient volcano, its steep slopes eroded with long gullies.

Mazelle moved her stool from behind the counter, kicked up the Oriental runner and paused to hike up her skirt and pull off her underwear. She keyed open the cash register and stowed the wadded panties in the dime compartment. When she lifted the trapdoor, light stumbled down the stairwell a step at a time. The familiar, and by now arousing, odor of limestone dust billowed up. She stepped down, holding the heavy door firmly, till she could grip the railing and allow the door to drop back into place. The stairs were steep and narrow. With the light from her shop window now occluded there was only her memory of each step, twenty-eight years of accumulated knowledge. Each tread held a worn hollow that fit her foot perfectly. Ten steps to the bottom and a small smooth floor of short boards. She'd arrived first. No light emanated from the cistern. She stepped down onto the rough limestone floor. She moved toward the center of the room and the dangling light cord, but misjudged and bumped into the bedpost, but then knew where she was and switched on the light. After all these years it was still hard not to look at the bare bulb. She held her hand over her eyes for a moment, then allowed the light to filter in through her fingers. She always expected to find the walls sweating, the floor covered with two inches of cold water.

It was a small room, ten feet square, with a vaulted ceiling, also of limestone, that was at most seven feet tall. Designed to hold rainwater funneled from the rooftops of the adjoining houses, it looked as if it had never been used. The mortar was powder dry. Perhaps, shortly after the houses had been built, the city had run a water line and the cistern had never been needed. The vault was buried two feet beneath the surface of her husband's garden. The room contained only two pieces of furniture, a small pine nightstand and the bed itself, a mahogany four-poster that Mazelle bought from Howard Dog-in-His-Path. It had been some work getting it and the mattress down the stairs and into the cistern. But it was the least she could do, since Charlie had done all the hard work of tunneling out the entrances and building the stairs. He'd discovered the cistern while digging out an old grapevine, back when all four of them worked on the garden. Working alone, he'd used an iron bar to break through the ceiling and then dropped a burning rag into the hole. He quickly repaired the ceiling with cement. Then, over a period of six years, he'd slowly dug out the two tunnels, breaking through the side walls of the cistern. The dirt removed from the tunnels was added to the garden, increasing the depth over the limestone roof by another six inches. And all this was done in free moments, stolen hours, when his wife was away from the house. He said she never once asked about the occasional dirt stains on his clothes. For six years their affair, Mazelle's and Mr. Haygood's, had been led aboveground. For another twenty-eight it had been led below.

Mazelle turned back the bedcovers. Her hands trembled. Whenever she arrived first she wondered if she hadn't made a mistake. Perhaps it had been a wrong number. Perhaps Mrs.

Haygood had returned unexpectedly. She tried to count her husband's steps, to visualize where he was at that moment. She could hear a phone ringing distantly and wondered if it was hers or the Haygoods'. All sound was muffled here, passing through corridors and stone. She'd once heard her husband digging in the earth above her as Charlie stroked in and out of her. It was a heartless, stunted sound, like knives thrust into pillows. She'd told Charlie to hurry, hurry.

"There's no way you could hear him, Mazelle," he'd told her, and continued to stroke.

But she'd heard him often, pulling at roots, scratching at the mortar with his fingernails. She'd often expected rocks from the ceiling to come tumbling down on Charlie's back and her own face, followed by a shower of topsoil, a shaft of sunlight, her husband squinting down at their nakedness.

"He's back, he's early," she'd whispered shrilly into Charlie's ear a hundred times. "He's lifting the trapdoor."

But it had never been so. They'd never been caught. She still owned this one sacred secret.

"Knock, knock," Mr. Haygood said.

"Who's there?" Mazelle answered. She sat on the bed.

"I've missed you, Maisie, dear."

She held out her arms. Mr. Haygood began as he always did, by unbuttoning her blouse, lifting it off her shoulders and hanging it on the bedpost. He slid her bra straps off her shoulders and then, kissing her firmly, reached around her back and popped the snap. With his free hand he held the stiff bra, and then drawing back, he caught Mazelle's prosthesis before it could fall free. He placed the bra and the prosthesis (which he'd picked out from among the many shapes and varieties) on the nightstand gently, and then he began to kiss the long scar of her fifteen-year-old mastectomy.

"Why do you do that, Charlie?" she asked. "Why do you always do that?"

"It's such a sad scar," he said, "turned down at the ends the way it is."

"Because it reminds you of the old breast? Rather than this one that's left?"

"Don't be silly, Maisie."

"I know that my scars are the only firm skin I have left."

"I'm just trying to heal it, Maisie. I'm just trying to tell you it doesn't matter."

She put her arms around his head and pulled him closer.

1:41 A white Dodge stopped in front of my house. A man, I would say about forty-five or fifty, unfolded a map and looked at it a good while, as if he didn't know <u>exactly</u> where he was! I would like to have a big bowl of salad if I were not sure I'd find a bug in it, which are always the same color as the lettuce.

1:44 I just called Verda's house and let the phone ring only once to let her know I'm not a fool. I don't think she is out with her daughter at all but is only trying to ignore me. Well, ignorance works both ways. I have never once told her of my feelings toward her tiresome elbows, which hang off her arm like an empty scrotum.

"Just to think," Louise said, "someone from Fort Worth has been to the Great Wall of China."

Arlen shook his head from side to side, equally appalled. The warm snapshots dropped singly onto a clear plastic tray.

"I wonder if the Chinese had an art deco period," Arlen said.

"I doubt it. I don't think their culture would have approved of naked women riding crescent moons, or holding up lightbulbs or offering themselves to an ashtray."

"Now, what brought that on?"

"Just look around the shop, Arlen. Everything we sell is either nude or it's a phallic symbol."

"Shhh," Arlen said. "I wish you wouldn't say that word in the mall."

"What?"

"Be quiet. You're in a public place."

"Arlen. We're so old no one listens to us."

"You think I'm hard of hearing and you speak too loudly."

"You *are* hard of hearing."

"What we sell is a period of design: geometric forms, symmetrical curves, streamlined shapes. There are as many flamingos and greyhounds depicted as nudes. And nudes are prevalent in every period, not just art deco."

"All right, all right. I didn't mean anything by it. You get too defensive. I like the nudes too. I love the things in our shop. There are so many things I wish we hadn't let get away."

"I still think about that chrome clock with the blue glass hands," Arlen sighed.

"We sold it too cheaply," Louise said, and rubbed the back of Arlen's withered hand. There were deep valleys between his tendons.

"At the time it was a reasonable price."

"I miss that cocktail shaker in the shape of a zeppelin," Louise said. She put her hands around an imaginary zeppelin and shook it.

"I don't remember it," Arlen said.

"We owned that years and years ago. I've been looking for another one ever since."

"I'll look too," Arlen said. "You never can tell when something will turn up. Maybe even down at the flea market at the Cattle Barns." He put his arm over her narrow shoulders and brought her closer. They both turned their attention to the slot in the developing machine.

Over the next hour they attended a thirty-year high school reunion, a photo shoot of a sixteen-year-old would-be model in western wear, a birthday party for eleven-year-old Shawn, a bridal shower and some sort of car washing service. They talked about how vacation photos had dropped off now that summer was over. It would be after Christmas before they saw many pictures that weren't taken in Fort Worth. They made a decision as to which direction they'd quick-march around the mall that afternoon and how many laps they'd make, two, before going home.

1:48 Tradio is not yet back, as if I care. How I know his shop is ripe for theft. Just listen to the radio and any thief would know he isn't at home. I tried to tell my son this but he said it was none of my business. So I went directly to my daughter-in-law, who will listen to me, and she said she would warn him as she knows I do not speak to him any longer. He is lucky that I cannot help but watch his house as it is directly across the street. I told my daughter-in-law to suggest that Tradio not park his truck next to the house, where I cannot see it, because I won't be responsible if some thief breaks into it. At least she realizes how hardheaded he can be. She seems, although, to have no feeling whatsoever about her father's man friend living with him, saying her mother is gone. But I can tell she disapproves of this lifestyle, even though she visits him regularly unlike my son. I have not received so much as a <u>go to hell</u> from him in several years, owing to the fact that he caused me to be abducted from my own front yard, coming with an ambulance and an orderly and a doctor with papers saying I was under their total control. They did hurt my arm. I also received rude statements from the orderly who would not tell me his name. My lawyers however secured my release in just two hours as they threatened to sue not only my son but the doctor. I hear that infernal carpenter.

✦

"She's just jealous of our relationship and of your relationship with your daughter, Tradio. I think she's still madly in love with you. You know she won't speak my name. Mazelle says she refers to me as your 'man friend.' "

Tradio put the truck in gear, pulled onto Highway 174 leading out of Cleburne.

"I never led her on, Arthur. It's time to move on. Don't you want a new place? We're bursting at the seams with merchandise."

"It's just that I've made such good friends: Aura and Mazelle and Nadine. The Postlethwaites treat me like a human being. You've been selling antiques on that street for so long. If we set up somewhere else it would be years before everyone found us. All of our old customers would be wandering the streets, lost."

"I don't like being watched."

"Is it because you're a homosexual now?"

"I was always a homosexual, Pie Bird."

"I know that. But it's out in the open now."

"That has nothing to do with it."

"All the people on the Row knew you as Tradio, husband of Alice, for twenty-five years. If you'd just admit that you're uncomfortable—"

"Do you not live in the same house I do? Do we not go grocery shopping together and do the yard work together?"

"You won't kiss me in public."

"Who wants to see two old farts like us kissing?"

"They make TV commercials around two old people kissing."

"Not of us they don't."

"Can't you understand how that makes me feel?" Arthur asked.

"Yes," Tradio sighed. "Alice felt the same way."

"Do you know what Howard called Alice? To my face he called her Alice in Wonderland, and I didn't have any comeback. She lived in a make-believe world. And I don't want to, Tradio. Now, how many times did you escort Effie after Alice died?"

"Half a dozen times. I don't know."

"She baked things for you, brought you food, for how long after the funeral?"

"Maybe a year."

"You taught her how to dance?"

"I did."

"Knowing what you knew about yourself?"

"Yes. But I knew who I was when I was married to Alice. There's something you should know, Arthur. I don't regret Alice."

"I wouldn't want you to. Still, I'm jealous. There's photos in the albums. You were never embarrassed to kiss her in public."

"No. Please, leave Alice alone."

"Do you love me?"

"You know I do. Isn't it all right for me to be an old man and not be affectionate in public? Lots of heterosexual men aren't affectionate in public. It has nothing to do with being ashamed. I just want to move through the world without people watching me. Every time I look across the street and Effie's making that eye shape in the venetian blinds, I feel like I'm falling into that dark hole, all my old doubt and half-lies. I'm past all that now. I just want to buy and sell antiques."

"She's a crazy old woman, Tradio. Let her live in her craziness. Let's us go about our business of love and honor."

"I shouldn't have led her on."

"You were lonely. You missed Alice."

"I was too afraid to look for you. I didn't know how."

"Moving away isn't the answer. You'd still be connected to Effie through Michael."

"He doesn't have anything to do with her."

"I don't think she knows yet about the kids."

"Why do you insist on calling them 'the kids'? You're barely five years older than Susie and Michael." Tradio shook his head. "I'm with a man who's the same age as my daughter."

"Crib robber," Arthur teased.

A half hour later they turned onto Worth Row and drove slowly up the slight incline, dodging the open wounds in the asphalt that bled red brick. Mose and Howard waved at them from their bathtubs.

"What do you suppose that's all about?" Arthur asked.

"First time I've ever seen that old Indian talking to anybody that wasn't a customer."

"Look, Effie's not out in her yard, or on her porch, and she's not peeking through the shades."

"She must be dead."

"Oh, Tradio."

"Maybe I should kill her."

"Stop that, right now."

Tradio pulled the truck up into the driveway and set the parking brake. Arthur jumped from his seat and met his lover at the tailgate.

"What about just a hug?" Arthur asked. "Here in front of Mose and Howard. For a start."

"This will not end up with us making out in a grope on a Saturday afternoon down at the Water Gardens."

"Of course it won't. This will end up with you apologizing to Effie and never feeling awkward again, and us living happily ever after with the memories of everyone we've loved."

"Jesus, Arthur, can't you leave anything unsaid?"

"Just a hug."

❧❦

2:00 Verda still not home and I have decided to erase her from my memory. I expect any minute my phone to ring and that voice to whisper, YOU HAD BETTER LEAVE TOWN IF YOU KNOW WHAT'S GOOD FOR YOU.

2:08 Red car—DZQ-888—ran red light at our intersection. License plate hard to read. Mose and That Big Indian were witness to this.

2:09 That train that used to come by every day at two o'clock sure didn't come by today and hasn't for five years now. I bet Nadine won't make the railroad mow their grass.

2:13 Tradio and his man friend home from their "work." Two healthy men such as them need a job and need to act like men and not women. Tradio hugged him like a woman would. If only Alice could see him now. I wish there was some way I could tell her. They did not see me as I was in my backyard looking through the peephole in my fence.

2:16 Nadine is on her porch looking over at that carpenter's. Why doesn't she just hike up her dress and point to the spot. I went out on my porch to adjust my sign and Nadine and Mose and That Big Indian and Tradio and his man friend all turned to look at me like I was the Second Coming. If my life is so interesting to them why don't they just say so. Not everyone can sell better things. I said BOO! and they all turned to their own business or lack thereof.

➤❈◄

When he was inside her no one could find him, and there was no secret he did not know, nothing he couldn't overhear. "Don't worry," he told Mazelle. "I'll never repair the muffler on the car; your husband will always be stupid." Mazelle was a stream of mercury beneath him, her skin no longer tied to muscle, but he enjoyed the chase. He came to her in the dim cistern like a cup of coffee he'd left a week earlier, and yet she was still warm. He marveled at her resiliency, her intransigent eagerness. They lived beneath the earth, a short time each week, for a simple consummation that had never become habit. Each mating was rapturous and new, made so by bitterness and an overwhelming joy of guilt.

"I love it that you don't wear panties," he said.

"Leave the mark of your teeth on my inner thigh," Mazelle whispered. "Make them last for a week. I don't let him go there. Do you hear him?"

"No, no. You've locked the door." Mr. Haygood bit down but couldn't apply enough pressure with his dentures. He hadn't expected this request. He needed fresh glue. Her skin simply rolled between his teeth. He looked up through the low gray copse to Mazelle's expectant face. "Have you made your payment this month?" he asked.

"Yes, yes. It's done."

"I will kill him someday."

"He's kept his word. Come up here. Forget him. We've only minutes left."

"It's as if I must pay to see you."

"We pay for each other. It's always been worth it. Come up here. You dug the tunnels for me. I'm worth it. Here there are no books, no toys, no husbands or wives, only our secret."

"I will kill him someday."

"Kill me now," Mazelle said.

Mr. Haygood moved up over her, bringing one of her thighs with him.

"There you are," she said. "Now work."

He'd dug the tunnels over six years for this privilege. Using a handheld pick and a gallon Folger's coffee can, he'd gone through soil disturbed a century earlier by the men who dug and built the cistern. He'd supported the tunnel with boards as he went and spread the dirt a thin layer at a time over the garden. He collected a handful of eyes in the digging. They appeared in a wall of the tunnel, or between his feet: always unexpectedly. At first he thought Mrs. Haygood was putting them there, and he became afraid of her for a time, but soon he knew he hadn't been discovered, he wasn't being watched. Along with the eyes he found a hinged rusty hook, a ball joint of hollow brass, an ear carved from pink soapstone. The eyes were only the spoiled casts, the uncentered pupils, the spalled and overglazed refuse of the old Worth Mill. The construction workers had built over the factory's midden. Worth Row lay over a vast field of vacant eyes and prosthetic replacements, all seconds. When he realized this, he dug faster. Still, when he came across the eyes he put them away quickly, stuffing them into the can or into his pocket. He wouldn't allow them to watch from the steps behind him. They rested now in a coffee cup in the drawer of the nightstand by their bed. Occasionally, Maisie would align them across the three-quarter-inch thickness of the headboard, each eye facing the mattress and their lovemaking. She would sit on him and move slowly up and down, not looking at him but at the eyes, returning their unblinking interest, till her movements rocked each eye off the precipice to the floor or mattress. It bothered him, the eyes bouncing off his pillow and around his head, but his view of Maisie was worth it, her hands in her hair, her glassy eyes.

Mazelle would not leave her husband. There were the children, and there was his lifetime of labor, and she'd told Mr. Haygood often enough that he himself was the kind of man who treated a wife badly. And of course then there would be no secret. Hers would be an ordinary life, an affair, a divorce. And Mr. Haygood, on his side, would have put all that work into the cistern for it to go unused.

Mrs. Haygood, while irritating, was dependable. Mr. Haygood could go for days without noticing her. She'd been agreeable to going without children, and so he'd saved a good deal, traveled widely in search of stock. His collection of toys was unrivaled in Fort Worth. One of the Bass brothers had visited his shop. He owned a train set once played with by Amon Carter. Mazelle had once applied her lipstick by initially daubing the thick red pencil around the base of Mr. Haygood's locomotive.

As they both bent over the side of the bed to lace their shoes, Mazelle whispered, "Do you hear him?"

"Do you want me to hear him?" Mr. Haygood asked.

"I want to take my secret to the grave, Charlie," she said. "I want to live my life and have my secret."

"I don't hear him."

"Help me make the bed."

2:20 Mazelle's husband pulling his cart, sure full of <u>something</u>, up the sidewalk.

2:21 Mose and That Big Indian seem to be asleep in their bathtubs. What has become of our neighborhood? I guess they have shared all the meanness they know, right sprang in the center of the street, uncaring of who sees or knows. The things I know and cannot tell for fear of my very life. I intend to call the FBI and warn them of the imminent daily danger I persist in, knowing full well they will be powerless to save me. I write it all down here. You who read this—a careful search of my house will reveal my tablets in chronological order dating from November 3rd, 1958. (They are in boxes in my attic—marked "Junkmail" to thwart thieves.) I leave this record so that when harm comes to me, justice will prevail.

"You awake, old man?"

"I'm awake now," Mose said. "If I wasn't so old, I'd move around a lot more. I'd get up and go home."

"You think I'm a bad man," Howard said.

"What do you care what I think?"

"You're right. But I want you to listen to me. Don't fall asleep again. When I got tired of shovels and dirt, I began to buy and sell the artifacts myself. I went to the reservations, the pueblos, and traded for rugs, pottery, old skins. I bought from pot hunters who dug illegally on government land."

"What about the war? Didn't you go to the war?"

"Too young for World War One and too old for World War Two. Don't try to redeem me. The way I see it, you sell white people's grave goods."

"I've never heard of anyone taking a radio into the coffin with them," Mose said.

"Every museum in the world is full of plundered grave goods. I sold to museums. They never asked where my merchandise came from. The British Museum is full of Egyptian tomb plunder. If the world doesn't agree with grave robbing, why don't they empty the museums, put the goods back where they came from? For all they know those Pharaohs are floundering around in limbo with no servants and nothing to eat. At least I plundered my own people. I didn't go halfway around the world to justify it. And I didn't do it for science. I was hungry. The scientists think if they put everything down on a sheet of graph paper, it makes everything OK. They're out to make careers and reputations. What should make it OK is being hungry."

"So why did you stop?" Mose asked.

"I told you, I was tired of dirt and shovels."

"You don't get tired. You said you woke up tired and it was your first time. Why lie now?"

"I could drown you in those leaves," Howard said. "They would find you drowned in a bathtub of dry leaves."

"No, you couldn't," Mose said. "You're tired now, remember?"

"I don't care what you think."

"Maybe you stopped after taking the fetish from the child."

"I have no sentiment for children. The child was long dead. The worst had already happened."

"Then maybe you thought of something worse you could do for a living. Something that paid better."

"You should have invented people," Howard told him and smiled. "Perhaps you are better at people than bells and wheels."

"You don't need to insult me."

"No insult. You're right. I knew every pueblo, every village, every reservation from Arkansas to California. I was taken in hand by a white man the Indians wouldn't trust. He taught me how to sell insurance."

"What kind of insurance?"

"The worthless kind. It amazed me. A few pennies each month from a thousand Indians and it adds up. I guess some of those people still try to collect on that insurance. They go along thinking it has value for thirty years or so and then they need it and find out they were duped almost three decades earlier. It might be happening to one of them today. Some old man dies and his widow thinks she has the extra thousand to bury him with. The company doesn't even exist anymore. That job was good for three or four years and then I wasn't welcome on the reservations either. I came here."

"You've lived here for almost forty years. I know the rest."

"You know nothing."

"For a while you sold Indian curios. Old guns. Saddles. Then you started tearing down the old houses."

"You know nothing. You sit in your house and fix radios and Victrolas. Your head is always in a box. You don't know your own neighbors, much less me. How many pets are buried in the back-yards of this street?"

"What?"

"I've been here for thirty-seven years and by my count it's seventy-eight. Unbelievable, isn't it? How things accumulate. Dogs, cats, birds, all buried and forgotten. You have to pay attention."

><

2:29 I heard the yelp of a dog and looked out my window to see that stray diving under the porch next door. Mazelle's husband was in his garden, still holding a stick over his head. I throw rocks at that dog but I don't hit him with a stick. I throw rocks because I know I'll miss. This made me mad. I'd like to hit Mazelle's husband with a stick and see how he likes it.

2:34 Mrs. Haygood drove past in her loud car raising the dead. She sure looked my way, trying to see no doubt my Lalique display in the window.

><

The dog Himself jumped over the threshold into the sawdust house and the Earth sprang up to meet his feet. No rest, he thought, no rest. He shook, and the flung shavings and dust displayed the furthest extent of his effect upon the world. He let the man approach as close as two feet before he Himself backed away. Then the man's hand opened. Across the street then, the rubberyness of bologna still remembered in his mouth, and he leaped over the short fence that kept Dideebiteya and Yeseedid penned. He visited this backyard a half dozen times a day, sniffing the moist craps of the Pekingese and eating their food, little difference between the two. If he willed it hard enough the bowls were consistently refilled. But today there'd only been the morning snack and no more. He saw the bowls empty but couldn't trust his eyes, and scanned with his nose and tongue. The bowls scraped along the concrete porch. The Pekingese were at the back window then, both of them standing on the kitchen table, their forepaws pressed against the glass in a white bloodless rage. He looked at them for an instant but couldn't understand their yapping, other than its insistent Mine, mine, mine.

Over the fence again, the ground snapping up and jarring his very bones. Up the sidewalk, cutting between the houses, when . . . he paused. Here. The soil swayed with tenseness beneath his feet. His muzzle plunged into the earth. At first he thought it was only an urge to defecate, but this was far more. Here was the thing that had held him hostage for so long, the very spring beneath the ground. He leaped and spun around in place, snapping at the air. He paused again, listened. He could even hear it, the rhythmic scuffling of compression and release. He leaped again. Yes, the ground came up forcefully here. His feet sank into the dirt. If he could dig up this spring, he thought, he'd be free of all responsibility, free from the Earth. When he leaped there would be no past tense, only leap, only escape. He could eat among the trees, piss into the sky, sleep on a cloud, free from worry. He began to dig in the very center of the spring, pausing occasionally to make sure he was sure. The soil broke away from the Earth loosely, crisply, peculiarly, without the fragrance of weeds. He Himself dug down a foot, a foot and a half, only his hindquarters visible above the rim of the crater. When his nails scraped against the very shell of what he was searching for, when his release was orgasmically imminent, a great howl filled the pit of which he was the center, rushing in to puddle every pore of his skin with fear. He huddled next to the warm Earth, remembering suddenly how much he loved it. The howl again, closer, and then above him, Mazelle's husband coming down with the stick.

2:37 Mrs. Haygood and Mazelle's husband are at home acting nonchalant. It sure doesn't take them long! Do their husband

and wife never notice that they leave and return simultaneously? I can smell it on her when she comes in my shop. Of course that's none of my business, but if they don't care what people think of them they ought to just do it right there in the garden with the peas so we can all get a good look.

When Jack and Steve pulled up in front of number eight, the dog Himself cowered under the porch, growled without realizing it made a sound humans could hear. He curled into a tight ball, ready to feel the stick again, as they stepped up onto the front porch. All the while the two men were in the house, Himself couldn't control his shaking, the constant uncompromising thought of Mine, mine, mine.

"You see what I mean," Steve said.

"But isn't this district historic? Aren't there limits to our actions? No one wants this place?"

"Yes, no and no."

"What is it, about a hundred years old?" Jack asked.

"Ninety-nine. You can see how the neighborhood is."

"My folks bought their dining room table and chairs on this street. My mother used to say, 'I'm going to the Row,' and my father would join her. It was the only time he'd go anywhere with her. That guy who sells house parts was there when I was a kid. Look, there must be six layers of wallpaper here. Maybe we're asking too much."

"I had it listed at thirty, then twenty, then twelve. The wiring's gone, the plumbing's gone. You can see that the roof leaks. The last Realtor who brought in a client won't bring another because of the dog crap on the floor."

"What about the neighbors? Maybe they'd be interested. My mother loved that table. My dad loved radios. I climbed up on that table once, and Mom beat the shit out of me."

"Yeah?"

"How much are we into this place?"

"We foreclosed with fourteen thousand due. We've sunk another eight hundred in taxes the last two years, plus another four hundred in plumbing contractors and having the yard mowed. Taxes are due again in January."

"Who was the officer on this loan, Steve?"

"Well, sir, I made the loan. Eight years ago. Before I was transferred to foreclosures. It was an older lady who ran a small tearoom here."

"Our insurance covers the risk?"

"Eighty percent."

"We'd still have the lot."

"I don't understand."

"We'd receive close to eleven thousand from the insurers and still own the lot if the house were lost?"

"Yes."

"It doesn't sound like we have a choice."

"Yes, sir. But the old house, sir. We could give it away. Write it off. I never meant that we should . . ."

"I never suggested we should. Let's get back to the office."

2:39 License plate—BSZ-367. Black German car next door. Two men wearing nice suits and ties used a key to gain entrance to Mrs. Martin's house. No Realtor sign on their car and I have never seen these men before so I took a picture of them. Possibly from bank? I will go over later to make sure they lock the door back.

When he first began building, he knew the old house couldn't conceal the whole boat. He had a spare two feet at stem and stern, but the bowsprit was almost nine feet long. He needed another seven feet. He'd considered for a time enlarging and closing in the front porch, but his measurements soon revealed that a simple hole between the peak of the porch roof and the peak of the front gable would suffice. After feeding the stray several pieces of bologna, he took on the day's main project. Following the line of the sheer he calculated the steeve, the angle of the bowsprit to the horizon, and marked an X between two wall studs. Measuring from the base of the bowsprit to that point where it would pass through the house told him the hole in the siding would need to be eight inches in diameter. Carl drilled a small pilot hole with a paddle bit, and finding it irresistible, since he knew Nadine's house was directly aligned, he put his sawdust-fringed eye to the opening. Nadine was there in her porch swing, smoothing the fabric of her dress over her thighs. He quickly cut the hole larger with a saber saw. Nadine turned her head when the circle of siding dropped onto Carl's porch roof and rolled down into the front yard. He put his face to the opening and smiled at her. Then as she stood watching, her hands splayed on her hipbones, Carl shoved the eight feet of gleaming spruce through the hole at the precise angle of twenty-five degrees. Nadine stepped back as though she'd been violated. Carl used a clamp to hold the sprit securely in place, then rushed outside. Nadine was already halfway across the street.

"What in the world?" she asked.

"What do you think?" Carl asked. The sprit was so heavily varnished it looked wet. He didn't wait for her answer. He ran back to his house and climbed a ladder to the porch roof. Taking the folded cloth from inside his shirt, he quickly made a flagpole from the sprit with a pair of half-hitches, then stepped back to give Nadine a better view of Old Glory. He stood next to the erect shaft and patted it as if it were a gun on his hip.

"It's too big," Nadine yelled from the sidewalk.

"I wanted it to last," Carl yelled back.

"It's an abomination, Carl. You can hardly see the flag for the flagpole."

"If you don't like it in a week," Carl said, "I'll take it down."

"You've gone to a lot of work for nothing then," Nadine said. "Come to my porch and I'll give you a cup of tea. Pat yourself off first, though."

Carl climbed down, stood in a shaft of sunlight striking down through the gap of a missing limb in a cottonwood and slapped at his pants. Soon he was enveloped in a bright haze of spruce motes that quickly reattached themselves to him as soon as he stepped out of the sunspot.

When Nadine placed the cup and saucer in Carl's hands, when she knew his hands were occupied, she reached up and brushed a curl of shaved wood, so thin it was transparent, from his eyelash.

"Do you ever want to go places, Nadine?" Carl whispered.

"There's no need to whisper, Carl, honey. We're alone," she whispered. "Did you know I spent my senior year of high school in Paris, Carl? Life was so rich there. Life was never meager the way it is here. Does your life ever seem meager? Isn't it a shame that anyone ever had to invent such a word? When I returned from Paris, all of my friends were sure I'd been sent there to have a baby. My name was on everyone's lips, but I had pictures of myself made throughout the year just for such gossip. Mother wanted me to see more of the world than Fort Worth. I was so silly that I thought the whole world came to Fort Worth every year for the stock show. You know, I can still remember a few French words, even though it's been more than thirty years. Would you like to see pictures of me when I was in Paris?"

"No, I like looking at you the way you are now, Nadine. Did you know there are French-speaking islands in the Caribbean?" Carl asked her.

"Carl, I've mostly forgotten my French. There's so many things, drink your tea, that I used to know which I can't now remember.

But I know I once knew them. For instance, I used to know the name of that movie with Jimmy Stewart, and that crochet stitch that tucks twice and then rolls and then what? What dehydrates me, though, is this: how many things have I forgotten, and also forgotten that I once knew them? I'll never know. I mean, how many things have I forgotten without knowing I've forgotten them? It's a double forgetting, that doesn't make a remembering. It's what true oblivion is. It makes me want to apologize to strangers on the street because they might not be strangers. They might be old lovers. Have we ever been more to each other than we are now, Carl?"

Carl looked into the bottom of his teacup. Still, he was whispering. "Nadine, don't think about the past. Think about the future. Even the stray dogs on the street think about what's next, not what's behind."

"Perhaps I have no desire to become a stray dog, Carl. I know I don't want to be compared to one."

"I didn't mean—"

"We think in a fundamentally different way, Carl. The past is more valuable than the future. It's richer, wiser, older. My momma lived in the past. I was in Paris in the past. I was beautiful in the past. The future only happens a squeaky little moment at a time. The past is as big as everything I remember."

"You are beautiful now," Carl said. "You are beautiful now."

"I won't be, in the future."

"You need to get away from here, away from these old clothes."

"Carl, I love this street. This is where I belong. My vacations are over anyway. I come out on my porch and talk to you for a vacation. You go on back to work now. I won't keep you. You've got cabinets to build and I've got clothes to mend. I never knew you were such a patriot. There's a romantic side to you, Carl. I can see it."

➤✦◄

2:50 That carpenter is walking back from Nadine's porch with his hands in his pockets. Guess he's still thinking about her.

2:51 Mazelle's husband and Mrs. Haygood are back in the garden, three feet apart and having a bitter argument. It is obvious he is threatening to hit her with his stick if she betrays their secret.

Mazelle's husband returned from his errand to find a stray dog digging in the garden. He struck him once on the shoulder with a broken hoe handle and raised the stick again but there was no need. The dog leaped from the hole as if on a spring. Six-foot sections of two rows of greens were either ripped from the ground or buried. The hole was at least two feet deep at its center. What could have gotten into an animal to expend such energy? The dog had been digging so furiously he'd allowed a human to walk up on him unaware. Mazelle's husband stepped down into the hole to retrieve half a head of lettuce. Beneath it was a cut stone. He brushed loose soil from its surface. On the face of the rock was the fossilized trail of a worm. He swept away more dirt and followed the trail, which wound so sinuously that it often circled back and crossed itself, leaving little islands of limestone. He was wondering how a cut stone came to be buried so deep in his garden when he came to its edge and found the mortar. Using both hands he clawed away more dirt from the side of the hole, his efforts so intense he failed to notice Mrs. Haygood.

"What are you doing?" she whispered harshly.

Adrenaline shot through his body and he leapt into the air.

"Jesus Christ, Mrs. Haygood, you scared the daylight out of me." He put his palm to his chest. "A dog did this, ruined eight or ten head of lettuce, but there's something here. Something manmade."

"It's a rock," she said.

"No, no, you see . . ." He bent down to show her. "There's more rocks with mortar between them."

"It's nothing," she said. "It's probably some old foundation."

"Well, I'll soon find out. I'm going to get a shovel." He turned back toward the shed.

"Get one for me too," she whispered. She'd come home to find the shop door locked. Looking into the bedroom window she saw that her husband had fallen asleep on the bed. She'd had a spare key made years ago and had hidden it in a crack in the concrete of her back stoop. She'd watched Mazelle's husband begin to dig the hole from there.

He returned not with the shovel but with a long iron rod and a sledgehammer. He pounded the rod into the soil three feet away from the hole. When the bar hit rock, he looked up at her. He moved two feet in another direction and drove the rod again. Again, he hit rock two feet below the surface.

"There's something under our garden, Mrs. Haygood."

She looked to her bedroom window to see if the rapping of the sledge to the iron bar had awakened her husband. She turned and looked at the empty windows in Mazelle's house.

"This is why our fruit trees never got a good purchase," he told her. "They were trying to root in solid rock. I don't understand what it could be."

"It's a grave," Mrs. Haygood said. "It's a vault. We should leave it alone. It has nothing to do with us."

He stepped down into the hole again with the sledge and bar and tested the exposed stone. It rang.

"I believe you're right. It's hollow. But it's too large for a grave. If we could make this hole larger, I could break through the roof and we could see what's inside."

"You're destroying our garden," Mrs. Haygood said. "It's sacrilegious. I won't be a part of digging up someone's grave."

"If we see that it's a grave, we'll stop," he said.

"Can you not see that I'm wearing makeup? Are you blind?"

He was taken aback. He stepped closer to her, put his hand on her sleeve. With his back to Mr. Haygood's house, he said, "Dorothy, I'll wait for you to go and take it off. I won't start without you."

She ripped her arm free from his grasp. "Please don't do this. Let's just fill the hole back in and salvage what we can of the vegetables." She felt something move behind her and turned to Mazelle's bedroom window. Perhaps it was only the curtains. When she turned back, Mazelle's husband was on his way to the shed.

"I won't disturb anything sacred," he said.

"I won't be a party to this," she told him, and stalked away.

The first few shovels of dirt brought back the old pain of heavy meat. As the blade scraped across the limestone, he felt the same uneasiness he'd felt after each of his flat tires: the feeling that it was somehow his fault. He'd run over something he should have seen, should have been paying attention to. He decided it was the noise of the shovel on rock that made him feel this way, this and Mrs. Haygood's burst of emotion over spoiled lettuce. She'd shown the same intractability when he'd wanted to install an automatic sprinkler system in the garden to save them the trouble of constant hand watering. She'd insisted watering was one of the few pleasures in life. At last he'd agreed with her. He dug and wondered why Mrs. Haygood wore makeup today. What was special about today? When half a dozen flagstones were revealed, he stood up and pressed both clinched fists into his lower back. I have never been afraid of hard work, he thought. When I die, my children will remember me as a hard worker. He turned to his house. Mazelle was at the window, the sheer curtains spread, her palms blanched against the glass. She looked at him as if she didn't know him, and then she was gone. He put down the shovel, chose a stone twelve inches square between his feet, and then he beat the Earth with a big hammer.

❥❈

2:54 Mazelle's husband is digging a big hole right sprang in the middle of his garden. I'd say he's digging for China.

❥❈

"The things I don't know are unimportant to me," Mose said.

"Surely not. How do you know?" Howard asked. "Knowledge is the mother of invention."

"No it's not," Mose huffed. "Necessity is the mother of invention. See, you don't know everything."

"I have invented my life," Howard said.

"Which part is true and which is invented?"

"It's all true and I invented it."

"A life isn't invented. It's lived. Or maybe stolen, in your case."

"I don't think anyone before me lived a life like mine. I'm new. I could be patented."

"I don't know if I should believe anything you say."

"You will."

"Tell me what you think of this, Howard: metal detectors built into the soles of your shoes. You could cover vast amounts of ground, searching for old coins, or pipes or electrical wiring."

"An invention I don't need."

"That's the difference between us. I'm thinking what other people might want or need, and you think only of yourself."

"I was thinking, since I am now tired, that my last act would be to tear down my own house."

❥❈

2:57 I record it here. When my sister Freddis Opal came down for a visit last summer from her home in Ohio, I had her call several of my so called neighbors and ask them sly questions of their feelings toward me while I listened in on my extension phone. Of course, Freddis Opal is familiar with my situation. She acted as if she was calling from Ohio and was concerned about my health in order to obtain truthful responses. This was a very scientific process which cannot be questioned. Aura told her that she felt for me and that I must be very "lonely." Tradio sided with my son and said she should definitely be institutionalized. (This is my underlining.) Verda offered to keep Freddis Opal notified should any of my "symptoms" reoccur. I had a list with eleven other people I wanted Freddis Opal to call but at this point she refused to consider any more telephone calls. I may have mentioned this in an earlier tablet.

3:05 I have telephoned the telephone company, desiring them to check out my two phones for wire taps. They are to come tomorrow afternoon if not earlier. In the meantime, I must be circumspect about what I say.

3:10 Tradio and his man friend are unloading a buffet from their truck. First they unloaded boxes which I could not see into but which were obviously heavy. Tradio had to rent nice shoes and a decent suit for his daughter's wedding. I was told this by one of my pickers, Hilman Davis, who attended the wedding. She said my son wore a powder blue tuxedo and looked very happy. I may have mentioned this before.

3:15 Tradio's man friend, Mazelle and Nadine peeked like stupid idiots would when I checked my sign. Mazelle actually came out on her front porch, fluttered her hands like dust mops, and turned around and went back inside. If that's not a signal, I don't know what is.

Nadine changed into a light wool two-piece suit originally purchased at Neiman Marcus in the early sixties. To this she added short white gloves, a pillbox hat and low gray pumps that were a size too small. She unpinned the price tags from each of these items before stepping outside. She was on her way to Effie's to collect her share of the *Star-Telegram* bill. A businesslike presence was called for.

For a week now, upon stepping out her front door onto the porch, she'd gotten the impression that the Row was somehow shrinking. The street itself seemed narrower and strangely bowed, the houses smaller and closer together, as if the whole neighborhood had been squeezed into one of those convex anti-shoplifting mirrors at Montgomery Wards. The leaves that fell from the trees were tiny, the gravel nestled along the curb looked like a photo of a river delta taken from space. She paused to peer through the glass into the abandoned car in front of her house. How could anyone drive such a filthy car? When she leaned away the reflections of Carl's and Howard's houses filled the car window, hovering over her shoulders like vultures.

Mose and Howard were still lying in the bathtubs. It would be impolite not to say hello, but it occurred to her that this would be the first time in her life that she'd spoken to a man in a bathtub, much less two at once.

"Isn't there a better place to hold your conversation, gentlemen?" she asked.

"Take a bathtub, Nadine," Howard said.

"Now, goddamn it, Howard," Mose said.

"Thank you, no. I'm on my way to see Effie. Mose, Momma never would have appreciated the GD word."

"I'm sorry, Nadine. That's a fine-looking suit."

"You better watch out for Effie," Howard said. "There's no making friends with that goddamn woman. I used to be upset about that so-called commission she took, but you can tell her I'm over it. She can keep the money."

"Well, Howard, she owes me now, and I'm a different story."

Howard tapped the rim of his tub. "You're not your momma, Nadine. I knew your momma. Effie never would have considered letting a payment slip to your momma."

"Well, goddamn it, Howard, guess what? You're not my momma either. Mose here isn't my momma. Carl's not my momma. Tradio's not my momma either."

Nadine turned and walked away, but she heard the old Indian twist in his tub of leaves and whisper to Mose, "I'd do her too, wouldn't you? Still a fine solid thigh." Against her very will her gloved hand fell to her hip. She grasped Effie's doorknob firmly and turned. The door was locked. She rapped on the glass.

"Effie, I need to speak to you right now." Nadine looked to her left and saw the tips of Effie's fingers draw back, as if bitten, through the closed venetian blinds. "Effie, I will call my mother back from the grave itself to harass you if you do not open this door immediately."

"I'm busy," Effie yelled back.

"Right now!" The deadbolt clicked and Effie pulled the door open. "Thank you," Nadine said.

"You're welcome, Nadine. Come right in. You look so pretty today."

"One hundred and twelve-fifty, Effie. I'll take cash or check. If you don't want to be included in next month's ad you can say so, but I need you to pay me for this month's as it's already been in the paper."

"Nadine, I was just in the bathroom for a moment. Of course, I'll get your check right now."

"Now, Effie, if it comes back with a stop payment on it, I'm going to hit the roof. You know that, don't you?"

"I wouldn't do that to you, Nadine. I know you're the only friend I've got on the Row. We've got to watch out for each other. There's been a lot of strange activities and I do hope you're keeping an eye on it. My sales have been very poor lately."

"Effie, you run off your customers. You act like they've come to steal from you, rather than buy."

"I know I've had some problems but I've been taking my medicine regular and I'm all better now. Here's my check and it's as good as gold."

"You need to sign it there on the bottom."

"Oh, all right."

"Thank you, Effie."

"Your momma would have been proud of you, Nadine. The way you handle things. I miss her very much and Lord knows nobody loved her more than I did. I know she had many sadnesses but she's resting peaceful now. Every secret she asked me to keep, I've been faithful to."

"Yes, Effie. I need to get back to my shop now."

"Of course you do, dear. Watch your step. That old grass does grow. You can count on me."

3:22 Check #1022 to Nadine for $112.50 for September Startlegram advertisement. Paid in full. I warned Nadine of the goings on nearby and reminded her of the secrets I keep. I believe she took my advice about watching her step. Hair stiff as a brush poking from her nose. No one wants to admit that I have lived here longer than any other. It was me and then Nadine and her momma and then That Big Indian and then the Haygoods and Mazelle and her husband. Mrs. Martin arrived then, but she is dead at the present time. The corner house was the home of Mr. and Mrs. Killebrew, who both now reside in the Panther City Nursing Center. Then Mose. The Postlethwaites came next, and Verda and Havis, Tradio and Alice, and years later Aura and now this carpenter. In that exact order. They know what I know and then I know some more.

By the time Aura reached the toilet, the cramp was ebbing. She peed a patter, soughed away a whirl of gas and decided a soak in the tub was in order. The hot and cold water issued from separate faucets into the old tub, commingled, became something between, something average, something acceptable. Before stepping into the tub she thought about beeping Marshall to tell him about her pain, but then she realized if she didn't step into the water at that moment the opportunity, the perfect temperature, would be gone. The water embraced her body like a lover. She felt sensuous, ticklish. Only her face and the great peach thermometers of her nipples rose above the water's surface. She flexed her toes, reached down and spread her cheeks so the water could find its way there too. I'll stay here till Marshall finds me this evening, she thought. Aura brought her hands and arms from beneath her body to her stomach, having to do so one arm at a time because the tub was an especially tight fit lately. There, with her hands clasped over her yodeling belly button, her body floating a half-inch off the bottom of the tub, she closed her eyes and bobbed.

Her parents had been athletes: her mother a tennis player, her father a track star, both polished, supple, bronzed. She thought the only thing she'd inherited from them was their skin, its ability to stretch and to take color from the sun. But when she was eighteen, they revealed to her that she'd been adopted, a baby from the Edna Gladney Home, and so she lost even her skin. Her parents seemed to be greatly relieved with their revelation, as if their secret had been a great burden to exercise under. "We're not going to hide this from anyone now, Aura," they told her. "We're proud that you're adopted. Now you know why we never pressed you into sports. Our lifestyle wasn't something you could have possibly been prepared for, and we understood that." She loved her parents, and when they died within six months of each other, her mother from breast cancer, her father of a coronary, neither having reached forty, she too felt somewhat relieved that she'd been adopted. She wasn't their fault, and they weren't hers. They'd left her with enough money to start her business, buy a new car. Years after the funerals her parents' lawyer mailed her the deed to the house on Worth Row. He called it a "misplaced investment" and apologized. So she'd moved to the old house. It was too warm in the summer, too cold in the winter, but was the best location an antique dealer could hope for in Fort Worth at the time. She was accepted into a larger family, adopted again. Nadine's momma brought all of her neighbors by, one by one, to introduce themselves, even Howard, the old Indian, who rarely spoke and even then mumbled some language that was like a windblown branch beating against the side of a house. He'd sat on her sofa, holding his hat like a dead pet squirrel, and that was the last time she'd ever spoken to him. But Verda was a good friend, and Mrs. Haygood was a treasure, and the Postlethwaites were always asking her to go to the mall with them. All her neighbors were old, and she liked to think of herself as having a dozen parents on the block, even though she knew they all had their own children, and she'd never be like them.

She'd been listening to the water cool for ten, fifteen minutes, when there was the faintest sensation of something giving way, and then, sure as Marshall's large hands down along her inner thighs, she felt a warm gush of fluid, and her body shivered violently with the loss of heat.

➻✷

3:27 I have just called Channel 5 News and told them they could expect a big story soon on the south side of Fort Worth. When they asked for details, I gave my name as Verda because it was the only name I could come up with on such short notice. They said I should sure get back to them when I thought events were coming to a head. Verda is still not home. I suppose she is off with her daughter talking to Jesus again. She implies very often that Jesus will take care of me too, but I insisted He would have to prove it first before I invest much of my time. I am not so worried about dying as who will get my things. I once told Verda I thought it was far strange that Jesus talks to her a lot more than her husband ever did and then she told me she had forgiven me years ago and I said I hadn't meant to bring that up and she said, Well, I had, so she'd brought up the forgiveness. Then I said there was nothing to forgive me for as I didn't have a guilty bone in my body, that her conscience must be bothering her and she said how can you say that you slut I caught you with your mouth around my husband's fatherhood and I said just the one time. This was more than several years ago and we are now friends again and often trade antiques. But I know she still has it in for me. I am tired of her forgiving me, knowing it does her more good than me.

3:36 Mazelle's husband, I believe, is digging a swimming pool in the middle of his garden. That will mean less vegetables for all of us.

Verda couldn't understand where her husband and girls were. How long had she been lying on this floor? Her dogs were sniffing broken figurines. There was the decapitated head of General Washington. Martha lay on her side, looking at her husband's head approvingly. That's right: Havis was dead these ten years, just like the President. Orene lived in San Francisco and Alma lived across town, but today she was making a white cotton dress. Maybe she'll give it to me for my funeral, Verda thought. I'd like to go to heaven in a white dress. Her heart began to beat arrhythmically, like car tires thumping over the black scars in an old road. It hurt. She tried to lie as still as possible but the pain didn't seem to have anything to do with stillness, or for that matter with quietness, goodness or faith. She knew God had an iron fist, but why use it on her? I should have run my car into a tree, she thought, instead of grasping at time.

She bent her elbow and dropped her forearm and palm to the smooth cypress floor. The door was closer. If she opened it, even just an inch or two, Effie would see and come to check. Verda brushed Martha and two eyes out of her path and used her palms to drag her body a few inches across the floor. With the pain, her breath fell out of her mouth as if clotted. I'm not asking for anything, Jesus, she thought. I won't even think about you. I know I'm not valuable. She rested.

Her husband had died holding both his daughters' hands. That must have been nice. He deserved that, Verda thought. I'll see Havis soon. She'd shared a Hershey's chocolate bar with him on their first date. In the darkened movie theater, she'd slipped the foil-covered bar between her warm thighs, and held it tightly there for the first half of the movie. When she felt the bar become warm itself, malleable, she took it from beneath her skirt, letting him see her do this, and then slowly unfolded the wrapper and guided his finger into the smooth pool of melted chocolate. They took turns, dipping their fingers, bringing them back to their open mouths, sucking the sweetness from beneath their fingernails till they tasted their own skin's salt.

Verda reached out, pulled her body forward across the floor.

3:37 My phone has not rung in over two hours. My son said to me that I never appreciated his patience with me. Whatever that means.

3:39 My blinds were closed when I came back into my shop from my bedroom. I know I left them open. I made a thorough search behind all my showcases but found no one. Another instance of objects being moved without my permission.

Often merchandise has been moved from where I intentionally put it.

3:42 It is the time of day when shadows are cast between the houses along the Row making me think I see things which perhaps do not exist, they being only shadows. Of course were I devious this would be the exact time I'd pick to sneak between houses. Things always happen when I least expect them. For instance, much to my shock, I just discovered a layer of dust has descended upon my better things without my approval.

3:47 You would think Mose and That Big Indian would have exhausted the subject of Effie by now but apparently not!

The Postlethwaites were warming up for their quick march in front of the developer when a flock of five birds swooped down to the mall floor, then banked tightly upward and settled in a tree a few feet from them.

"They're still here," Arlen said, sitting on the low wall, reaching out with his taut fingers for his equally yearning toes. "I hope they never catch them."

The mall maintenance crew had been trying to trap the family of sparrows for over two years. Janice, the photo technician, told Louise they'd about given up. "Those birds are smart," Janice said. "They know this mall better than anyone." Still, it seemed unnatural to Louise, birds in a building, not to mention the trees.

"I wish they could catch them," Louise told Arlen. "It's not the way it's supposed to be. You shouldn't spend your whole life in one place. You know what Janice told me? That in the winter the birds move down to the south end of the mall by Neiman Marcus. It's the saddest thing I've ever heard."

"It's warm here, though," Arlen consoled her. "They get all those crumbs down at the food court. No predators."

"Janice said they found a baby bird once outside the Gap. It had flown into the display window and died. Poor little thing never knew it."

"That could have happened anywhere."

"Arlen, it's not supposed to be the same temperature twenty-four hours a day all your life long," Louise snapped.

"But that's why we come here. Because it's always the same," he said. "Do your stretches, Louise."

"I want to see that roll the man brought in a few minutes ago. Then we can start. He looked like he's been somewhere. I think Janice is about caught up to his roll of film."

"All right. I was thinking about getting a pretzel before we leave."

"Lot of good the walking does if you're eating extra pretzels."

"I'd give you half," he said.

"You've worked your way around it again," she said. "Now be quiet. Here they come."

The roll began with pictures of a dozen balloons floating out of a blue sky into the ground.

"It's another birthday party," Arlen said.

"Don't try to guess the end," Louise said. "Try not to figure it out."

Two photos of an older man standing next to a gravestone. His hand lay on top of the brown granite. A picture of a fancy speedboat behind a truck that was the same color. Three little girls hunched over a cake with five lit candles. The cake said MARCY.

"What'd I say?" Arlen asked.

There were two more photos of one of the little girls. In the first she was in the bathtub, the water up to her elbows, a party hat still on her head. She was laughing. In the last picture she was standing in a room in low light. She was standing on a small bed, naked, her hands gathered over and hiding her genitals. She was looking straight into the camera. There wasn't a recognizable emotion on her face. There was a final picture of a boat.

"All right, let's go," Louise said.

"This way, Louise," Arlen said.

"No, I'm going home now."

"Please, don't let that bother you."

"I'm old enough to make that decision if I want to. I want to go home. I don't want to exercise. Go home right now."

"We can still quick-march on the way," Arlen said. "We'll still get something out of it."

"I'm going to walk at my own pace," Louise said.

3:54 A woman just called (I picked up the phone on the third ring). I'll say she was in her early thirties. She asked if I carried any Fostoria in the American pattern and I said No, because people like that are hoping you'll say yes, and then will come to steal these items. I won't take the nails in my hands.

Dear Diary,

Tradio and I unloaded the truck this afternoon. Just a buffet, table and chairs, a few boxes of glassware, a trunk, and he began to breathe so heavily again. The twenty years' difference in our age is finally beginning to tell. I worry about him all the time now. Twice in a week he's forgotten to take his cholesterol medicine and so I've put a bottle of pills in the truck along with his nitro so we'll never be without it. He's having a nap now.

Today, I talked to him about hugging me, not just here in the house, but out in the front yard and when he knew two of his old neighbors were watching. I know it wasn't easy for him and it's a big step for his emotional health. It's easy for me. Who am I. But he's known throughout the antiques community and I know our relationship, even though it's been in the open for four years now, troubles him. He has a public image to maintain. He's a radio personality. But I know it's not just these things. He feels he's betrayed Alice by being true to himself. She never knew, although I can't help but think she did. He tells me they weren't always physically affectionate, at least not in the same way he is with me. I felt a little thrill of victory when he said that, but then I remembered that Alice was dead, dead of that old cancer, and I felt a little vain then, a little tramp. I know I'll always be second. You can't change what's come before. He won't apologize for loving Alice, and I don't expect him to. I just tell him his heart is enormous. He was able to live with and love a woman he felt no sexual attraction to. I tell him that's like a heterosexual man living with and loving someone who's gay. He sees the difference though, even though he never tries to deny it. I think he could live with his memory of Alice if it weren't for the memory of Effie. She's all the bad things Alice could have been, and what's more, all the things he feels Alice had a right to be. He still thinks he stole a life from her, used her as a place to hide. He's too hard a judge on himself. I wish I'd met him years earlier than I did. We'd be so much further along now.

I've called Susie and asked her to come see her old daddy and she promised she would. I asked her politely as I could about her and Michael. It's for the best. Every time Michael came over he talked about his mother, constantly peeping out the windows over at her house. Lord knows she was peeping right back at him. You'd think they'd blind each other with their peeping. I can't begin to fathom that relationship. I've stopped asking Tradio to broach that subject with Effie. I don't think she knows, because she and Michael never speak. I'm just so grateful that Susie has accepted her father's turn in life. It would have been so much harder for him if he lost her too. That man loves his daughter and grandson.

I've called Nadine to come look at this trunk full of old clothes we bought in Cleburne today. I think we can double our money easily. In the bottom of the trunk was a candy box with four or five old pieces of plated flatware. I think I'm just going to give them to Aura. She's been trying to keep her pregnancy a secret, as I've told you before Diary, but I can tell.

I'm going to make a Caesar salad for dinner tonight, with some garlic toast on the side. Pulse: 65. I am fifty years, three months, two days and fourteen hours old right now. My father died two years ago next week. I still have not received my October issue of *Antiques*. We have $11,462.58 in savings and praise be to God for it. Temperature: 65 degrees.

4:09 Street very quiet. Very unusual.

Mrs. Haygood knew it would come to this. She'd been putting it off for some thirty-four years, and with skill and some luck she'd been successful. She stood with her arms clasped to her own body, stood in the very center of her kitchen, and listened to the scraping of the shovel as if it were biting into her own skin. She crept to the bedroom door, and even though she was completely silent, she put her hand over her mouth. Her husband slept soundly, his mouth open, his fists clinched. There was a round stain on his pants that continued to spread slightly. She could pour a bottle of Clorox through his open lips. The kitchen clock was ticking too loudly. She moved to the window casing and looked directly across the garden at Mazelle in her window. She was watching her husband, who seemed to stand in a shell crater. Mrs. Haygood knew he stood in the rubble of their garden. When she looked back, Mazelle was gone. They never met each other's eyes. He struck the earth repeatedly. She imagined the hot dust of stone reaching his nostrils and urging him on. She wondered if she should start packing but then realized her clothes and bag were in the bedroom and she'd wake Mr. Haygood.

Suddenly, beyond the hammer's coming down on the stone, through the tended Saint Augustine grass, Mazelle was striding away. She had her purse in one hand, something else under her other arm. She's scurrying, Mrs. Haygood thought. She's not going to face it. The striking ceased. She turned from the vanishing Mazelle, back to the crater, and found it empty.

4:10 Mazelle's husband, digging in his garden, just fell straight through to hell. I knew it, I knew it. There one instant, gone the next, and Mazelle actually <u>running</u> down the street (Only one boob bouncing, poor thing). That's more like it. I ran out on my porch and yelled, Where's the fire, Mazelle? But she just kept on hurrying. She tried to take the corner too fast right in front of Nadine's house and bowled right up against a tree, legs spread up in the air and skirt over her head. Last time she opened her mailbox that wide moths flew out! Mose and That Big Indian sure took notice, both of them sitting up in their bathtubs.

4:16 Postlethwaites have come home. They must be pretty rich to shut down their shop on a Friday and take the whole day off. One day their daughter will come home and they'll be at the mall and never know she tried to contact them. It's a terrible thing when a family doesn't speak to one another. I wonder if their daughter is waiting for them to die the way my son counts the minutes till my death and his inheritance.

✽✦

For an entire hour Howard has gone on, Mose thought. He has talked for an hour about tearing down his own house, where he'll start, where he'll end. But now he is getting to the point and I'll be able to get out of this bathtub. I may need some help.

"I've gone into houses," Howard said, "knowing there were ghosts there. I knew when I tore those houses down, the ghosts wouldn't have anywhere to live. Each nail gripped for its life, and screamed when I tore it away from the lumber."

As Howard spoke, Mose came up with the idea for a new swizzle stick, one especially for iced tea served at restaurants. It would have a little sign on top that said, "Please don't top me up, I'm sugared just right." Get those formed in plastic, sell them by the gross to cafeterias. The lady with the cart would never have to interrupt a conversation to ask if you'd like more tea. I'm about to wet my pants from that glass of iced tea, he thought. He's still talking. I don't believe a word he says.

"A house is a living thing," Howard said. "It breathes. It has a past. I go in and I find phone numbers in pencil on the wall around a bare spot where the phone used to be. How do you think that makes me feel, to be the last person who sees those phone numbers? It makes me feel like an executioner. Children's measurements on a door casing, their names next to the numbers: Bobby, Theresa, Juan. Lots of times I put my crowbar behind that board and the board splinters into a dozen spears. The deep scratches in the bottom of a door that some dog or cat put there over the span of his life. All he wanted was to come in. Let me in. Worn spots in the linoleum, right in front of the old stove. How many pairs of shoes did she wear out standing there frying eggs and boiling oatmeal? The marks of a woman's feet. Bloodstains on a wood floor, vomit between the cracks, the sweet smell of old urine that waits to get deep inside your nostrils before it curdles. Then you're stuck with someone else's piss in your nose for the rest of the day. Dents in the plaster walls where a headboard knocked out the rhythm of children. It's difficult work, tearing down a house. I can't tell you how they try to hang together."

"Then why do you do it?"

"It's a living."

"But why tear down your own house?"

"Just to finish things. Just to round things off. I deserve it. Why should I let someone see the inside of my house once I'm gone?"

"You act like it would be a privilege for them, something special."

"I've always felt that way about other people's houses, such pleasure in walking through them, tearing them down."

"You said you felt like an executioner."

"Yes."

Mose frowned. "Are we through now? I think you're going to have to help me out of this tub. My knees have gone solid."

They both heard then the clapping of Mazelle's feet to the cracked sidewalk across the street, followed her with the slow turn of their heads.

"Where's the fire, Mazelle?" Effie yelled.

They turned to Effie, then back to Mazelle to watch her fall at the corner.

"You all right, Mazelle?" Mose yelled out.

She lifted one hand to them, a simple signal to stop, to come no farther, then she picked up her purse and five or six books she'd been carrying under her arm. She turned the corner and continued walking down Hemphill.

"There's more," Howard said, taking up where he'd left off. "I have a gift for you. A piece of business that won't do me any good after I'm gone. I want you to have it. I've been blackmailing Haygood and Mazelle. They pay me fifteen dollars a month for my silence, seven-fifty each, cash, every month, right there in the mailbox."

"What?"

"I know. It doesn't sound like a lot now, but thirty years ago it was good money, good pay for simply keeping my mouth shut. They asked me then how long they had to pay and I told them just as long as they didn't want their husband and wife to find out. Who'd have figured they'd want to keep a secret for so long? It's been a real windfall."

"But what have they done?"

"They deepened the dents in the walls of each other's houses."

"But why would they pay so long for something they did thirty years ago?"

"In part because they didn't want anyone to know. It's a secret. In part because they still do it."

"But how did you, how do you, know?" Mose asked.

"You see, you haven't been paying attention. It was just something I noticed. I'll tell Mazelle and Howard that when I die, they're to continue making the customary payments to you. Now that you know. I don't think they'll balk. I think they like paying. It's such a little bit of money these days. Every time they open my mailbox and slip in their envelopes, a five, two singles and two quarters in each envelope, it's like a little act of sex, like they're having sex with me too."

"It's disgusting," Mose said. "I want no part of it. I don't want their money. I don't want to have sex with Mazelle and Mr. Haygood."

"What if I set it up to be more? They might be willing to go up to ten dollars, maybe twelve-fifty each. But they're both retirees now. On a fixed income. They haven't got a lot."

"No, no, no," Mose said. "Leave me out of it. I don't want anything to do with it."

"There's been times when I needed an extra fifteen dollars. You shouldn't be so proud."

"I don't want to hear any more."

"But there's more."

4:22 I just went out to check my mailbox in case I'd missed anything this morning and heard That Big Indian say the word <u>Blackmail</u> and Mose gasp and then they stopped talking because they noticed I was walking real slow up my sidewalk. I came inside then shivering with fear. Well, just see how much they get out of me!

4:24 A blue car with rust spots turned around in Aura's driveway and left the Row without stopping at any shop. The driver intentionally did not look my way. Could have been a man or woman. Could have been anybody.

The dog Himself sprawled under the porch, holding down the ground with as much weight and body surface area as he could muster. Then rolled over, felt the dirt work its way up between each of the bones in his back. Work, ceaseless effort. With his nose in the air, the knowledge of approaching rain puddled at the back of his skull again, and a soft growl guttered in his throat. Rolling over a bit farther, he licked the tip of his burning penis, licked a pink itch on his hind foot where a toe had once been, licked the cool dirt beneath his muzzle. This was all comforting. His tongue was one of the few things that reminded him of his mother. Between his paws, an ant stumbled along on five legs. He watched the ant, his ears locked forward, and when the bug was a half inch from his paw he dipped and snapped, worked the shell back and forth between two teeth, then swallowed. The voices of the two men in the bathtubs were vaguely unsettling, as if the men were on the verge of chasing him. A car passed on the street, mesmerizing hubcaps, the noise of rubber on asphalt exactly the same as a squirrel's fear. But he knew they were not the same. Before he realized it, he was whining, the whine without reason, the abysmal anxiety of being alone under the porch. He barked. He watched Mazelle's husband digging, watched him there, there, there, not there, watched him drop through the Earth and then felt the same uneasiness of watching another, bigger dog dig up a bone he thought he'd hidden better. It was his bone.

4:26 I was here first. The rest of them are foreigners.

4:27 What Verda needs is some device to prohibit her pants from entering the cleavage of her rear, a butt bridge. I'll get Mose to work on that. That is an invention the world needs. I was in her bathroom once and found a big fat religion novel on her toilet tank. You could tell she turned down page corners by the creases they left. You could tell she read that book while she sat on the toilet, and you could tell how long each of her bowel movements were by how many pages she'd read. There was one forty page section without creases that must have been a particularly unpleasant episode! That novel was so fat it's going to take a bout of constipation to finish reading it.

4:31 The wind is blowing against my house.

4:32 It is possible Mazelle's husband has collapsed with a heart attack in his garden, since I still cannot see him. It serves him right. I should call 911. It will take forever if Mazelle has gone after the ambulance on foot.

❈

The boat is the body of Nadine: the keel her solid backbone, the ribs her ribs, the wineglass transom her bottom beneath cloth, the white sails her breasts, the varnished spars her tanned arms, and in the sheer strake aft of the stem, Carl gouged out her eyes. He used a spoon-shaped knife to deftly hollow out a socket in the cypress plank, paused from time to time to test-fit the eye, and finally worked it deep into the orbit with his thumb.

He found the eyes, the same hazel as Nadine's, in the soil beneath the flooring. He found also, beneath the flooring joists, that several of his piers were hollow cypress human thighs. One still retained its leather harness and brass buckles. When digging the pit to pour his lead keel he excavated a number of pins, cables and D rings, all oddly familiar because they were similar to marine fittings. At first he thought someone had built a boat here before, but when he found the eyes, and a partial set of ivory dentures, he realized he was digging up the remnants of orthopedic appliances. He'd then walked down to the Daughters of the Texas Republic historic marker on Nadine's property and read it for the first time. His house was already destroyed by that time, or, as he rationalized, was transformed.

He'd had no idea he was taking apart history. But he would have done the same even if he'd known. There was no way he could have afforded the house, cabinet shop, and the site and lumber to build a boat if each were a separate entity. And there was no way that Nadine would have simply moved across the street to live in a house exactly like her own, that looked back at her own. The break would have to be complete and traumatic.

Using a dollop of West Marine epoxy, Carl set Nadine's new eyes into the cypress looking forward. And then he kissed them.

The only thing that emanated from the past was his love for this woman. It was the only thing he remembered from yesterday. Everything else was new, was to come, was arriving. Nadine always *would* be his. He lived his life in expectation, in the anticipation and glory of almost now. He was a man holding a six-number lottery ticket. The first five numbers matched and in the moment that lived between the next-to-last number and the announcement of the last, he understood that suspense was more acceptable, more sustainable, than gratification, that it might be more exciting. Still, after the eyes were in place (the epoxy set almost immediately—no time to manipulate them) he began to loosen the clamps and bolts that held the four flimsy walls of his house to the roof in preparation for the arrival of the boat hauler. He'd decided to give Nadine an hour to make her decision: to go or stay. He'd kept the boat a secret from everyone so her decision wouldn't be tainted by advice. He'd lived the life of a recluse to save Nadine from her life as a recluse, trading his past for her future. She'd saved everything, he thought: her clothes, her mother, her memories, and there was now no room for anything else unless she did away with it all in a moment's catharsis, an acceptance of forgetting.

Carl himself cannot remember when he did not love Nadine.

4:33 Nadine, in a different dress than what she wore to my house, has closed her shop early and walked up to Tradio's. She should have figured out by now he has no interest in our kind. That he just teaches us how to dance. She's not her momma.

4:35 I called 911 but they took my report and filed it away as they said I could be prosecuted for calling them with false reports, saying my address shows up on their screen when I call and that I have called nine times in the past month, but I responded that each and every call was a dire emergency and it would be on their heads if Mazelle's husband died of a heart attack. I have done my duty and will turn my attention elsewhere.

4:39 Mose and That Big Indian still talking about me in those bathtubs. They could be touching themselves for all I know as I cannot see below their shoulders. It has just occurred to me that Nadine and Tradio have something in mind for Effie and are at this very moment discussing their plans. Nadine is ignorant of the secret I keep for her momma. Effie doesn't forget. Effie keeps notes.

4:45 I marched right over a little while ago and checked the front door at the Martins' house and found the door completely unlocked, an open invitation to thieves. I walked in but the house is as I suspected completely empty. I didn't see any use in the lightbulbs waiting to be smashed by vandals so I took all I could reach from their fixtures for safekeeping. Mose watched me all the way home as I had to lift my skirt to hold all the bulbs, revealing my knees. He must have been a gentleman because That Big Indian never turned around to peek.

Mose turned to Howard. The old Indian was working dead leaves between his hands, washing his hands, sweeping leaves like lather up his arms to his shoulders and wrinkled neck, letting them fall to his wide chest. Then, beyond the tub and the old man, he watched Effie waddle out of Mrs. Martin's empty house, her skirt gathered and held high, so that her jostling inner thighs, her clockwork knees and her plastic underwear all vied for his attention. He found himself unable to hear Howard speaking for several minutes, and finally came out of the miasma of his embarrassment by thinking about the technical requirements of a pair of pants whose zipper was continuous from the crotch to the belt loop in back. Then you wouldn't have to take them down to go number two. You'd have to sell matching zippered underwear. You'd sell the set, the underwear and the pants. You could wear legs from separate pairs of pants if you wanted too. Kids might like that. If you had a broken leg with a cast you wouldn't have to cut up a good pair of pants. But this reminded him of an earlier idea he'd had, one that Nadine and her mother had both reproached him for, his false cast invention. It had hinges on the inner leg, and snaps and buckles on the outer thigh and calf. Each cast would have to be custom made, but once the initial expense had been incurred the wearer had a cast for life, unless of course they gained weight. With a snap-on cast one might get bulkhead seats on airplanes, ringside seats at fights, special placement at concerts. Then, when the cast was no longer needed, it could be used as a suitcase. Nadine and her mother had questioned its morality and so Mose had only built the one working model.

He couldn't think where he'd be without the influence of Nadine's mother. In prison, probably, the result of some invention or course of action of which he'd never understood the complete moral implications. He was no different from Howard, really, except that he'd accepted, relied upon, a good woman's guidance. For a moment he missed Nadine's mother intensely, as if she were his own mother and not the great love of his life. As old as he was, he found himself questioning whether the things he remembered about her were true, or were only sterile constructions built in the vacuum of his radio tube mind. He could recall no impurities in her formula.

Howard touched his arm, and Mose drew it back with the action of a lever and hinge.

"What?" Mose asked.

"You're drifting again."

"I'm sorry," Mose said. Howard's face, Mose thought, was a face that moved away in all directions from its nose. The corners of the mouth turned down, the eyebrows pulled away like accents over eyes that seemed to be on the verge of spurting from their sockets. Even the shaved hair of his mustache and beard radiated from the nostrils, the apparent aftermath of a hurricane-force sneeze. The nose itself, ostracized, remained in some way haughty and proud, as if it were too good for the face attempting to abandon it.

"You look at my face as if you think I stole it," Howard said.

"I'm not accusing you of anything."

"It's my face," Howard said.

"OK."

"I've lived with it for eighty-three years and it's done all right by me."

"You were born with it. You don't have to apologize."

"I'm not apologizing."

Mose ducked. Howard's voice seemed to fall out of the sky like gravel dropping on a tin roof, gathering in iron furrows, gargling down copper gutters, ravishing below a galvanized bucket. "Well," Mose ventured, "you can't be proud of your face either, because you were born with it. You had no say. I only say this because some people are proud of their faces."

"I just want you to stop looking at me. Stop trying to take me apart."

"I don't want to know what you're made of," Mose said.

"Sure you do. I'm the man who made Nadine's momma lose her language. Her breasts farted, spit sweat up into our faces. Then she got fat so I left the door locked at night. She used to lie on my porch and cry, an hour, two hours, till the light began to come and she'd walk back across the street, afraid Nadine would wake up and miss her. I think of her often now, how nice it was to have her offer ways I'd never thought of. Of course, this was after Nadine's father died. I am proud to say I've never screwed another man's wife, put myself in that vulnerable position. I'd have hated to give up my blackmail money to another blackmailer."

By this time Mose was falling over the rim of his bathtub. He had to spread his legs, work himself back up on his knees, before he could fall over into Howard's tub. He fell and flailed, his first swing missing and landing on the porcelain, but his knee landed in Howard's midsection so that hot vapors issued from the Indian's open mouth and Mose breathed in, feeding on the air that was once inside Nadine's momma. As Howard fought him off, his great hands encircling Mose's wrists, the old Indian said, "That's more like it. That's more like it. Now you care."

Mose began to cry, and tried to pull free, but finally he collapsed on the broad chest beneath him and lay there as Nadine's momma once had, and then through clinched teeth wheezed, "You've gone too far."

"No," Howard said, "we're not there yet."

4:51 Tradio traded Effie in on a man.

4:52 Aura has a face like an oven door and plainly there's nothing cooking behind it. My sign needs adjustment. There's a spoon she has I'd like to call mine. Marshall might give it to me if I were to ask. If Aura weren't around. I guess she is pleased with her position as the <u>sweetheart</u> of the neighborhood, everybody's special friend. The truck Marshall drives is owned by the company he works for, not him. She keeps her house like the bottom of a well, perfect habitat for a Walrus. I've seen her and Marshall do it, and would have seen more if my arches hadn't cramped. That's all this neighborhood needs is a little kid running from door to door soliciting.

5:00 Time for the news.

5:02 At the commercial break I just by merest chance saw Mose getting <u>out</u> of That Big Indian's bathtub, and That Big Indian still in it! The man friend disease is catching! I can't think of anyone to call, and hardly want to go back to the TV. In the middle of the street! I hope Mose isn't being forced upon. I should go out and clap my hands to startle them. I can't keep my hand from going up to cover my open mouth. Oh, Oh, Oh! That I have to record such things! It makes me want to take a bath!

⋙⋘

Nadine wore a pale green sleeveless flapper dress, cropped at the knees, sequined in gold at the waistline, Paris label. Her headband was covered in rhinestones. A heavy metal-beaded purse hung on a long chain from her bare shoulder. She smelled Mazelle's perfume loitering in the air as she walked up the sidewalk, her perfume and another, thicker odor that she couldn't recognize.

Arthur met her at the screen door. "Where did you get that outfit? You're a goddess."

"One of my buyers brought it by yesterday. She bought it at a yard sale in Ridglea. I'm going to keep it." Nadine picked at the dress hem and pulled it taut on both sides.

"You don't have any choice. Of course, you'll keep it. Who would it look better on? No one. Come on in, but be quiet, Tradio's having a nap. He worked so hard today."

"How is he?" Nadine whispered.

"Always tired. You know. It wears him out, having to be nice to everybody, to always be on parade as a celebrity. He's getting too old for it."

"He's lucky to have you, Arthur."

"No he's not. I'm lucky to have him."

"I always felt the same way about Momma."

Arthur thought, Well, it's really not the same thing, but I'll let it pass. I know what she means. "I'm sorry I came so late to the Row that I couldn't know her, Nadine."

"Well, you would have adored her. Everyone did. But look here." She snapped open her purse. "Look what I've brought you." She held up a small porcelain blackbird, its head thrown back and its yellow beak bellowing at the sky.

"A Pie Bird," Arthur squeaked, and couldn't keep from reaching out and snatching it from Nadine's hands.

"It was Momma's. I wanted you to have it. It has that little collar to support the pastry. When I was a kid, I'd sit in front of the oven door to watch the steam pour out of that little bird's mouth. She called it a pie vent. Momma made such good pies. She never would tell me her chocolate pie receipt. I used to try to get her to write it down and put it somewhere safe, but she never would. I think it had something to do with a touch of almond extract."

"Oh, Nadine. Thank you. I'll treasure it."

"How many does that make now?"

"One hundred and eighty-eight. You'd think I'd have them all but they keep turning up, just like this little fellow. Look at his little yellow beak. I'd say he's from the early twenties. Nobody worries about their pies boiling over anymore. Why do you think that is?"

"Tinfoil," Nadine said.

Arthur paused, his mouth sewn shut. "I've never thought of it that way before. You're right. That's so unsettling. They stopped making Pie Birds because of tinfoil. It doesn't seem like a fair replacement. Oh Lord, why do we save old things, Nadine? Why do we collect these old precious things?"

"I don't have a one-word answer for that one, Arthur."

Arthur carried the bird back into the bedroom, with Nadine following like a student. He placed it on a specially constructed shelf, along with the one hundred and eighty-seven other Pie Birds, a silent chorus of steam, a whole flock waiting to be fed.

"There," Arthur said quietly. "He's safe now."

"It's unnerving," Nadine whispered, "all those open mouths." Tradio lay sprawled on the unmade bed, his mouth open, his arm over his eyes. Nadine could count the fillings in his yellowed teeth, and thought of the uneasiness Tradio would experience chewing on a wad of tinfoil.

Arthur crooked his finger and led Nadine back into the shop. "If you'll just help me with this," he whispered. They carried a trunk out the front door to the porch, setting it down between two pressed steel chairs. "We bought this at a farm outside Joshua this morning. I think we'll more than double our money on the trunk, so I thought maybe you could sell the contents and maybe give Tradio and me twenty-five percent?"

Arthur lifted the domed lid. Inside, in a choke of wrinkles, in an entangling odor of dust, were the fifty-year-old white linens and underthings of a middle-aged woman. Nadine had gone through the discarded clothes of so many estates that she thought she could tell not only the age of the person when they wore the items but also their state of mind. Who'd wear a blouse like that if they weren't desperate in some way? Would a man sport such a tie if he didn't feel inadequate?

"It all needs to be washed and pressed, of course," Arthur said. "This tablecloth must be eight feet long and four wide, but there's a stain on one end."

"Wine maybe," Nadine said.

"All that's left of that party," Arthur said.

"Look at these table linens. Each one is embroidered on the corner."

"They're nice but there's only three of them."

Nadine drew a long slip from the trunk by the straps, standing up as she pulled, as if she were rising from the trunk too. "I love these old things. Back when silk meant something."

"Oh, there's a stain on it too, Nadine." The slip curled in the wind, subsided. Halfway down its length, in the shape of the Red Sea, an old bloodstain ebbed. Nadine held the slip higher, turned it to the evening light.

"I'm pretty good with stains," she said. She dropped the slip over one arm, swung it up, caught it with her free hand and doubled it over, folded it a third time and set it aside. No one could see the stain now. It was slightly embarrassing.

"Look at these," Arthur said. "Fifty-year-old dishrags."

"Momma used to have some just like these, but in red," Nadine said. "I was scared to death of them."

"Why were you scared of a dishrag?"

"Didn't your mother ever give you a dishrag whupping?"

"Well, no," Arthur said, his hands momentarily caught in the clouds of loose clothes. "What's a dishrag whupping?"

"Well, Momma, and everybody's momma the way I remember it, used to work in the kitchen and around the house with at least one and sometimes two dishrags draped over their shoulder. If you crossed her, she'd snatch, first thing, that dishrag, and sometimes it was wet, and start whupping you with it. It stung. If you were across the room, she'd ball it up and throw it at you. She'd chase me around and around the kitchen table, that dishrag popping and flinging spray. Last dishrag whupping I got I was seventeen. Momma told me she'd signed me up for a year of school in Paris and I said flat out that I wasn't going. The hell you say, she said, and then those dishrags were popping all around my head. That was the last one I ever received, but I went to Paris. It was silly to argue with Momma and I knew that. Of course, I loved Paris once I arrived."

"I've never been to Paris," Arthur sighed.

"If you ever decide to go, I still have all my maps and brochures and pamphlets, and you're welcome to use them. They're more than thirty years old now, but I doubt if Paris has changed much. They're not going to move Notre Dame or the Seine. Some things don't change."

Nadine looked up from the old clothes, stared out into the street. Arthur watched her gaze go glassy, her fingers slacken. She was such a pretty woman, he thought. The skin along her jaw was still firm, her lips weren't weathered. But she was wearing too much makeup around her eyes. She must be trying to hide something.

"What's in Nadine's closet?" Arthur asked softly.

"What?"

"What are you thinking about?"

"Oh, I don't know. I see a customer on the Row anymore and it's like seeing an alien from another planet."

"Tradio wants us to find another place to set up shop, Nadine."

"Oh, I hope you don't leave. I'd miss y'all so much."

"I've tried to talk him out of it and we've compromised. Twice a month we're going to load up the truck and set up at Canton and Grapevine. We'll be away from the Row for two weekends a month. They say you can do pretty well at the flea markets."

"But there's all that loading and unloading and working out in the weather."

"I know. But there's two of us and that makes it easier."

"I suppose it does."

"Nadine, why won't you take Carl to your heart? It's plain he thinks the world of you."

"Arthur, you're the only man in the world who'd say something like that to me."

"I'm your friend, Nadine."

"I haven't lived with anybody since Momma died. I don't know if I'd like it again. Carl is a sweet nothing of a man. He loves me far more than I do myself. He's out of proportion. Look at that flagpole he mounted today. No sense of scale. Its lines are completely at odds with his house. I couldn't live with so much sawdust."

"Love accepts contradictions, Nadine. You wouldn't believe what I have to put up with. Tradio is a man unable to demonstrate affection. You know how I like to hug. My Aunt Marfa says I am by far the best hugger in our family. And Tradio doesn't know the meaning of the word. He hugs the way a pair of pliers do."

"I'll hug you, Arthur."

"I know you will, sweetie, but it's not the same thing, if you know what I mean."

"Oh, Arthur, I'd like to get half a dozen letters today that all begin with the words 'Please find enclosed.' I love that phrase. It must be as old as Fort Worth. It wouldn't have to be money that was enclosed. Perhaps something I've lost that someone's returning, or a pressed flower, or a key to a room in a town I've never heard of."

The mail's already come today, Nadine, Arthur thought.

5:05 Nadine was welcomed into Tradio's house by his man friend. Of course, it's been several years since I was in there and I'd hate to see what's been done to Alice's nice decorating.

5:05 Nadine and Tradio's man friend are pawing through something in a trunk. I can't hear what they are saying, but it is plain from here that Nadine has too much makeup on her eyes and mouth. It makes her nose look like it wandered onto her face. Makeup won't do anything for Tradio's man friend, I can tell her.

5:05 I was just called by a woman who said she was in my shop a week ago and saw my Wedgwood Powder Box. She wanted to know if my firm price really meant firm, in other words, would I take any less. I told her firm was a four letter word that began with an F and I meant it when I said it. She hung up about one split second before I did.

5:05 My clock is broke.

5:16 Everybody knows I wear a wig.

Fighting the knowledge of pregnancy, ignoring the thick issue of mucus and palest blood that hung immobile in her bathwater, Aura imagined cancer, seasickness, kidney failure, a diseased gallbladder, a rupturing appendix. She left her phone number dangling on Marshall's hip. She mouthed the oval sound of her mother's name, but instinctively understood that this was something she couldn't help with, that it was something she never knew. She skidded down the precipice on the far side of another pain, then patted herself and the phone dry. The sheets of her bed were so cold. Nothing seemed to be coming together. Each of her breaths sounded as if it were from a different person. Her thick legs didn't match. She slid her sweating palms across her slick belly and found it not symmetrical but misshapen, as lumpy as a cantaloupe crated under the weight of a thousand other cantaloupes. She found that her belly button was no longer tufted, that it had become bulbous, like a seed about to burst. She imagined a thick green stem erupting from her stomach. As another pain grew, as it twined around the length of her backbone and worked its way toward the light through the narrow passages of her intestines, Aura understood that something inside was coming out. She tried with all her might to keep it in. She refused to breathe, clinched her legs, did not hear, feel or taste. It could not happen without her. She tried to match pain with her conviction of ignorance. And failed. Tears brimmed in her eyes as the contraction drew her knees vainly toward her chin. What was cold in her rolled to warmth. Her opinion turned a hundred and eighty degrees: she wanted it out. But now it wouldn't come. She compressed, contracted every muscle she had control over and screamed. As the pain subsided once again, and the warmth receded to a chill, Aura heard the tentative knocking of a customer on her shop door. Someone has come to match a silver spoon, she thought. Then it was all clear to her: someone wants in, something wants out, an exchange. All she had to do was answer the door.

5:17 Mr. Postlethwaite is watering his front yard. Looks like he is down in the knees. One more day has passed without his daughter coming home and everyone knows why.

5:19 Car still parked—three days now—in front of Nadine's. I'll do my best not to satisfy her by asking.

5:25 Harold Taft says rain and he should know.

5:26 No sign of a police car all day long. Our neighborhood is completely unprotected. I will turn my sign around in three minutes, no matter how many customers are marching up my sidewalk. Business hours are business hours. I have a life of my own to live. Some customers don't understand that we live in our shops and must have time to ourselves.

5:29 Tradio's man friend and Nadine are still talking about me on Tradio's front porch. They glance my way in a very suspicious manner every few minutes. It's almost more than I can stand. It's possible they've killed Tradio in a plot to inherit all his things, as I haven't seen him since he came home. He usually checks his mail as soon as he comes home and he hasn't done so yet.

Every ten or fifteen minutes Verda gathered the strength to pull herself a bit closer to the door. It was only three feet away now. The blood on her temple had become crusty, but the pain in her chest and shoulder was still liquid, an acid sloshing through her body as she lurched across the floor. In the valleys between peaks of pain she heard footsteps pass on the sidewalk in front of her shop. The first person's steps were a lizard's skittering, the second a careful, moderate pace, a lesson from God. She yelled at both passings but her dogs' barking swallowed her cries. Still, she was able to forgive her babies. They were only protecting her.

She saw how dirty her floor was. Her shallow breath blew dust a few inches away from her face. Strange, how dust tumbled. She'd never noticed this before. The leg of a ballerina figurine lay against the base of the door, its pink foot still pointing. It reminded her of her husband. I'll die, Verda thought, and Effie won't return the plate I took her that fish on. I'll die and she'll keep my plate. She'll throw out the tinfoil the fish was covered with, and she knows I save my tinfoil. It's so expensive. Verda thought of writing a note to her daughters in the dust of the floor. EFFIE AND YOUR FATHER. But that was a secret they didn't deserve to know. They didn't deserve that old pain. It was separate from them. Their father didn't deserve that legacy. Jesus would make everything even. And as for Effie, it was hard to stay mad at a person for something she'd had in her mouth fifteen years ago, even if it was your husband's penis. Still, she knows I save my tinfoil. But if I can just get to the door, she'll be the one who saves me. If I hadn't been so greedy. If I'd lowered my prices more, the way Nadine and her momma told me. Then all these broken sweethearts might have sold long ago. I'd have saved their little lives if I hadn't been so greedy. I shouldn't have held Havis so close. Orene wouldn't live in California now if I hadn't tried to keep her at home. Alma wouldn't tell me it takes all day to make a white dress. I've been selfish with Jesus too. I keep telling Him how much I love Him and He just stays away. There is a kind of light coming through my window.

❧❦

5:33 I know that Verda is trying to make me jealous, staying out all day with her daughter. As I was turning around my sign, her awful dogs barked at me through her front window. I have often thought of stomping on both their pitiful necks. If there's anything I hate it's a dog that yaps without anything to say.

5:36 I have put my cash drawer in its secret hiding place known only to me and my tablet (Under board in closet).

5:37 Nadine on her way home with an armload of dirty laundry. What a woman will do for male company of any sort.

When Mazelle fell, she realized, looking back at the crack in the sidewalk, that a tree had grown there thirty years earlier. The tree was long gone but the hump and break in the sidewalk remained. The root of a tree long dead had tripped her. It didn't seem fair. She looked down at her knee. A round scrape oozed blood and a clear fluid. It reminded her of her children's school lunches. They complained that their apples and oranges sat on their peanut butter and jelly sandwiches all morning in the bag. By lunchtime their sandwiches had a jelly bruise working up through the bread. So she'd bought each of them compartmentalized metal lunch boxes. Her knee looked like a jelly bruise. What would her children think? They'd think she'd made another mistake.

When she saw her husband digging over the cistern, saw his curiosity and determination in the face of stone, she knew her world was collapsing. She'd envisioned the moment for so many years that now it seemed rather unsportsmanlike that she had to live it as well. She'd turned away from the window, walked out the front door to her porch. Then her hands seemed to take flight, to leave the nest like fledglings. Her fingers fluttered on the air, swooned, then caught on an updraft that came up the porch steps. She thought, I need something to carry. She went back to the window, pressed her palms to the glass. He was still digging. She didn't want to live with a man from whom she had nothing to hide. She wouldn't be like Mrs. Haygood, who wore the wet weight of her marriage like a dishrag draped over the neck of a kitchen faucet. Mazelle stood in the middle of her shop, surrounded by books. So many of them were unread. Every one of them had a secret but her. As she moved back through her house toward the front door she gathered up an armful of books. Now that she no longer had a secret of her own, now that she and her husband shared nothing, she'd once again need something to read.

Effie yelled at her as she skipped away. Verda's dogs barked. When she fell on the hummock of concrete giving her knee the jelly bruise, Mose called her name. Two blocks farther away it occurred to her that she'd forgotten her car. Her whole body fluttered then, like a weathered scrap of paper tearing free from the world. She turned around to see where she'd come from, but every direction seemed unfamiliar. What was that noise of a shovel scraping stone? There were books in her hands: a geography text, two novels named after states, a diet manual.

5:39 I can't help what I know. I am a bird of knowledge. The time Mrs. Postlethwaite hit me with her cane. My lawyer said if I had not been in her yard I could have surely sued. She was only using a cane for a short time and took this opportunity to use it as a weapon against me. I was severely bruised. See my account for July 25th or thereabouts, 1977. Very few believe me because I'm old, but the truth can't be replaced, no matter who tells it. My upper leg was severely bruised. See my account. Just like your husband, I guess, I told her. She raised her cane a second time and I decided to leave. Needless to say words don't often pass between us in the recent past.

5:45 Very little action down at Mazelle's.

※

After watering the yard, Mr. Postlethwaite knocked on Aura's door, but she didn't answer. He waited for a moment longer, putting off the moment when he'd step back inside his own house. Mrs. Postlethwaite would be in her mood for at least an hour and there was nothing he could say to draw her from it, but he knew he couldn't stop himself from trying. He walked back across the yard to his front door, passed through the dark shop and into the bedroom. She was still sitting in her recliner, where she'd composed herself into an art deco figurine by crossing her legs and raising her arms above her head, where her hands grasped the top of the chair. He could not stop himself from speaking.

"Maybe losing Margaret made our marriage stronger: the way the loss of one arm makes the other stronger, or the loss of sight makes hearing more acute."

"What a stupid thing to say," she said. "I can't believe it's been twelve years now."

"Why do you have to bring it up now? Can't you let it rest?"

"Arlen, we've been twenty years deciding if we want muntins in these windows, whether we want to see the world in one piece or four or twelve. Why shouldn't it take us twelve years to discover our only daughter, our only child, is gone? We've lost something we can't replace."

"At what age was I supposed to stop touching her? I gave her baths from the time she came home from the hospital, didn't I?"

"I'm not accusing you. I've stayed, haven't I? I just want to grieve. I want to say that it wasn't fair: having to choose between my husband and my daughter. I look outside and the street seems so empty."

"That was Margaret who forced that decision on you. It wasn't me."

"I'm not accusing you."

"I'll deny it again, though. Because you make me feel I have to." He stood in front of the windows without muntins. "Yes, I put her to bed. Yes, I sat on the bed with her. I told her good night. I told her stories. I told her I loved her. I never, never, put my hand on her private parts. She can say it's so a thousand times and I'll deny it a thousand times."

"She doesn't say it anymore. She stopped saying it a long time ago. She stopped saying everything."

"Louise, it never made sense: when she's twenty-five years old she remembers something that happened to her once or twice when she was five years old?"

"It was repressed. She didn't want to think about it. I understand that now. I don't like to think about it either."

"She was the one who said you had to believe her or believe me. She was the one who said there was no middle ground, no compromise, that I was a child molester, and that if you stayed with me you condoned the actions of a child molester. She was the one who cut us off."

"Why would she have done that if she wasn't sure?"

"I believe she believes what she remembers. But she's wrong in her memory and wrong in her belief. She's made the horrific mistake of renouncing her parents. She couldn't forgive me and I've lost interest in forgiving her."

"Stop talking like that," Louise cried. "I chose you."

"You'll never know, Louise, whether I touched her or not."

"I do know. I believe you."

"I can't believe that I'm still suffering for something I allegedly did more than thirty years ago."

"I believe you. But you have to let me grieve every once in a while." She brought her arms down and wiped the tears from her face.

"She's hurt us far more than we could have ever hurt her."

"Before she left, when she was waiting for me to decide, she said she couldn't trust anyone anymore, because of what she remembered. When I decided to stay with you, I imagine her faith was resolved. She hurt too. At least you and I have each other."

"She's probably married by now, Louise. She probably has children of her own. Maybe she'll do a better job. She's not alone. That's probably why she's never come home. She wouldn't want me to be with them."

"It's disgusting. You're a good man."

"I never touched her that way, Louise. But I'll always feel dirty because she said I did. I loved my baby daughter. I feel guilty when any of the neighbors' grandkids say hello to me. Simply because I'm accused. I could never move away from this street because it would be admitting my guilt. So I stand out there and water my grass knowing the neighborhood is watching, and I know they're thinking I'm either guilty or I'm not. It's as simple as that. I'm either guilty or I'm not. It almost doesn't matter what I think. What's more important is what you think, what Effie thinks, what Mose thinks."

"I just want to sit here in my chair for a while, Arlen," Louise said.

5:47 Bowel movement. Nothing special.

5:49 Here comes Tradio. He thinks I don't have a gun.

How did this come to be, that you owe someone you haven't talked to in four years, that you not only owe them but have to apologize because other people think it's good for your health? Her relationship with her son is none of my business.

Tradio knocked on Effie's door.

Even if he did marry my daughter. Not my fault he doesn't

speak to her and doesn't let the grandson speak to her even if it's not right. But there's been the whole week now with her not knowing and I'm standing here. She will think I've come court-ing and it serves me right.

Effie pulled her hair behind her ears and opened the door.

"Hello, Effie. It's me."

"Long time no see," Effie said.

"You've been taking speech lessons from Howard," Tradio said, and left his lips at that juncture between smile and apology.

Effie held her door at her cheek. The hand at her side still held an unsharpened pencil. "You've interrupted me," she said.

"Oh, I'm sorry. Should I come back? Are you on the phone?"

"I just never thought you'd cross that street again. I had a way of thinking and you've interrupted me."

"Well, Effie, there's some things I need to tell you, things you should know. Can you come out here and sit on the porch?"

"Everybody will be able to see," Effie said.

"That's all right."

They took seats in white wicker chairs. I've sat in these chairs before, Tradio thought. He groaned as he sat down.

"We're getting old," Effie said.

"Well, I don't know about you, but I arrived and set up house a long time ago."

"I heard you on the radio today. I listen every day except Wednesday. I can't get that Weatherford station."

"I didn't know that, Effie."

"Well, I'm in the business. There might be something I want to buy."

"Effie, Arthur thinks I need to apologize for—"

"Who's Arthur?"

Tradio paused. He took his hands out of his pants pockets and clasped them. "Well, Effie, he's that man who lives across the street with me. He's been there for four years now. I'm sorry you haven't learned his name."

"I've learned a lot of things in my life," she said, and pushed her hair back over her ears. "I run out of room for learning new things a while back."

"Arthur is a good fellow, Effie. He'd be your best friend, just like he is everybody's, if you'd only let him."

"Like me and Alice?"

"I know you've said that to cut me, but it's true. He'd be just as good a friend to you as Alice was."

"It wouldn't have made a difference, the fact that my son was married to your daughter. We could have married. There wasn't blood between us."

"That wasn't why, Effie."

"I know there would have been tensions."

"That wasn't why. I wasn't in love, Effie. You wouldn't have wanted somebody who wasn't in love."

"You taught me how to dance."

"I know."

"That wasn't fair."

"I know that now. I've come to apologize."

"How could a person be so stupid as to teach another person how to dance?"

"I wasn't stupid, Effie. I was lonely and afraid."

"You traded me in on a little man."

"I used you, Effie. It's a fact. And I've come to apologize."

"Who's going to apologize to Alice? How many times she came to my house in tears because she had no understanding of your ways. She could have had a real life with a real man."

"I loved Alice. She knew that."

"You deceived a person for their entire life."

"That's for me to live with. I don't need you to keep an account of it. I've crossed the street to correct a fault. We only accompanied each other for that few months. I need you to let me live in peace, to stop watching me all the time, stop peeking."

"When Alice died she gave me her eyes," Effie said. "It's not just me."

The old wicker chair swayed just enough to accept Tradio's swoon. He let his own eyes close, let the air escape from his open mouth. You're next, Caller. What do you have to sell? He drew back the crumpled brown skin of his eyelids.

"Effie, you don't know so I've come to tell you: Michael and Susie have been separated for six months now, and last week they were finally divorced. David is living with Susie. I expect she'll let him visit you now, now that your son doesn't have any say. That's what I've come to tell you."

"Divorced because you did me wrong? Divorced because you have a man friend?" Effie said these things listlessly, as if they were the last place in the house she'd look for something she'd lost.

"It was between them, Effie. I've taken my daughter's side because she's my daughter."

"Why hasn't he come home?"

"Who?" Tradio asked.

"My son."

"He'll never come home, Effie. But you'll be able to see David now. I like him a lot. He's a good boy. We're both his grand-parents. We'll have him to share."

"I never had to live alone till my husband died," Effie said. "We never would have gotten a divorce."

Tradio watched shadows gather in the folds of Effie's face, the relentless onslaught of evening. For minutes they dissolved into the silence of their porch chairs. I don't know what to do if we can't apologize and start over, Tradio thought. There's no time for time. This is my wife's old friend. They've come to look like each other.

"I was thinking I might come over and mow your lawn," he said, then realized he'd said this aloud.

✦✦

6:09

6:13

✦✦

Mrs. Haygood couldn't hold her tongue. When Mazelle's husband disappeared from the face of the Earth, she yelped. Her husband snuffled in his sleep and cupped his hand over his crotch protectively. She skipped by the bed without breathing and arrived in the toy shop as if she'd been blown in accidentally. She scanned the room quickly, quite certain of the possibility that Mr. Haygood had arrived there before her, even though she'd just passed him. The carpet runner behind the counter was worn threadbare over the handle beneath it. The bronze D ring in the trapdoor had a lustrous patina from three decades of consistent use. She lifted the heavy door, let it rest gently against the counter and then hurried down the stairs. A shaft of light slanted across the cistern. Mazelle's husband lay in its penumbra on the bed, his body oddly jumbled. What she first thought were throw pillows were chunks of limestone. The rocks had fallen in on the mattress and he'd bounced among them. She heard a whimper, looked up at the bright hole in the darkness and saw the dog.

"It's OK," she whispered.

She lifted a stone from Mazelle's husband's chest and he coughed. She moved another rock from beneath his thigh. There was dirt and stone dust on his face until she blew lightly across his eyelids and lips.

"You've fallen," she told him. "The ceiling gave way."

"Oh, Lord."

"Do you think you've broken anything?" She ran her hands

along his arms. "Do you understand when I tell you you've fallen?"

"Yes," he answered. "Fallen into where?" He lifted his head. She didn't answer. "How did you get down here?" He looked up into the pale blue sky, at the dust still swirling down, at the head of the stray dog. He'd never had a dog look at him with this much interest. "Mrs. Haygood?"

"I came down the stairs," she said.

"What stairs?"

"The stairs that lead down from Mr. Haygood's toy shop."

"Why didn't you just tell me y'all had a cellar? I wouldn't have broken into it."

"Sit up."

He rolled over and sat on Mr. Haygood's side of the bed. "Why do you keep a bed down here? Why didn't you tell me you had a cellar under the garden? We could have kept potatoes here."

"I'm not supposed to know about it," she said. "Are you all right?"

"Yes, yes, I'm fine. I think I had the wind knocked out of me. What does it mean, Mrs. Haygood?"

"Mr. Haygood used this place to carry on an affair."

The tracks of Mazelle's husband's mind crossed. The only thing he could think to say was "I'm sorry."

"I wish you hadn't been so obstinate about digging," she said.

"I would have covered it back over if you'd only told me," he whispered. "I didn't know. How long ago was it?"

"What?"

"The affair."

"An hour or two," she said.

"What?"

"If you'd been much earlier you would have ended up in bed with them."

"Where are they now?"

"Mr. Haygood is having a nap. He always does, afterwards. She's gone."

"You know her?"

"Yes."

"You knew about the affair and you let it go on?"

"Yes."

"For how long?"

"About thirty-four years."

Mazelle's husband put his hand over the lower half of his face. He stood up and walked through the shaft of light to the bottom of the steps that led to Mr. Haygood's shop. He could see toys at the top of the stairs. He turned back to Mrs. Haygood. The cylinder of light, with the silhouette of the dog's head at its base, obscured the far end of the room. He walked through the light, felt its warmth, and eased into the darkness beyond. He paused to allow his eyes to adjust. The last few steps of another flight of stairs were at his feet. They turned up into a deeper darkness.

"I'm behind you," Mrs. Haygood warned him, and clasped his bicep in both of her hands.

"Where do these go?" he asked.

"I've never been up them" was the only true answer she wanted to give.

"Let go of me," he said. He moved up the wooden steps on his knees, waving his hand above his head till it bumped into the door. He pushed. His arm felt weak. He pushed again and heard something topple, then he pushed harder and the door swung up a few inches, lifting the throw rug. He looked at the bottom row of books on a shelf behind Mazelle's counter, and then let the hatch close back slowly and quietly, as if he'd stepped into the wrong apartment. He sat in the darkness, hunched over, aware only of the darkness and the odor of limestone.

"Please come back down," Mrs. Haygood said. "Don't stay up there."

He crawled down the steps and she took the weight of his

body into the light, helped him fall against the cistern wall. The shadow of the dog's tongue lolled in his lap.

"I need to give him a flat tire," he said. "I need to drive a nail through his skull."

"I will help," she said.

"If you knew, why didn't you divorce him, Mrs. Haygood? Why didn't you tell me?"

"I wasn't afraid of losing him. I was afraid of losing you. It was enough to live next door to you. I didn't want to jeopardize the garden."

"I need to find Mazelle."

"She's gone. I saw her leave. She realized what you were about to find. You and I could leave too. Mr. Haygood is still asleep."

"I can't just leave. There's the children. Our children. She's the mother of my children."

"This was what I was afraid of. That you'd stay with her. Shall I say the sentence that will convince you? I will. She isn't the mother of your children. She is the mother of Mr. Haygood's children. You have toiled to raise his children, not yours. He watched you feed them and clothe them and send them off to school. Then when you went to work, he would slide up into your wife's body and put another child there. And you would raise it too, like some misled duck warming a clutch of chicken eggs."

"They're my kids. Even if she did . . . with him. We did too."

"There were no children before you moved here. You were married for five years before you moved here. The children don't look like you. I suspect you are the last of your line. Perhaps I was wrong in not coming forward sooner."

※

6:16 Very clever of him to ask me out on my porch where there would be witnesses and his confession out of my tape recorder's range. I thought of stabbing him with my pencil but it was dull.

He has gotten so old, I could have hung a paint bucket on the knob of his chin.

6:18 Car still parked in front of Nadine's. It has been there for three full days now. Possible bomb.

6:19 Everyone knows I have provided for myself, a lady by myself.

※※

Mose crawled back over into his tub, burrowed into the camouflage of dry leaves. His tears still hung in the wrinkles beneath his eyes.

"Don't feel bad about it," Howard said. "She strung you along."

"No she didn't," Mose confessed. "I always knew there was nothing in her heart for me. But I thought she didn't care for anyone after her husband died. It's hard to accept that she could love someone else, especially you. Are you telling me the truth?"

"It never meant enough to me to lie about it."

"She was so valuable and you squandered her." Mose wiped his cheeks with a leaf that crumbled on his skin.

"Strangest thing," Howard said, "when you got mad at me, I felt bad. Why do you suppose that happened?"

"Go to hell, for all I care," Mose said. "I should get up and go home."

"I'm afraid I can't let you do that," Howard told him. "I need you to stay awhile longer."

"Don't tell me anything more," Mose said. "Tell me how it was."

"I don't understand you."

"Tell me how it was to be kissed by her."

"You don't want to hear it from me."

"Well, her husband's dead, isn't he? There's only you left. You're my last chance."

"Her mouth was wide. It tasted of raw vegetables cut up and left in the refrigerator for a week. At first I liked the looseness of her lips, the slackness of her jaw, the way I could mold them with my own mouth. Her muscles adapted to mine so completely that I began to forget she was there. Occasionally, I'd draw blood by accident. She went to her coffin with a quarter-inch scar on her tongue that I put there. I thought about apologizing but she didn't want me to. She kept her scar like a trophy. But I had put it there. It was mine. Often I tried to take it back, but the meat of her tongue had toughened. Her whole mouth became less flexible, more resilient. Instead of yielding, she stood her ground. It was like kissing my reflection in a mirror. The taste of her saliva became coppery. Her teeth collided with mine. Her taste buds grated against my inner cheek. I had to push her away with my hands. She was like a bird trying to fight its way into my mouth." Howard paused, turned to Mose. "It was a fluke of nature that she was attracted to me. Everyone knows you're a better man than I am. Even I know it. Who could have invented such a thing?"

"But she was strong. Why was she so weak?"

"I wasn't there to understand or explain. I was there to take advantage."

"She was better than you," Mose said. "She deserved more than you."

"She got what she deserved."

"She was strong."

"She was weak and conniving. She cared too much. The only way to conquer someone is not to care. She tried to make me care with the baby, but again I was beyond temptation."

"What baby?"

"I'm sorry. I sometimes forget who knows what, who came when. A year or two before you came. The year Nadine was sent to Paris. She had the baby that year."

6:20 Very strange and rare that Verda misses an entire day on her roost and watch post. I have almost missed her pushing back her curtains and staring over my way every time I adjust my sign. It's very rude approaching vulgar but I have become used to her ways. Two or three times a day she takes a big bowl of <u>something</u> to someone on the Row as a way to ingratiate herself and be the first to hear the latest gossip pertaining to Effie. I'm sure the phone lines will be burning when she finally gets home tonight. How she's able to stay away from the scene of such intense interest is a tribute to her willpower. No doubt she will be on my doorstep bright and early tomorrow morning with all her daughter's news dripping out of her dentures.

6:25 Verda says she doesn't eat any more than her God tells her to. First time I ever heard of God selling donuts.

He knew there was a God because he sometimes cringed with fear for no reason. But just as quickly he'd forget. The ring of dirt around the hole in the garden was cool but unforgiving. It shifted. He heard voices. The loose soil would drag him to the opening. Still, to be able to just peek over the edge was almost irresistible. He whined with uneasiness and anticipation. He felt that something delicious was escaping. The man might strike him again at any moment. The dirt curdled under his paws as he worked his way down the concavity like a roulette ball. At the edge of the hole, each toe still vibrating with fear, he dipped his head into the darkness. The burrow was huge. It smelled of anxiety, but whether this was his own nervousness or another's, he couldn't tell. He whined again and the woman in the hole answered. His back paws were caught in the undertow of loose soil. The sky itself seemed to pass over the hole uneasily, as if it might be drained away. He looked down again. There was the head of another dog nestled in the man's lap. This seemed unforgivable. Here, plainly, was a hole. It was not that power for which his four paws were an equal and opposite force, holding the surface of the planet in place. He let his long tongue loll from his mouth, sure that he could retrieve it.

6:26 If she expects me to raise her son for her she has another think coming. I've driven down that road before and had to walk back home. She should have thought about that before she got a divorce. I have a business to run. A teenager around the place would scare off all my customers. I don't know the boy.

6:28 Marshall's work truck parked in front of that carpenter's.

When Marshall climbed into the truck at the end of day, he found Aura's number on his beeper, but since he was on his way, he didn't go back into the office to call. He'd be home in a few minutes anyway. But as he turned the corner onto the Row the idea of Carl's pregnant shop caused him to pull up in front of the carpenter's house. There were two bags of sawdust, like great moldy oranges, on the curb. For eight or nine months, Marshall has had the feeling that more material went in the building than came out. He had a contractor's curiosity. He moved the wing bone from one side of his mouth to the other. As he stepped out of the truck, the notion of a fall weekend collapsed onto his shoulders and he sighed. There would be little need for air-conditioning or heat over the next couple of days. If he was lucky there wouldn't be a single call. He looked up toward his own house and from a distance realized he'd need to mow the yard that evening. That would please Aura. He waved at Mose and Howard in their bathtubs and thought, If I'm able to do that in thirty years I'll be a lucky man. I'll lay in a bathtub all day long. The flag on Carl's new staff snapped in the wind. It still made Marshall nervous to approach another human being. He was so tall. People looked at his bone. But he was learning from Aura, trying to include himself in the world. He was finding that people would rather answer a question than not. They were generally kind if you took an interest in their work, if you pretended you were stupider than you were. Marshall felt there was something going on inside this cabinet shop beyond cabinets, in the same way he'd recognized Aura, knew she was more than the surface area of her skin. He could estimate the time and materials required to build a set of cabinets in the same way that he estimated ductwork and plumbing. For all the noise, for all the edges of light that escaped from the windows at night, for all the sawdust that sat on the curb, there were too few cabinets. He stepped quickly and quietly up the short sidewalk and onto the porch. I'm here already, he thought. He put his hand on the doorpost to steady himself as he balanced on one leg and leaned over to peer along the curled yellow edge of the window shade. Only a thin strip of darkness. Before he knocked, he squatted down and put his eye to the keyhole. As if he'd been stabbed, he fell back on his haunches and the palms of his flailing hands. His chicken bone caught in his throat and he had to cough it out. On the far side of the keyhole, Carl's own batting lash had blown sawdust into Marshall's eye an inch away.

"What do you want?" Carl asked through the door.

"You scared me half to death," Marshall answered.

"What do you want?"

"Why don't you get a peephole in your door? Then you wouldn't have to look through the keyhole like that," Marshall said.

"Why don't you learn how to knock? Then you wouldn't have to spy through my keyhole. Step back down to the sidewalk." Marshall stood up and took two long backward steps down to the walk. Carl opened the door, climbed up out of his house and closed the door behind him. "What can I do for you?"

"I live down at the end of the street." Carl nodded. "I'm married to Aura." Carl nodded. "I'm a heat and air contractor." Carl didn't nod. "Which isn't of any real importance because I was peeping through your keyhole to find out what's going on here besides kitchen cabinets and it's plainly none of my business and I'm sorry."

Carl looked across the street at Nadine's shop, at the hand-lettered Closed sign in the window. He looked at the bone in Marshall's mouth. "You've got a bone in your mouth," Carl told Marshall.

"Yes, sir, I know."

"Your name's Marshall?"

"Yes, sir."

"I knew that. Yes, I did. Marshall, I'm at my wits' end."

"That can happen to just about anybody," Marshall said. "And I'm sorry for my part in it."

"Oh, it's nothing to do with you." Carl put his hands in his pockets and found a small drill bit and a number-eight bronze wood screw there.

"I'm a pretty good hand with tools if you ever need a hand."

"You're in love with your wife, aren't you?" Carl said.

"I am," Marshall answered.

"Must be nice, I mean, living in the same house."

"Well, she likes it real cold so I generally have to wear a jacket. It's give and take. I hate to brag on it because I know I'm lucky. Why don't you come up to the house sometime and have a bite to eat? We eat real good. I sure would like to know what you're doing in there, but I know it's none of my business."

"I've built a thirty-two-foot oceangoing sloop. A sailboat. I've taken my house apart from the inside out for the materials to build it, all in the hope that a woman will go away with me."

"I guess I deserved that," Marshall said.

Carl shrugged. "I haven't let anybody know because it's possible she'll say no. I've got too much pride."

"I was just trying to be friendly."

Carl looked over Marshall's shoulder. "Care to have a look?" he asked.

6:30 I can't see what Marshall is saying to the carpenter because of the hedge. That hedge has always thwarted me in the spring and summer and fall. A little root poison this winter should settle that score.

6:32 Tradio's man friend, <u>ARTHUR</u> sweetie pie hug ums, is putting gas into their lawn mower. Always the busy-bee. They have agreed to mow my lawn without pay, although I'm sure I'll pay for it in the long run.

6:34 Time for dinner but I'm not hungry, too upset by my neighbors. Stress for which I have no responsibility but am forced to endure. I am sure they are snickering.

"I don't believe you," Mose said.

"I don't care."

"Nadine's never mentioned a baby."

"Nadine was sent away so she wouldn't know."

"I don't believe you."

"Ask Effie. She knows. She was here."

"Why would Effie keep such a secret all these years?"

"Because Nadine's mother kept one for her."

"What secret?"

"I could never get Nadine's momma to tell me. She was afraid I'd blackmail the old bitch."

"If there was a baby, where is it? What happened to it?"

"She carried the baby hoping I'd relent. But it just pushed me further away. I was forty-eight years old. Who wanted a baby? When the baby was born, when Nadine was about to return home, when I wouldn't have any part of it, she gave it up. Then she thought the giving it up would convince me, but when you're tired of it you're tired of it. You take the same kind of sandwich to work every day and one day you can't eat another bite. I was honest with her."

"So you're telling me, Nadine has a brother or sister out there somewhere that she doesn't even know exists?"

"I don't know about out there. I think it's probably Aura."

Mose didn't sit up, didn't turn to look at Howard. The light between the branches above him was the palest blue, a weathered fabric of sky. It seemed as thin as the glass of a vacuum tube. There was very little separating the entire world from a void eager to expand. If only Howard would stop talking. I wasn't put on this Earth to discover, but to invent, Mose thought. There is a difference. There are things I don't need to know. I am healthier not knowing them. The molecules of a secret are dispersed when it's told. The world is made somehow less. That is discovery. Invention is a gathering up of vagrant molecules. But either way we are doomed to mystery and knowledge. We will forever not know then know. We are doomed to understanding. Why then does the word *obvious* never surface before knowledge but only after? It's so obvious. Of course, Aura is Nadine's half-sister. How could it have been any other way? There is no need to feel ignorant. This isn't a new way to raise blinds or flush a toilet or even a clockwork perpetual motion machine. It's something that was always there, that existed independently, and now it's even less than it was because it's visible. It doesn't have the authority or the effervescence of secrecy. Now it's just something I know. Now it can't be denied. Now it's not nearly as important.

"She looks," Howard said, "like Nadine's momma, doesn't she? Not so much like Nadine. She'd be the right age. She's an Edna Gladney baby. I've never checked into it, but it would be like Nadine's momma to set her up here on the Row. That house sold and sat vacant for a year before Aura moved in. It was her way to set the girl up two houses down from me. Spite."

"So Aura won't have anything to do with you?"

"Oh, she doesn't know I'm her father. Doesn't know who her mother was. Doesn't know Nadine's her sister."

"She thinks her parents left her that house."

"They did. Or I should say her momma did. You don't think she looks like Nadine's momma? Fat as a bleach bottle, skin like a thin sheet of stainless steel? Every time I see one of those bulbous wind deflectors on a semi truck I think of Nadine's momma."

"Why do you have to be so hard on people?" Mose said. "Why do you have to say things?" he asked, as if he were asking the leaves he sat in.

"They were always hard on me. I don't expect you to understand. I just want you to listen. I don't care if anyone understands anymore. People treat you differently than they treat me. I only handle folks the way they handle me. I do unto others as they do unto me. Nadine's momma never screwed you but she treated you like a human being."

"Who said she never?" Mose said.

"Good God, old man, let it go. There's lots of women I've never been with. If you'd known her that way, you'd have less than you have now."

"I'm not going to ask why you haven't approached Aura. You'd just say she has no more relevance to you than any neighbor. But why not let them, Aura and Nadine, why not let them know they're sisters? Nadine's been a lonely person since her momma died."

"One, it's none of my business. Two, who's to say either of them wants a sister? Three, they'd both expect something from me. Four, it was a twenty-year-old mess, all but forgotten, when Nadine's momma brought it all back. That's how long her spite lasted. That's the kind of woman she was. Now, you can see my side of it."

"Maybe she didn't care about you at all. Maybe after Aura's parents died, Nadine's momma wanted to give Aura something, set her up in life before she passed away too. Maybe she wasn't thinking of you at all."

"I find that hard to believe. She wanted to help her but felt no inclination to reveal that she was her mother?"

"She was ashamed."

"She was shameful. She didn't want Nadine to think she'd ever lost control. She didn't want to lose control of Nadine, to lose that worship. Now it's your burden. You think it's easy. Go ahead and tell Nadine about her mother if you think it's the right thing to do. I've passed the burden to you. How have your feelings changed about Nadine's momma in the last few minutes? How will Nadine's change? Take that away from her, will you? All-powerful secret teller Mose."

"I didn't say I was going to tell her."

"You can't wait to cross the street."

"That's not true. I don't have any desire to rise out of this tub. I'm tired and old and dirty. I know too much."

"Now you feel like me. You've had a bath in my water."

"Why did you do this to me?" Mose asked.

"Because I was jealous. Because I thought I might die when I got up this morning. And when I saw you mowing your grass I knew you wouldn't."

"Of course I'll die."

"I mean, I'll die before you. I hate everyone who'll go on living after I die."

"Then you've got a lot of people to hate. That would be almost everyone."

"The older I get the madder I get. It's true. So I have one last thing for you to hear."

"I don't want to hear it."

"I couldn't help it then and I can't help it now."

"Take it to your grave."

6:38 There's an ant using every method known to man to get into my house via my front window.

Nadine finished off her low-cal frozen entrée, then washed her fork. Arthur's clothes waited for her in the darkened shop. She passed through her brightly lit bedroom, passed her own and her mother's single beds covered in matching pink chenille spreads. The drawers of both their dressers were full. In the shop, she opened the venetian blinds a quarter inch so she could see through the narrow slats to the darkening street while she tried on the clothes. It was so exciting to change clothes in the dusk, in the semipublic area of her closed shop. Carl stood in his front yard talking to Marshall, but Nadine was sure they couldn't see. She thought the pleasure she received by looking outside while she stood naked inside was unusually perverse. She'd only been able to experience this feeling since her momma died, which only added to the overall pleasurable sense of wickedness. She wiggled out of the flapper outfit, draped it over a chair and then ran her hands down her sides till they rested on the smooth slope of her hips. She'd never gained the weight her mother had put on in her forties and fifties. She snapped on a black bra whose support structure was a spiral of thin copper wire surrounding each breast, shaping them into sharply pointed cones. She was sure that if she wore the brassiere alone into the yard she'd snare birds and small animals on the tips of her breasts. But the bra was from the same period as the first ensemble, an early forties two-piece wool suit with enormous shoulder pads and a tailored waist. She buttoned up the skirt and blouse, ran her hands down her woolly thighs and slowly turned. She never needed a mirror. She knew exactly what she looked like, able to call up an encyclopedia of her mother's discerning comments and criticisms. Marshall was following Carl into his house. She'd never seen anyone but Carl go into his house. He'd never invited her in, not that she'd have accepted. All that sawdust. She watched them close the door, but they didn't turn on a light. The edges of Carl's windows were still dark. She unbuttoned the blouse and stepped out of the skirt, steadying herself with one hand on the chair. Next was a long silk nightgown. She pushed her panties down with two thumbs, sprung the bra from her chest and then threw the gown with a flourish high above her head, to let it cascade over her bare shoulders. It hung at her left ear. It was a tighter fit than she'd thought it would be, pleated over the breasts, with a tufted button between them, and a real cinch at the waist. How could anyone have ever slept in this? she wondered. Then she wondered how many of these things Arthur had already tried on. She was sure he wouldn't look nearly as good as she did. There was no way he could fill out the pleats. The sleeves and lower half of the nightgown were sheer. When she finally felt herself fitted, she let her hands roam over the fabric. It wasn't a gown for sleeping in, after all. It was a gown for slowly removing before making love. And almost fifty years old. Nadine leaned over toward the venetian blinds, a hand cupped under each breast so they wouldn't fall through the slats. Effie's kitchen light was on. Mose and Howard were still lying in their bathtubs. Then she watched Aura tumble off her front porch and collapse onto the lawn as if she'd been coughed out of a clothes dryer.

※

6:40 Tradio's man friend sure taking his time.

※

"No, I mean it." Carl turned around and kicked open his front door. "Get in here right now."

Marshall hesitated for a moment. He'd have to duck when he went through the door. He'd be at a disadvantage for a moment. It was dark beyond the doorsill. The floor was completely gone. Carl, refusing to wait any longer, stepped to the sill and jumped into his house as if he were leaping from a moving truck. This was too much for Marshall and he followed, holding both hands over his vulnerable head as he dropped down to the dirt floor. The boat seemed to rise up above him like a whale broaching, filling the entire interior of the house. Marshall hadn't yet removed his hands from his head, expected a heavy stick to come crashing down. He clinched the chicken bone tightly, crushing it.

"Over here," Carl whispered harshly.

"Where are you?" Marshall asked.

"Here, at the window."

Marshall followed the voice. As his vision became accustomed to the available light, he could make out the cabinet builder squatting on a sawhorse before his front window. He was holding the shade back, gazing out at the street. Marshall crept under the hull, aware that he was beneath an immense weight.

"You were telling the truth," Marshall said. "It really is a boat."

"That's not what I wanted you to see. Look."

Carl held back the shade an inch more and beckoned. Marshall took one hand from his head and leaned over the sawhorse, leaned into Carl's odor of sweat-soaked sawdust.

"What?" he asked.

"The window," Carl said.

Then Marshall saw. He thought of turning his head to acknowledge that he saw, but then he thought he wouldn't look away from what he saw. He simply said, "Oh." Through the slatted venetian blinds of Nadine's front window, he could see her nude silhouette, backlit from a light beyond. She was trying on clothes. He watched quietly for a few minutes. He watched her breasts fall from a bra like Jell-O from a mold. She raised her arms to let a dress slide down over her body. Again, without turning, Marshall said, "Does she know?"

"I used to think she knew, that she was doing it for my sake, but now I'm not sure."

"Every night?"

"No, only once in a while, when she gets some new stock in."

"You wouldn't think that a quarter-inch gap every two inches would give you such an idea of the way she is. She's remarkable. Not the kind of woman I prefer, but shapely. You oughtn't to torture yourself like this."

"I've noticed you haven't turned away," Carl said.

"I can't seem to help myself. Look, she's coming outside."

Carl yelped, "Quick, close the shade!"

⇥⇤

6:41 There goes Nadine!

6:42 I thought Nadine was barefoot for Tradio's man friend, but she passed him doing ninety. Now Mose and Howard are running across my grass, and Arthur has left the lawn mower in the middle of the street. They're trying to peak my interest. I won't be drawn outside my house. I can't see.

⇥⇤

Gathering her strength, and with the impetus of small dogs humping each of her knees, Verda pulled herself up and sat with her back to her front door. She swatted at each of her dogs weakly. "God'll get ya," she told them in a pang of despair and frustration. She looked across her shop, at the armageddon of figurines and the trail of her own blood and urine through them. There's a mess I won't have to clean up, she thought. This door will be hard to push open with my dead body up against it, she thought. Her heart dangled in her chest cavity like a dead bird on a string. I smell so bad. I'm ready to go to a better place, ready to leave this body, this old house, this street. I don't understand why no one's come for me. Not even a phone call. Where's my dead husband, my mother and father, my Jesus, my little lost puppy, Wheresyurbone? Why am I forced to struggle? Why can't my babies come with me? "Babies, babies," she called, and the dogs, with lolling tongues the size of infants' earlobes, crawled up in her wet lap and pawed at her breasts. She stroked them, completely encircled each dog's throat with her hands, and lifted them up into the air. When they began to gasp, their paws struggling with the air, she realized she couldn't have done this moments ago. Her strength was returning. Her arm didn't hurt as much. She dropped the dogs on the floor and they skittered away like drops of water on a hot skillet. Verda placed the palms of her hands on the floor and tried to push her body up, but her legs were too heavy just yet. She'd wait. She'd gather more strength, let it accumulate. And in the meantime, she'd decide what to do once she was up. Whether she'd call each of her girls to tell them she was dead—but she wouldn't be dead, so she could only tell them she should be dead, no thanks to them—or whether she'd cross the street to slap Effie's face, or whether she'd have a twenty-five-percent-off sale on her broken figurines. She could think of nothing more pleasurable than slapping her best friend's face, but she worried that she wouldn't have the arm strength. Perhaps that would best be saved for a later day.

Verda picked up an eye at her hip, allowed her fingertips to form a manipulative socket. It blamed her. There was no place in the world where she could deposit, throw or hide this eye that it wouldn't be looking back at her. Then she had an idea. She lifted a six-molar bridge off her gums with her tongue and spat it into her lap. The dogs took it greedily. Her fingertips dropped the eye into her open mouth. Its texture took her back almost seventy years. It tasted like a marble. She slid the smooth glass across her still-lithe tongue, filled the eye's cavity with darts and jabs of her tongue's tip, till the eye hung on it with moist suction. This feat accomplished, feeling as if she'd molded the glass to her own form, she snapped the eye over her bridgeless gums so that its only view was back down the dark tunnel of her throat. She had to fight the urge to swallow. Her hunger begged for the eye. I'm famished, she thought. The only things edible, within range, were her dogs. She called them to her side. Maybe they would bring her something to eat. Dideebiteya and Yeseedid took her instructions with only a slight banking of their skulls, but brought back from the kitchen a sock and a rubber Minnie Mouse. I'm in the middle of a famine, Verda realized. It's not just Africans anymore. I'm being visited by God. She thrust her back against the door and pushed with all her accumulated fear until she once again collapsed. Just before she fell asleep she recalled that her front door opened in. Her dogs whined for moments then nestled in the hollows of her armpits, and they too fell fast asleep.

⇥⇤

6:43 I'm being left out.

⇥⇤

Mrs. Haygood helped Mazelle's husband up from the floor. She saw the indecision in his face. "I've always been afraid," she said.

"But the only thing I'm afraid of now is that you'll forgive them. Perhaps I let it grow so it would become so monstrous you couldn't forgive them."

They sat on the stony bed for an hour, two hours, neither of them speaking, in the same way that they'd sometimes weed their garden.

"There's a dog I have to apologize to," he said finally. They stepped up on the bed, climbed the headboard and bedpost, and clawed their way out of the cistern. The dog backed away from them. Mazelle's husband looked it in the eye and said, "I'm sorry." And the dog turned uneasily and trotted back across the street, occasionally turning and looking over his shoulder. Mrs. Haygood took Mazelle's husband to her bedroom window.

"He's still napping," Mrs. Haygood said. "You're stronger than he is."

"I've carried carcasses around on my back for too long. You go inside. Close the door between your bedroom and the toy shop. Wait for me in the shop. I'll be along."

"You will come? You won't go searching for Mazelle?"

"Mazelle will end up at one of the kids' houses. She's been replacing me with them for years now. She'll be all right."

"But I'm worried about you. What are you going to do?"

"I have one more load to carry and then I'll be free."

"I mean about me. What about us?"

"Will you help me? Will you close the door to your husband's bedroom?"

"I will slit his throat for you. I will."

"Wait for me. Just close the door."

"What if he wakes up?"

"We'll serve him to the neighborhood dogs."

Mazelle's husband entered his house through the back door. The box of black plastic garbage bags was under the kitchen sink. His home seemed suddenly quieter than it ever had. The books made no noise. How softly the past wafted down to silence. He looked at their made-up bed in the corner of the kitchen and then remembered he'd slept his last night there. Still, it would go on being a bed. He started to walk into the two front rooms of his house, then didn't. Everything forward of that door belonged to Mazelle, and he didn't want to confront the hatch to the cistern from this side. He'd carried so much meat, so many books, to raise someone else's children. Strange, how none of this affected his love for them. He knew they'd always looked upon him as a vacant but kind draft horse, but he also knew they respected him. One of his sons truly loved him, and his daughters still sought solace in his arms. He had no fears of being rejected by his children. They'd always accepted him as their father and always would. In a sense, it was the children who'd been cheated, and it was for them that he slapped the box of garbage bags on his hip and pushed his way back out the door. Striding through the loose dirt of the garden, he let the notion, fresh and vibrant, poke its head above the soil: perhaps he'd gained more than he'd lost.

Mrs. Haygood opened the front door to the shop softly and let him in. Neither of them noticed, as they closed the door, that Aura was falling off her front porch across the street. They didn't notice that Nadine was the first to reach her, then Arthur, then Mose and Howard. When Effie pushed her way into the circle of onlookers standing over Aura's body, Nadine shoved her back toward her house and said, "Effie, run back to your phone and call 911 right now. You keep calling till they're here. Go. Right now."

6:47 I have called 911 and informed them of the situation. I am unsure as to whether I should become more involved. They are all gathered around her so as I cannot see from here. I guess Aura needs her attention, her time in the headlights.

6:49 I have called 911 again. There is a strange buzzing in my phone.

※

On the wall above the recliner in which Mrs. Postlethwaite sat hung a framed black-and-white photograph, an art deco nude by Hart. The woman in the photograph was curled into a large hoop, her arms and legs outlining a fine crescent, a new moon. The oblique lighting highlighted the swell of her hip, her biceps, the curve of her breasts, her neck. The expression on the portion of her face that remained in darkness was clear to Mrs. Postlethwaite. She was afraid she was going to fall.

Mr. Postlethwaite stared at the photograph while his wife congealed into a ball in the recliner. It seemed as if they hadn't spoken for years. He stood next to the window, looked from one object in the room to another, looked at everything but his wife. The dresser he bought at the auction on Camp Bowie Boulevard: she found dirt dauber nests on the back of the mirror when he brought it home. I found that ashtray at a yard sale on Eighth Avenue, he thought. It has gained a lot of value since then. Some things are worth more than what they're worth. Maybe she'll go to the mall this evening alone. Everything in this room is ours.

He turned to Mrs. Postlethwaite. "I'll admit it. I'll admit I molested her if she'll take you back. She doesn't have to take me back. I'll tell her I'm sorry. I'll tell her I haven't touched any more children since I touched her. I'll find her and tell her she was right, that I needed help back then but I'm all right now. I'll admit what I did and you and she can have each other again. I'm sure there's some way we can find her."

"But you didn't touch her," Mrs. Postlethwaite said.

"But I'll admit I did. I'll say she remembered it all correctly. I have nothing to lose. She already thinks I'm a child molester.

Then, you at least could have her back. I know she probably wouldn't want to meet with me again. So you can say anything to her. Tell her you're staying with me out of compassion. Tell her you're sorry you believed my lies. Tell her I didn't want to lose both of you so I lied. Tell her I lied to keep you because I was afraid to be alone."

"But you didn't touch her. I won't let you admit it. None of it is your fault. It's her memory that's in error."

"But I don't mind. I'll admit it."

"You won't. I won't let you. I'll deny it."

"I'll cut off both my hands to prove to her I'm sorry. To prove I won't use them again."

"No. Be quiet."

"I—"

"Be quiet. There's voices outside."

6:50 There goes Tradio. He ran right past that lawn mower with nary a thought to his promise. Somebody ought to go tell Marshall that his wife is laying upside down in their front yard.

"Aura, we're going to turn you over, honey," Arthur said.

"She's cut her elbow," Mose said. He and Howard stood behind Nadine, still panting from the climb out of their tubs and the run across two yards.

"We've called an ambulance, Aura. They'll be here soon," Nadine told her.

"I don't think she can hear you," Mose said.

"Let's turn her over."

"I don't think you should move her," Howard said.

"She just cartwheeled right off the porch," Nadine told them.

"Did anybody else see her fall?" She pulled a film of nightgown across her own cleavage.

"I hope she isn't losing the baby," Arthur whispered.

"The what?" Nadine said.

"The poor thing's pregnant," Arthur said.

Howard backed up.

"She would have told me," Nadine said.

"She doesn't have to get your OK on everything," Arthur said. "I could see it from a mile away," he insisted.

"Well, I've never been pregnant, have I?" Nadine shrieked.

"Well, neither have I," Arthur yelled.

"She's moving."

"Aura, honey, this is Mose." Mose went down on one knee next to her face. "Can you roll over, honey?"

A drop of water splashed on Aura's flushed cheek. At first Mose thought he'd spit on her, but then he felt a drop on the back of his shirt. The blue sky above them had been breached by a long dark boil of cloud that stretched across the northwestern horizon. In the folds of the front a green light was tucked.

When Tradio heard over KRLD that there was a tornado watch across the Metroplex, he pushed himself up from the kitchen table. It would be best if Arthur finished mowing Effie's lawn later. He opened his front door and saw the lawn mower in the street, and then the group of people huddled around the body. He knew then that Effie had killed Arthur in a jealous fit, that she'd shot him in the middle of the street and he'd staggered up into Aura's front yard and died. He should have mowed Effie's yard himself, but Arthur had insisted he rest. He ran down his steps, across the street, past the abandoned mower. What he thought was the roaring of the mower over asphalt turned out to be his own heart thudding against his lungs, the flailing of weak valves. When he finally staggered up into Aura's grass, and could see beyond the broad expanse of Howard's back to the stunned expression on Pie Bird's face, he knew he was going to collapse, and not wanting to be alone when he died, he flung himself into the kneeling group, knocking Mose to the ground and coming to rest lying full length alongside Aura, who rolled over with his impact, thrust her hips toward the roiling sky and screamed as her baby crowned.

6:52 See my notes for August 11th, 1975, where I explain in detail how my husband died, how my son (not my son any longer) treated me. And so my son's son is not my grandson, but a way to get at my things. Someone needs to stay in my house during my funeral to protect my things, as thieves often read the obituaries. And I mean to tell you my son can read.

In a shrieking fear of capture, Carl pulled Marshall from the window and dragged him back through the dark house toward the remnants of his kitchen. He was sure that Nadine had caught them peeking and was charging across the street to pound on his door and shame him for the pervert he was.

"Get under this table," Carl hissed at Marshall.

"I'm almost seven feet tall. I can't get under that table."

"Crouch behind the refrigerator then."

"I can't even see the refrigerator. How's she going to see us?"

"Then be quiet. She'll hear you."

"She couldn't have seen us." Marshall stood with his hands at his side, his head brushing against the hull of the sloop. He could hear Carl breathing heavily. "There's no need to be afraid," he said softly.

They waited quietly, minutes passing.

"I guess she would have been here by now," Carl whispered.

"I think you can come out from underneath that table," Marshall said. "I keep bumping my head. Can you turn on the lights?"

Carl complied.

"She doesn't know about the boat, then," Marshall said.

"Of course not."

"Why not?"

"I didn't want to overwhelm her."

"Then you should have brought her in here before you started."

"I've been trying to get her used to the idea of the Caribbean. I thought that when she saw the boat and I told her I built it for her . . ."

Marshall moved the bone over his tongue, brought it completely inside his mouth. He lifted both palms and clapped them to the smooth planks and began to walk along the faired hull. "How will you get her out of here?" he asked as he walked.

"I'll tell her I love her."

"I meant the boat."

"Oh. The house is just an eggshell now. I'll cut out a few key pins and the walls will fall away. Then I can saw up the roof, break the boat free. Now that it's come time, I almost hate to finish."

"You're just nervous. Hell, I'd go with you if you'd built this for me."

"It's kind of you to say that."

"Nadine's a fine woman. And I don't just mean what we saw of her. She's forthright, and honest, and she works hard, and she's always dressed in a way that my wife admires."

"What do you suppose it is that makes a person latch on to a single idea, or a way of doing things, that makes them focus on one person, one boat, when the world is full of so many other possibilities? There must be hundreds of other women I could love. Even though it's hard for me to say it, I know Nadine isn't the most beautiful woman in the world. There's probably thousands of women who already live on old wooden boats in the Caribbean. I could have just gone there in the first place."

"I don't know. I love my wife. I want to have five little girls that look just like her. She makes me want to be wiser and friendlier. I'd have spent my life in front of a TV if it hadn't been for her. You don't know that Nadine doesn't need you. She's been in that old dress shop a long time. As far as I know, she's got no family to hold her here. Don't accept defeat yet. I wonder, if Nadine wasn't coming over here when she came running down her porch steps, where was she going?"

"Let me peek out the door before you go out."

6:54 Just a big crowd in Aura's front yard now, a regular block party.

"Is he still abed, Mrs. Haygood?" Mazelle's husband asked. The darkening sky had shaded the toy shop a restful umber. Even though the shelves and showcases were without dust they seemed dull, blunted, as if the room had been chided.

"He's asleep still. Where will we start? There's knives, but suffocation might be better. If you could hold him, I would hold the pillow. Or is that what the plastic bags are for?"

"It's too late for that," he said. "It's thirty-four years and four kids too late. If you'd only killed him then, the first hour you knew."

"Then what?" She put her hands at her own throat. "We could simply maim him."

"No."

"Why? He shamed us both. He took from both of us."

"He's the father of my children."

"He's not."

"He is in that way. And I want my kids to come talk to him. So they'll see what I was. So he'll see what he missed. I've got good kids."

"Then what are we here for?"

Mazelle's husband pointed to the sign above the bronze cash register. HE WHO DIES WITH THE MOST TOYS WINS. "What do you suppose the value of these things is?" he asked.

"It's his retirement fund. He thinks maybe close to half a million. He's never told me that, of course. But he brags when he makes a good buy. He can't keep from telling me the profit."

"All of these things should have been played with by his kids. It's a shameful thing for a grown man to covet toys. We're going to make sure that when Mr. Haygood dies, he loses. Do you know which toys are especially valuable?"

"The Marklin ships, the Ives toys. I know."

"If I hold these plastic bags open can you slip them in quietly?"

"I can."

"We'll sell a few of them, open up accounts for the kids. The rest you and I will take as reparation. We'll find some place where the soil is deeper than it is here. I want to tell you, Mrs. Haygood, that I have often looked at your leg in the garden."

"I couldn't help but think that you had," she said, and handed him an Arcade moving van.

"Does anyone else know," he asked, "other than the four of us?"

"He's given Howard seven dollars and fifty cents every month for over thirty years. He's always been afraid of Nadine."

"They've been blackmailing him?"

"Howard, I suppose. Mr. Haygood's afraid Nadine knows simply because she's not afraid of him like everybody else. I don't think she knows."

"How do you know these things? I mean, what Mr. Haygood thinks."

"Because he thinks I'm stupid."

"He'll know you weren't when he wakes. Just scoop every-thing up. We'll bring the car around."

"I'll want some herbs in the new garden," she said.

"I was thinking about—get that little airplane—a brick border and slate stepping stones."

"Did you ever love anything more than you love a garden?" she asked, knowing she asked about all the time he'd spent with her.

"I love my kids more," he said. He placed a Hubley sleigh quietly into the bag. "But not as consistently. And I've loved nothing that returned my attentions with such reward."

"Me either," Mrs. Haygood said.

"I'll get another bag."

"It's starting to rain."

"All these old cast-iron toys," Mazelle's husband said, "all their little rubber tires have flats."

"What was that?" Mrs. Haygood whispered. She stiffened in midstep, her arms full of toys. "Did you hear something?"

"Someone screamed," he said.

Mr. Haygood heard the scream too, rolled over uneasily and winced as the tip of his penis pulled free from where it had stuck to his shorts.

＊

6:55 Take, take, take from Effie, but when Effie wants something, when Effie needs something, it's <u>Katie, Bar The Door.</u> I often think of my poor little brother who at thirty-five years of age found out he was born with only one lung and his heart on the wrong side, and from that day to his death was only fourteen years. A person is born with two kidneys for a REASON!!! Aura is turned over now and her special spot displayed to the leering eyes of Mose, That Old Depraved Indian, and even Tradio's man friend (who must be looking out of scientific curiosity). They are all looking as if a train is about to come out of her tunnel. Her head is in Nadine's lap and Tradio is laying flat out next to her with his arm thrown across her bosom! It's a mighty good show that Effie won't try to compete with. Dogs do it, why can't we, I guess.

"She doesn't have any underwear on," Howard said, but before Mose could even look up, Tradio had sideswiped him. It was all Mose could do to keep himself from falling on Aura's face. His own cheek bounced off the Saint Augustine grass as he rolled, and he came to a stop coated in dry lawn clippings. The grass smelled of grocery bags. The impact had forced snot from his nose. He ran his sleeve across his upper lip as he pushed himself up to his knees and couldn't help but think that shirts and coats with terry cloth handkerchiefs sewn to the sleeves would be a good seller in winter. As he twisted back around to see who'd hit him, he heard Arthur squeak Tradio's name, then he saw the body lying next to Aura's, and then Aura woke up and screamed. Another raindrop pecked the back of his hand.

"Get up, you old oaf," Nadine yelled at Tradio.

"Tradio? Tradio?" Arthur knelt at his side.

"He's out cold," Howard said.

"He was clutching his chest," Arthur said. "Somebody call an ambulance."

"They've already been called," Mose said.

Howard pushed Arthur aside.

"Don't touch him!" Arthur screamed.

"Give him CPR," Nadine said. "Are you OK, Aura, honey?"

Howard slid his enormous hand under Tradio's collar, looked away as if he were searching for keys between seat cushions, then looked back at Arthur. "He's still got a pulse, little fellow. Better leave him be till the bus comes." Howard stood back up and took a step over one of Aura's knees. "Baby's coming," he said, matter-of-factly.

Aura snapped her knees together and glared at Howard. Tradio was lying on one of her arms, but with the other she tugged the hem of her shirt down over her crotch. Nadine's face was over her face then, blocking out the sky.

"Are you OK, honey?" she asked.

"We're sick," Aura cried.

"Why didn't you tell anybody you were pregnant?"

"We're not pregnant."

"All right, baby. You just lie still. We've called the ambulance."

"Ow, ow, ow," Aura said, then thrust out her legs. They snapped back up against her stomach almost as quickly.

"There's more baby now," Howard said.

Mose and Arthur joined him between Aura's feet. They put their hands on their knees and bent forward.

"Get this person off of us," Aura shouted, and then, using a compact, leveraged stroke of her forearm, rolled Tradio over onto his back.

"Where is that damned ambulance?" Nadine yelled.

"Put your jacket down there, Arthur," Mose said.

"Where?"

"Between her legs and sort of under there."

"Better get some towels and a pair of scissors," Howard said. He crossed his arms over his chest.

"You get down between her legs and help her, Arthur. You'd be best at it," Nadine said. "We all trust you."

Aura lifted her head out of Nadine's lap and asked Arthur, "Are we really having a baby?"

He looked down. "Yes, honey," he answered. Then he told Howard, "You check on Tradio again." He began to cry as he adjusted his jacket under Aura's wet, grass-matted cheeks.

"I'll get blankets," Mose said, and turned toward his house.

I'm in good shape for an old man, he thought. I can run. And so he did, leaving a brittle trail of dried grass in his wake. He felt the clouds looming over his shoulder, cringed when fat raindrops stung the back of his neck, but still concentrated on each running step, lifting his feet over the curb, leaping over an inch-wide crack in the pavement, avoiding the root-heaved sidewalk and crossing through the grass of Tradio's yard and his own, judging his own porch steps as if it were the first time he'd ascended them, and measuring the length of his outstretched arm so it wouldn't misjudge the doorknob. Still, he couldn't help himself, at his open door he turned to Nadine's front porch to see if her momma wasn't sitting there, watching him run. Strange, he thought, how his yearning to be loved didn't age with his feet, his ability to hurry. He tore the blanket from his bed, yanked open a drawer and pulled out scissors, and then picked up an opened bag of pork skins and its attached chip clip. Only then did he hear the insistent tone of his weather radio, the wail of a tornado warning. He couldn't wait for instructions. As he stepped back out of his door, forcing himself not to look at Nadine's porch, it occurred to him that Aura's baby was part Nadine's momma. Then he saw Carl and Marshall peeking out of Carl's front door, and as he ran he waved at them to follow.

6:59 Mose running back to his house in a guilty manner. Runs fast for an old man. I guess his parts are all excited. Now the Postlethwaites are out in Aura's yard too, having to see for themselves, take my word on it. They'll listen to all the gossip you can tell them but never tell you any of their own. Real quiet when it comes to family business. At least she doesn't have her cane weapon. Bruise on my leg. Just before my husband died, when I had all those tests, my knees swelled up real big and I could see the resemblance to my sister, Saravette, who was always heavy. She sent me a box of nuts for Christmas, knowing my teeth aren't good. Just like her. Mose again. And there goes Marshall and that carpenter right across my grass, all worried and wild-eyed. Marshall took two big steps and was across my yard. Lucky it's not a Saturday as this would not be good for business. Everybody gets sick. I've done my part. I never told my son what his father did. He can't thank me for that even though I deserve it. Lots of yelling now.

Under the porch, the dog Himself was already uneasy at the sight of so many running people. When the first gust of wind grated through the weathered lattice, he felt the need for a den, a hole in the ground, a better place to hide. When he heard the scream, he leaped to escape his anxiety, and a cypress board hit him on the head.

7:04 Note time. 15 minutes since I called 911 and still no ambulance. Taxes I pay but when I want services, well it's <u>Katie, Bar The Door</u>. Nadine's momma said if I ever mentioned a word of that baby to Nadine or anybody else she'd make public the fact that it belonged to my husband (see my notes for December 19th, 1963). I never asked my husband about it because I knew he'd deny it. But Nadine's momma never left the street and who else was there to make that baby? Only That Big Indian and even Nadine's momma wouldn't have him. She always abused him in my presence. I never accused my husband, I just lived with it, and saved my son from the knowledge of it and what thanks did I get? And now, and for the last thirty-five years, there's been the threat of that safety deposit box, and letters to lawyers inside it, that Nadine's momma left if ever I were to tell Nadine about the baby, which I wouldn't anyway because it would probably qualify for my support since it was my husband's. It could get my things even though I had no sexual part in it. My son hates me and he doesn't even know this thing his father did. Of course I don't want to get on Nadine's bad side in case the affair and baby become known in some other way. Nadine's momma left instructions with her lawyer to give the key to the safety deposit box to Nadine should any questions of wills, or heirs, or patrimony ever arise. I don't understand why people won't understand that my things are my things.

7:10 Now it's a big argument. I can't hear. The wind has come up. Big raindrops. That Big Indian's nostrils are so big. If I were a cat I'd think a mouse was hiding in there. They are all very interested in Aura except for Tradio who's obviously napping, but not so interested that they don't steal a glance my way every once in a while. I won't leave my house unprotected. Mrs. Postlethwaite's ear lobes all wadded up and hard like chewing gum under a table.

Mr. Postlethwaite stood over Nadine and Aura, spreading his jacket wide to keep the rain off them. The first shingle torn loose came from Verda's house, careened off Tradio's truck and skidded into the street. Marshall seemed to arrive in three long strides from somewhere far away. They all cleared a path for him. He waited for Aura to speak.

"We're having a baby," she said. "We didn't know." Then she stared intently at the bone in Marshall's mouth, wondered where her own was, took her husband by the collar and screamed into his face.

"That's it," Arthur screamed back at her.

"We've got to get her to a hospital," Marshall yelled.

"Not now, Daddy," Nadine said. "It's too late now."

"Can't we at least get her inside?"

"Don't move us," Aura whined. "We've come here for a purpose."

"I'm going to kill Effie," Nadine said. "Go tell her to call the ambulance again, Carl."

"Help me hold this blanket up, Mrs. Postlethwaite," Mose yelled. "It's really coming down now. We've got tornado warnings too."

"Push hard this next time, Aura," Arthur called out. "Can't somebody take care of Tradio? He's getting wet."

Howard looked down from the sky and said, "I'll get him." He hoisted Tradio up on his back in one sweeping movement and carried him toward his own house. Only Mose saw him lay Tradio down in the yard, then overturn a bathtub to cover his body. This didn't startle Mose. What startled him was Howard turning a second tub over himself, the four claw feet sticking up into the air with rigor mortis. Leaves thrashed the air. A bird tumbled by. Asphalt shingles plowed into the grass.

"She needs to hurry," Mose warned.

In the roar of wind and rain, Mr. Postlethwaite thought he could hear a siren far away. He was almost sure it was coming for him.

Mazelle's husband and Mrs. Haygood stepped out on her front porch. Each of them carried two large trash bags.

"Put these in my car, Mrs. Haygood," he said. "I'll see what's going on." He ducked his head into his sloped shoulders and ran toward Aura's lawn. A tree limb, short but thick, struck him in the back, and he struggled to stay on his feet. Before he could ask, he saw the baby's head erupt into Arthur's hands.

"That's it," Arthur screamed. "I've got its little head. Push again, Aura."

Knowledge pulsed in Mose's mind. He held the blanket taut above Aura and the emerging baby. Still, water soaked through the wool and dripped on them. There's no room to think about the past now, he thought. There's only the next few minutes to have the baby and find shelter from the storm. Clapboards were springing loose from old Mrs. Martin's abandoned house. The air around them was green, water gone bad in an aquarium. The blanket jerked in his clinched fists like an animal trying to break free. "Hurry, Aura, honey," Mose yelled.

Marshall and Nadine crouched over Aura's upper body, their faces close to hers, breathing her worn breath.

"We're getting colder," Aura said. "We've never been this cold in our life."

A brief intense light, a bulb burning out inches from everyone's eyes, and before their vertebrae could compress upon one another, the thunder cratered the air. All the breath was being drawn from Mrs. Postlethwaite's body and so she screamed, "Where's my baby?" before the last of it could escape. She and Mose dropped to their knees, still holding the blanket.

"It was just lightning," Mazelle's husband yelled at her. "It was just thunder." Even as he spoke, Verda's front porch broke loose from her house, stumbled down the steps and then glided into Tradio's yard.

Aura gathered herself, drew in Nadine's and Marshall's last breaths and applied pressure to the storm. Arthur twisted the baby slightly and it came fully into his rigid hands. "There," he yelled. "There."

Mose and Mrs. Postlethwaite let the wind take the blanket. He took his scissors and snipped the umbilical cord that Mrs. Postlethwaite held toward him. Then, throwing the bag of pork skins to the sky, he used the chip clip to clamp the baby's end of the cord.

"Let's go," Mazelle's husband yelled. "The houses aren't safe. Help me with her, Marshall." They picked Aura up, Marshall under her arms, Mazelle's husband between her legs. "Everyone follow me," he yelled.

"The baby," Aura screamed.

"I've got her," Arthur said. "I'm right behind you."

"Where are we going?" Marshall yelled as they started across the street.

Aura concentrated on catching her breath, waiting for her vision to clear.

"To my house," Mazelle's husband huffed. "I've got a basement."

Mrs. Haygood sat in the car, waited in the car, sure that the storm was Mr. Haygood, but understood immediately when they all started toward Mazelle's house. She slid over into the driver's seat and started the car. She watched Mazelle's husband, holding tightly to Aura's thighs, kick open his own front door. A section of picket fence caromed off the windshield taking the wipers with it. Mrs. Haygood backed up to the end of the driveway, then gunned the car over the curb and up into her garden. When she stopped, the body of the car rested over the man-sized hole in the cistern ceiling. As she opened the door, she realized the car was hubcap deep in mud. It would never provide a means of escape. She took off her shoes, held them firmly in one hand and ran.

7:13 Cannot see as I am under my sales counter. Loud car noises. That carpenter knocked on my door real hard, but I would not let him in. Very dark all of a sudden. Loud noises. I do not have insurance. We have been given no thunderstorm protection by the city of Fort Worth. If only my house will get through this storm I would buy insurance. I need to go to the bathroom too. My pot plants swinging very wildly.

Mazelle's husband led the way down into the cistern.

"Be careful with us," Aura reminded.

"I've never been so wet in all my life," Nadine said.

"Bring the baby," Aura screamed.

"Here, you take her, Nadine," Arthur said loudly. He handed her Aura's daughter, wrapped in his jacket. "I've got to go see about Tradio." He was yelling now, even though they stood in the stairwell. The storm vibrated in the air between them.

"Don't go back out there, Arthur," she pleaded, but he was already through the hatch. She watched him take the knob of the screen door in his hands, turn it slowly, and then be pulled outside by the wind-caught door, followed by a dozen flapping books. Carl reached past her, and with one arm around her shoulders, pulled the hatch closed.

"Come downstairs, Nadine," Carl said. "Bring the baby downstairs."

"I can't see," Nadine said.

"Just keep stepping down until you can't any longer. It's not far."

From the darkness below them, Aura yelled, "Where's our baby?"

"I'm coming, Aura, honey. I've got her."

"Everybody stop moving," Mose said. "I've got a lighter." Sparks struck once, but the second time a short flame rose. "Fire," Mose said.

Aura lay at the foot of the stairwell, Marshall and Mazelle's husband at her side. The Postlethwaites sat on the limestone floor next to the bed, holding each other. Mrs. Haygood stood alone in the middle of the room. Nadine bent down and put the baby in Aura's arms. When she stood up she was almost naked to the waist. The old, delicate fabric of the nightgown was in shreds. Carl took off his flannel shirt and put it around her.

Even in the cistern, the flame of Mose's lighter was buffeted by drafts. A brown stream of water flowed under the car and fell through the hole in the ceiling onto the bed, but for the most part the floor was dry.

"Everyone should sit next to a wall," Nadine said. "It will be safer."

Mazelle's husband left Aura's side, went to Mrs. Haygood.

"I'm going to let the lighter go out now," Mose said. "I'm not sure how much fuel there is."

No one spoke for a few moments as they listened to the wind spew through the undercarriage of Mazelle's car.

"Arthur went back out there," Nadine said. "I told him not to but he didn't listen to me. He went to Howard's to help Tradio."

"No," Mose said. "He won't find him there. Tradio and Howard are under bathtubs in the front yard. That's how I knew the weather was going to get really bad, when that damned Indian got under a cast-iron bathtub."

"What about Effie?" Mrs. Postlethwaite asked.

"She's in her house," Carl said. "She wouldn't answer the door. I could see her under her counter, but she wouldn't come to the door."

"That's Effie through and through," Nadine said. "Has anyone seen Verda?"

"I think she's gone to her daughter's. I haven't seen her all day," Mose answered.

"What about your husband, Mrs. Haygood?" Nadine asked.

She wouldn't answer.

"I'm sure he'll make it, honey," Nadine finally said.

"I don't know where my daughter is," Mrs. Postlethwaite said.

"What about Mazelle?" Aura asked.

"She's gone to one of the kids' houses," Mazelle's husband answered.

"I never knew you had a cellar," Mose said.

"Neither did I," he answered.

Above them, the body of the car rocked as it was struck by something heavy. The dog Himself, shivering under the bed, growled into the darkness.

"Oh, Jesus, there's something in here with us," Aura said. "It can smell our baby."

The Postlethwaites scrambled across the floor on their hands and knees until they both rammed into a stone wall.

Mose lit his lighter and walked slowly around the room, revealing the second stairwell on the far side, Mrs. Haygood in Mazelle's husband's arms, but no growling animal.

"It must be under the bed," he said.

Water dripped from the dust ruffle, formed dimly reflective pools, each with a tiny flame at its center.

"Opossum maybe," Mr. Postlethwaite said.

Carl left Nadine's side.

"Oh, don't, Carl," she said.

"Opossums don't growl," he answered. "Give me the light." He took the lighter, which blinked out for only a moment during the exchange with Mose, and dropped down on his knees at the foot of the bed.

"Careful, man," Mr. Postlethwaite said. "It's frightened, whatever it is."

Carl lifted the thin, dust-laden ruffle, as old as Nadine's shredded gown, and holding the lighter close to the floor, peered under the bed.

The baby cried for the first time, a light trickle of water gurgling down a drain.

"Come here, boy," Carl whispered.

"What is it?" Mrs. Postlethwaite asked.

"Come on," he said.

The dog Himself, looking at the hands which had often held food, crawled out toward the light as the light and the hands retreated. He sat, unsure of himself with so many humans so close, and alternately growled and whined.

"Oh, thank goodness," Nadine said. "It's that stray. He's safe from the storm."

Here and now, Carl turned to her, holding the light above his head, unable to control his fear, and said, "I love you."

⋙⋘

7:16 I have lived seventeen years longer than my husband. All my lights are out. I crawled to my kitchen to get a flashlight, given to me, not loaned, by Verda. There is a leak over my stove. Crawled back to my front window. Too dark to see except when lightning flashes. I think pieces of peoples' houses are damaging my house. They must have insurance.

"Isn't that sweet," Aura said.

"Would you like me to go upstairs and find some towels or blankets, Aura?" Mazelle's husband asked.

"We don't want anyone to leave this cellar until the storm has passed," she answered. "The baby seems fine. Look, Marshall, we were two and now we're three. Carl, could you bring the light so we can see our baby?"

Carl held the flame close to the baby's face. Everyone scooched closer.

"Just a little miracle," Mrs. Postlethwaite said.

"We love her so much," Aura said, and she began to cry. "We're so happy you were all there. We guess she wanted everybody on the street to be there when she was born."

"Marshall," Mose said, "you'll have to get her a little chicken bone."

"Yeah," Marshall said. "But when she's older." He smiled.

"It's not just us anymore," Aura said. "She's included us all in her life."

"When was the last baby born on the Row?" Nadine asked. "It's been years. Careful with that lighter, Carl."

"My daughter was born in 1949," Mrs. Postlethwaite said, "but we didn't live here then."

"Our youngest was born in 1964," Mazelle's husband said.

"When were you born, Aura?" Mose asked.

"Nineteen fifty-one," she said. "But Nadine's asking about people born here on the Row, Mose."

"I went to Paris in nineteen fifty-one," Nadine said. "Everyone thought I was pregnant. It wasn't true, of course. But if I'd had a baby then, she'd be your age, Aura."

"This little baby would be your granddaughter, then," Aura said.

Mose put his hands over his face. "I'm so confused," he said.

Nadine petted his shoulder. Above them, the car swayed again on its springs.

"Wind's really blowing now," Mr. Postlethwaite said. "I hope something's left when it's finished. We had all our clocks on that high shelf."

"That roaring just gets louder and louder," Aura said.

They listened to the guzzling of the wind, looked up at the rocking undercarriage of the car. The lighter burned out.

"That was a good idea, pulling the car over the hole," Mazelle's husband told Mrs. Haygood.

"Where does that other staircase go?" Nadine asked. "Can we get somewhere safer?"

"It goes up into my house," Mrs. Haygood explained.

"You know, Mrs. Haygood," Nadine said, "I never believed a word of Effie's gossip until now. She always said you and Mazelle's husband were always leaving the Row about the same time."

"That's because we were sent away," Mazelle's husband said. "Mrs. Haygood has been true, and I've been true. We were never down here in this cistern together before today."

"I'm sorry," Nadine said. "I didn't mean to pry. I was just shocked that Effie might have been right about something. I should have known she was making it all up."

"She wasn't wrong. Our spouses were having the affair, but it was Mrs. Haygood and I who were in love."

"I'm very confused," Mose said.

"I feel water," Mrs. Postlethwaite said.

"There's more coming in," Carl said. "We might want to move onto the steps. If this room is a cistern, it's designed to hold water."

"We're going to need a boat before it's over with," Nadine said.

"I love you," Carl said again.

"I wish you'd stop saying that," Nadine told him.

"I've only said it twice," Carl said.

"Oh, we can feel the water now too," Aura squeaked. "Help us into the stairwell everybody."

Nadine took the baby, as Marshall, Mose and Carl helped Aura stand up. Then they moved as a group into the stairwell, sitting two to a tread.

"What are you going to name the baby, Aura?" Mrs. Postlethwaite asked.

"Momma always liked the name Winnow," Nadine said.

"We don't know," Aura said. "We haven't ever thought about it."

Himself whined uneasily. He jumped up on the bed and barked at the wind. A limestone block, weighing twice as much as the dog, dropped from the ceiling and bounced on the bed. The shock wave in the mattress sent Himself a foot up into the air, where he was lost in the darkness. When he came back down to the still-bouncing Earth, he knew the world wasn't the same as it once was. He leaped from the bed into six inches of water and crawled over the ten people in the stairwell to the niche formed by the last riser and the hatch.

"Did he bite anybody?" Nadine asked.

"I think he's just afraid," Carl said.

"We'll never get through all those heavy books if Mazelle's house falls on us," Mrs. Postlethwaite said.

"We can go out through Mr. Haygood's shop," Mrs. Haygood said.

"We may have to swim there," Carl said. "That dog's belly was wet."

"I still don't hear any fire engines or policemen," Mose said.

"I don't think we could hear them even if they were on the front lawn, what with all this noise," Nadine said.

"I'm sure they're plenty busy," Mazelle's husband said.

Aura took Marshall's hand and placed it on the back of the baby's head. Even though he couldn't see either of them, his wife or daughter, he could feel the baby feeding. He held the baby's head up. His hand felt as if a thousand volts were being funneled through it. He began to shiver.

"It's OK," Aura told him. "We told you it would be like this."

7:19 My tongue does not fit in my mouth anymore, plus which all my hairs are avoiding each other. I feel a whole lot more like I do now than I did a little while ago.

Verda woke as the roof of her front porch was ripped from her house. Her dogs sprang away from her as if she'd made the noise. She tried to coax them back through the darkness. "Come to Momma," she said. "It's a big storm." Dideebiteya and Yeseedid held their ground. Verda felt the wind sucking at the back of her blouse through the crack in the door. The interior of her house seemed unnaturally still, as hollow as her own stomach. The sound of the wind and rain was powerful but not oppressive. Even though she could hear shingles and trim being torn away she came to accept the destruction quite easily. It's what's inside that counts, she thought. I'll think of Jesus and all He's done for me. Now I'll think about my dogs. She called them again, calling them to her side, wanting them to be with her when she died.

Lightning revealed them hiding under her Hummel showcase. They barked at her as she called, high-pitched howls of betrayal. Finally, Verda screamed, "Trust me, you ungrateful little . . ." but she couldn't finish. "Just come here," she moaned, and first Yeseedid, then Dideebiteya, came skidding up into her lap. "I just love you," she bawled. "I just want to take care of you." She clutched both dogs under one arm and slid her body away from the door, pulled herself to the windowsill eighteen inches away. In flashes of light she saw the roof of her front porch lying on Tradio's lawn like a big dead bird. A group of white plastic lawn chairs chased a man down the street. All the houses were dark. The wind buffeted the windowpane that was only an inch from her nose, sweeping the glass dry for moments till another wave of rain splashed up against it. "It's the end of the world," she whispered to the dogs. "There's nowhere to go. This was the time we had to prepare." She sighed. In the vast noise of uprooting, the dogs heard Verda's stomach growl and they growled back. This made Verda giggle. "Silly dogs," she said.

She looked across the street to Effie's dark house. Effie doesn't have storm windows, she thought. She's always been jealous of me for my husband and storm windows. Jealous of my having not one daughter but two. How is it that I feel bad because she's jealous? In the scale of things, I don't have much. My husband is dead too, and the memory of him stained by Effie's mouth. I mark my things down too much when she wants to buy them because I feel sorry that she's jealous. I bet she has a bank account the size of Fort Worth and it's just her cheapness that wouldn't let her have storm windows. I should go over there as soon as I'm able and see if she's all right. Stubborn, stubborn, stubborn. If she'd just get a dog or even a cat to keep her company, but she's too tight to buy a tinful of cat food. And it's awful how she treats her customers. I don't fault her for her husband's death, though many do, including her son. But her son is worthless anyway. My husband wouldn't let him come near our daughters, not that they ended up marrying gold anyway. After I caught him in her mouth, I thought all those horrible things, that maybe he and Effie had been doing it for years and that Effie's son was his son too and that's why he didn't want him dating our girls, but those were just horrible thoughts. Effie didn't come after him till her own husband had died. She never wanted two of anything, plates, figurines, men. As long as she had one she was satisfied, unless, of course, it was kidneys.

Across the street, in the windows of Mrs. Martin's abandoned house, a flash of lightning seemed to linger. "Oh, it's on fire," Verda told her dogs. Famine, flood and fire, she thought, and this reminded her the world was ending, so she lay down beneath the window, along the baseboard, and listened to her dark house moan, the old lumber swaying as it once had a hundred years earlier when it was part of the living tree.

7:20 My lawyer may think I was born yesterday but he doesn't know I stayed up all night. My tongue is still oversized. My hair is singed for good. The phone is once again out of order, but I have paid my 89 cents monthly fee in case the cause is inside my house. Funny shadows on my shop walls. All thieves know a storm is an ideal time for breaking and entering.

Mazelle's husband moved his hand through darkness and found Mrs. Haygood's breast. Her only response was to put her cheek against his shoulder. They sat on the bottom step of Mr. Haygood's stairway, their feet awash in the watery soil of their swirling garden.

"Half of our garden will wash down into this hole," she whispered to him.

"We'll make another garden," he said. They'd walked through

water to reach the far side of the cistern. He unbuttoned the top half of her blouse and slid his hand across the taut wet skin of her breastbone and into the damp cup of her bra. Her breasts were smaller than he'd imagined.

"Your hands are warm," she whispered. "I'm afraid he'll come down,"she said. "He must be awake by now. He must have seen the empty shop by now."

"I can't help myself," Mazelle's husband said.

"I don't want you to help yourself," she said. "I'll move farther up the stairs."

"Move farther up the stairs."

"Are you two all right over there?" Nadine yelled.

"We're all right," Mrs. Haygood said.

"Do you want to come over here with us? There's room."

"We're all right," Mrs. Haygood said.

"It's the storm," Mazelle's husband whispered in Mrs. Haygood's ear.

"I'd rather it be me," she said as she lay back against the stairs.

"It's you," he said, crawling up over her. "We should have realized long ago."

"It was my fault. But we had our garden."

"And now we'll have this," he said.

"Now we'll have this too."

"Is it him?" he grunted.

"It's the storm," she said.

＊＊＊

7:23 I hear sirens far away. That means the storm is passing. My house is still standing. That time I called my son on the phone was a mistake, as I had a number written down on a piece of paper and since I couldn't remember who the number belonged to, I called it, and it was my son and so I hung up. His voice sure sounded the same.

✦

After work, Steve went home, changed his clothes, went to Luby's cafeteria, where he had a LuAnn Platter: chicken-fried steak, two vegetables and a bread choice for less than five dollars. The matches at the cash register were free. While he ate he calculated that if he skipped these dinners for two thousand eight hundred days he could just buy the old house from the bank and save his dignity.

He parked three blocks away, put the matches in an inside pocket of his coat, pulled a baseball cap over his face and stepped out into the driving rain. The thunderstorm would be perfect cover, and if anyone saw him wet they'd be hard-pressed to identify him dry. He'd decided to enter through the back door, and so he walked along the railroad tracks to the Row, where he climbed over the Postlethwaites' fence and slipped through Aura's. Once inside the Martin house, he slumped against the kitchen wall, grateful for the shelter. He sat there for almost half an hour, through the worst part of the storm, listening to the house come apart, watching water dribble down the walls. He struck fifteen matches and let them burn out between his fingers, dropping them to the floor at the last instant. Each one burned out ineffectually at his feet. At last he stood up, thought, All right, I don't care, it's not important enough, my job, to become an arsonist. And his knees buckled when the lightning struck. He dropped to the floor in the midst of overwhelming light and sound. His mouth opened and from it poured a wail of fear that he could only contain by placing his hands over his face. When he finally looked up, still rocking on his knees, he saw half a dozen small fires, each born at an electrical outlet. He took off his wet coat and slapped out the flame nearest him, slapped out a second and a third and gave up his coat to the fourth. By then the far wall was ablaze. Fire skipped across the old wallpaper. "I've got to go," he screamed at the old house and kicked open the front door. He ran through a field of plumbing fixtures, chased by Aura's lawn furniture.

⊁⊰

7:26 I just crawled over to my side window and Mrs. Martin's house is a sopping wet dishrag on the outside and burning up on the inside. It was that lightning, the same that made my tongue swell.

7:28 I am watching it burn.

7:29 This will give me a much better view into Aura's side windows.

⊁⊰

"Does it sound like it's easing up?" Mose asked.

"I still hear things falling," Mrs. Postlethwaite said.

"Before the storm's over," Mr. Postlethwaite said, "I want you all to know I molested my daughter."

"It's not true," Mrs. Postlethwaite snapped.

"That's why she hasn't come home in all these years," he said. "Because I touched her."

"It's not so," Mrs. Postlethwaite said. "Why do you say such things? It's something only she remembers. He's saying it's so for my sake. So she'll come home again. He was a good father."

They sat on the treads of the dark stairwell, shoulder to hip.

Finally, Mose said, "It seems to me this isn't any of our business, Mr. Postlethwaite."

"I want my daughter to know I've admitted it," he said. "If any of you have contact with her, you can tell her. Tell her to come home to her mother. I won't be there. We're going to have an auction. Sell off all the stock."

"You've lost your mind," Mrs. Postlethwaite said.

"None of us know where your daughter is, Mr. Postle-thwaite," Nadine said.

"Howard might know," Mose said. "He knows everything."

"What does he know?" Carl asked.

"He knew that Mr. Haygood and Mazelle were having an affair."

"Shhh," Nadine said.

"They can't hear us," Mose said. "They're on the far side of the cistern."

"I thought it was Mrs. Haygood and Mazelle's husband who were in love," Marshall said. His lips seemed uncoordinated, unusually loose, then he realized his bone was missing. The only other time he'd lost his bone was in a car wreck.

"Not according to Howard," Mose said. "He's been getting a payoff every month from Mr. Haygood and Mazelle for thirty years."

"He's been blackmailing them?" Nadine asked.

"He wants me to take up the payments after he dies," Mose answered.

"He's going to die?" Carl asked.

"I don't know."

"Is that what you two were talking about all day?" Nadine asked.

"Partly," Mose said.

"Partly," Nadine said. "Mose, on my momma's grave, what else?"

Mose felt his skin part from his body, form a loose bag over his muscles, bones and bowels. He thought if he got up and ran he'd simply collapse, his skin rolling around to the wrong side of his body, leaving him unable to see, speak or even defecate without making a mess, leaving his elbows poking out of his stomach and back, his knee hung in his scrotum. How stupid Nadine's momma was, how unfairly she'd treated him all those years. He didn't mean that at all. How lovely she was. How much he loved her. And now he not only had Nadine to remind him of her features and character but Aura too. Then, quite suddenly, after almost eighty years of missing it, he invented a method to obfuscate the truth. Instead of lying badly he could simply expose a personal weakness or fault and misdirect everyone's attention. "Howard wants to learn how to fix radios," Mose said. "But I can't teach him. I don't so much fix radios as replace their parts. I cannibalize old radios for parts or simply put new parts in a broken radio till it works."

"But that's what surgeons do," Carl said.

"I've got two new knees that were done that way," Mrs. Postlethwaite said. "I don't even walk with a cane anymore."

"Do you know what the last thing I said to Howard was?" Mose said. "He asked me what he should do to make up for the way he's been and I told him to sign the back of his license, to donate his organs when he died."

"But he's so old," Aura said. "How good would his organs be?"

"That's right," Marshall said.

"What else has he done, Mose? That's the worst thing I've ever heard you say to anyone," Nadine said.

"Oh, Lord," Mose said.

"Mose."

"I don't know what to say."

"Mose."

"I've passed some wind."

"Mose."

Another failed invention, Mose thought. I don't want to be the only person who knows. Damn that old Indian. He was right: it's too heavy to carry. But he realized that once he told, everyone would understand that Nadine's momma spurned him fully, that she hadn't refused all men, only him. Well, he thought, the old thing's dead. She won't be hurt. And Nadine deserves a sister. I'll just be less important. She won't rely on me anymore.

She'll ask Marshall for favors, since he's her brother-in-law, her family. I will give up my way of life so they'll be happier.

"Why are you making that sound, Mose, honey?" Nadine asked. "I wish it wasn't so dark. I can't see your face." She reached up two steps till she found his knee.

"What sound?" he asked.

"You're moaning, honey. Are you sick?"

"Things aren't going to be the same," Mose said. He paused. The sound of the wind filled this gap. "Nadine, honey, Howard told me that he and your momma had a baby together, and she birthed that baby the year she sent you to Paris, and that baby became an Edna Gladney baby, and that baby is Aura here, which would make her baby your niece, not your granddaughter, and your momma untrue to both of us."

A moment passed, another, and then the stairwell echoed a soft patter of weeping. It was Carl who cried.

"Why are you crying?" Mrs. Postlethwaite asked.

Marshall explained. "Well, he's built a boat out of his house, hoping to carry Nadine away because he loves her. And I guess now he figures she won't go since she has family here."

7:30 House still on fire. I burned my finger bad once on a cigarette my husband left on the kitchen counter. Still, he did not die of lung cancer.

Tradio woke gradually. The bathtub drain was directly over his face and water dripped into his eyes. He moved his head to avoid the water and banged it into the cast iron. The pain was slight compared to that in his shoulder and chest. He lifted the arm that didn't hurt and felt for the thing he'd banged into. His body was covered with wet leaves. His hand touched the cool porcelain, traveled up the wall, slid over the bottom of the tub and back down the other side to the ground. The darkness was total. They've buried me alive, he thought. I missed the ambulance and the hospital and the mortuary and my own funeral to wake up from a coma in my casket. He put his hand back up to the ceiling of his vault and pushed with all his might. It didn't even begin to budge. He started to roll over but his chest hurt. What the hell kind of casket was this? They didn't even buy me a casket. I'm in some kind of cheap metal box with my back in the muck. Goddamn it, I paid for a plot and a two-thousand-dollar casket five years ago, so my daughter wouldn't be bothered. I'd have thought Arthur would have seen me into the ground with some decency at least. Tradio moved his hand down his aching chest to his crotch. I'm not even in a goddamned suit, he thought. Water dripped in his ear and he put his hand up to the stopperless drain. Some kind of pipe or tube. I can hear the wind blowing across it. It must go all the way to the surface to let the gases escape. They didn't even goddamn embalm me.

7:32 Fire working its way from Mrs. Martin's kitchen to her bedroom. The dining room will be next. I never ate there. You never do eat at the restaurants close to home. She was another one never too busy to look my way. She wanted to sell me her house and it's a good thing I didn't buy it. My husband thought she served a good lunch. Now she's dead and I can't tell her her house is burning down.

Mr. Haygood woke from his nap when a trash can burst through his bedroom window. At first he was furious with Mrs. Haygood. She must have dropped something in the kitchen. And she hadn't woken him at the usual time. He'd slept all the way to dark. Now he'd never get a good night's rest. But when he pulled the covers from his legs, glass fell to the floor. Something dripped off the end of his nose. He put his hand to his forehead and found blood there. The wind blew through his house freely. He couldn't understand why Mrs. Haygood hadn't woken him when the lights went out. He called for her. He called again. "I've been cut," he added. He yelled this again. Still, the worthless woman did not come. He bolted into the kitchen, sure that he'd find her sitting at the table so immersed in one of her gardening books that she ignored him. But the kitchen was empty. He put a paper towel to his forehead and then looked at the blood on the paper towel. Mazelle's house was dark too. Her car was in the garden between the two houses. He picked up the phone to call her, but it was dead. The wind corkscrewed around his body. There must be another door or window open, he thought. "Mrs. Haygood," he yelled again, and walked past the broken window, through the incoming rain. He opened the door to his shop but the wind jerked it back. He pulled harder, and saw that his front door had been yanked from its hinges. His shop was in tatters, papers everywhere, boxes on the floor. Water dripped from the ceiling and flowed off the light fixture. Then he saw that his shelves and showcases were empty. The toys weren't on the floor. They were gone. For a moment he thought they'd been sucked from the room by the storm, but the Buddy "L" trucks would have been too heavy, and most of the showcases had been locked. He'd been robbed. Mrs. Haygood was gone. He walked toward the cash register, expecting to find her bludgeoned body on the floor behind it.

7:35 I tried calling 911 again but no matter how hard I mash the buttons no one answers. Everyone in Fort Worth comes before Effie, I guess.

7:37 The wind is pushing that fire right through that house, opening doors and welcoming it from room to room. I can smell that old nasty smoke now. I hope I don't have to get out my water hose.

Even though he had chosen his largest bathtub for himself, Howard was still cramped beneath it. He knew this was a bad storm coming. Bare minutes after he turned the tub over himself he heard objects striking its sides. Water cascaded through the drain, washed over his face and soaked into the grass. This didn't bother him. He'd been wet before. In fact, he hadn't felt as secure in years. The storm raged without, but all he knew of it was cool water and the occasional ringing of his cast-iron cocoon. He clasped his hands and brought them up beneath his cheek for a pillow. The baby had interrupted his confession. There was the one thing more to tell Mose, a thing which was his fault and wasn't his fault. The night was still young, he reminded himself. The storm will pass, and if Mose survives it, he'll hear me out. Twice he'd felt the pounding of running feet across his yard, but he heard nothing over the roar of the wind and rain. Strange, how much stronger he felt now than he had that morning. The storm would provide many salvaging opportunities. Strange, how easy it was now to fall asleep.

7:40 Rain slacking off. No one on the street. There'll be no saving of Mrs. Martin's house now. Verda has missed the big show. They're all peeping from their windows and doing nothing about this fire.

7:43 I wish this fire was further away. Somebody ought to come and put it out.

"You can't believe that old liar," Carl said, and wiped his nose.

"Nadine?" Aura asked, not knowing what she asked.

"I can't believe you said those things, Mose," Nadine said.

"I'm just the messenger," Mose said hurriedly.

"But I am an Edna Gladney baby," Aura said. "What month did you come home from Paris, Nadine?"

"June."

"I was born in April."

"Every lie has some truth in it," Nadine said.

"You don't want to be my sister?" Aura asked.

"Aura, that's not it, honey. It's just impossible. Why would Momma hide something like that from me?"

"Howard said she did it because she was ashamed. She wasn't married. She thought you wouldn't mind her anymore," Mose explained. "He thinks she even set Aura up in her house here on the Row."

"But my parents . . ." Aura began and stopped.

"The baby does sort of look like—" Marshall began.

"Shut up," Nadine snapped.

"I was going to say 'Howard.' "

"Howard's my biological father," Aura mused. "Marshall, we've collected a daughter, a sister, a sister-in-law, a father and a father-in-law all in one day. It's the biggest family we've ever been a part of. Oh, Nadine, we hope it's true."

"Howard's only saying it all because he knows he was the only other person on the Row at that time."

"Effie was here, Nadine," Mose said.

"You see," Nadine said, "how could that old gossip keep such a secret for all these years? If Momma had a baby she couldn't have hidden it from Effie."

"Howard says your momma had something on Effie."

"But Momma's dead now. She could have started blabbing years ago."

"Maybe Effie thinks Howard knows whatever your momma knew," Mr. Postlethwaite said.

"It's awfully complicated," Aura said. "But here's how it stands with us, Nadine. If you're our sister we're really happy."

"We'd just be half-sisters," Nadine said.

"We don't want anything from you. We just want us to be sisters, a matched set."

"You'd want Howard as a father?"

"Your momma brought him to our house once. He didn't insult anything we had."

"I can't believe everyone's ready to drag my momma through the mud for something somebody said. There's no proof. You can't just change her after she's dead. She doesn't have a chance to have her say."

"Her say was to deny it," Mrs. Postlethwaite said.

"There were other neighbors back then, not just Effie," Nadine said.

"But there was a pretty good turnover on the Row in the early fifties, Nadine," Mose said. "Everyone respected your momma. They may have been able to keep a secret for just a few years. I guess they're all dead by now."

"How'd you come by your house, Aura?" Carl asked.

"Our parents left it to us. We always thought it was strange, because it came to us so long after they'd passed away."

"Your momma never owned Aura's house, did she?" Carl asked Nadine.

"Of course not."

"A house would have been a lot of money," Carl said.

"You could check her bank statements," Aura said.

"For the last thirty years? Momma always threw away her receipts in case she got audited."

"Maybe there was another reason than the IRS," Mrs. Postlethwaite hypothesized.

204 • Joe Coomer

"I've heard about enough speculation," Nadine said.

"Howard seemed pretty sure of himself, Nadine," Mose said. "And you're going to hurt Aura's feelings. This thing bothers me as much as it does you, honey."

From the far side of the cistern, Mazelle's husband called out, "Can you keep talking? We're coming across and we'll follow your voices."

"We're over here," Mose yelled.

There was the sound of sloshing water as Mrs. Haygood and Mazelle's husband waded by the bed to the crowded stairwell.

"Sounds like it's beginning to let up," Mazelle's husband said. "We, Mrs. Haygood and I, Dorothy and I, want to say good-bye to everyone. We're going away."

"Going away?" Nadine said, as if she had been personally insulted.

"But why?" Mrs. Postlethwaite asked.

"I'm leaving too," Mr. Postlethwaite said.

"You are not," she cried.

"We won't be able to let anybody know where we are," Mrs. Haygood said. "I've enjoyed knowing all of you. You were good neighbors."

"I've got to get out of here too," Nadine said. "I've got to go speak to Effie and Howard."

"I'd like to get Aura and the baby to the hospital," Marshall said.

"We're all right, Marshall."

Carl asked, "Doesn't anyone want to see my boat?"

7:45 I am not going to look at that burning house anymore. It can burn and crack and pop and smoke all it wants to and I'm not going to concern myself. I didn't set it on fire. My taxes support a fire department. I'm worried about that old dog.

After a thorough search of Howard's house, Arthur ran back through the storm, narrowly avoiding his own lawn mower, which was racing down the street, to Tradio's. Neither Howard nor Tradio were to be found. He couldn't understand where they could have gone. All the cars were still on the street. An ambulance couldn't have come and gone in the short time he was at Mazelle's. He went back out into the driving rain and yelled Tradio's name into the wind. His voice was carried up and away from him, the sound snatched from deep in his throat before it even made it to his lips. I'm not going to cry, he told himself. I've made some mistake and I've just got to figure it out. He'd seen Howard pick up Tradio, but then the baby had come, distracting him. Howard wouldn't have carried him all the way to the hospital district. That was miles away, two or three miles away. He went back into Tradio's bedroom, took the crumpled sheets in his hands, then curled up on the bed. It was seven or eight minutes before the thought of Effie struck him. He's at Effie's. Howard took him to Effie's. Her house would have been closer. Or at least she knows where he is. She never takes her eyes off him. Arthur made it halfway across the street before an eight-by-ten-foot section of Carl's house siding fell on top of him, pinning him to the wet pavement. He tried to move but several rows of nails pierced his skin, and the weight of the siding, although endurable, was far too great to move. He laid as still as he could, and hoped the wind wouldn't pick up the siding again. He didn't know which he was more afraid of, flying away with the section of house or being torn suddenly from it. One nail had pierced his cheek, and to divert himself he repeatedly touched his tongue to its rusty point.

7:47 They all came streaming out of Mazelle's house like the movie just ended and then they all saw the fire like it was the first time they've seen a fire. I can see the expressions on all their faces in the firelight. They thought it was a flood when it was really a fire. I was the one who saw it first. It's my fire. Now they've decided to put it out. Aura is the only one staying put in Mazelle's front yard. Everyone else has a job to do. Aura has something in her arms. I guess everyone was invited to Mazelle's for the storm but Effie. It's real still now and the fire is going straight up like it's the only thing in the world. Mose is using my water hose—<u>my water.</u> That dog is trying to get under Mrs. Martin's porch but that carpenter won't let him.

Of all his repairs, of all his inventions and insights, Mose never felt more satisfaction than he did at that moment, placing his thumb over the bib of the hose so the water would reach out farther into the fire. I should have put things out, he thought, I should have been a fireman. I should have saved people, saved houses, saved furniture. I should have put myself at risk, rather than have spent a life worrying over details, a better way to lace up shoes. I should have fought something that could fight back. I should have pushed that storm back with a trash can lid. He advanced on the fire, turned the arc of water into a window. Embers floated around his ears, and small leaves of flame cartwheeled through the Saint Augustine grass. The smoke was the flavor of mud, of bottom fish. Fighting a fire was a much finer life than thinking about women while you turned a screw back into a hole it had made fifty years earlier. There were other shapes around him, bending into the smoke, rolling away, but they all seemed unimportant, unconnected to him and his hose, his thumb pressed into the fire.

7:51 Now comes Mr. Haygood to join in the fun. He has his wife by the arm, trying to save her. Mazelle's husband has a hose now too, and Mr. Postlethwaite, but I can't see Marshall or Nadine. They ought to stay in my view.

Nadine took off Carl's shirt and began to beat the burning grass that was working toward Marshall and Aura's house. Occasionally, a shred of her nightgown would glow or begin to flame and she'd reach down and squeeze the fabric in her palm as if she were crushing rose petals. She felt the heat in her hair, and it was hotly cupped between her breasts. The grass steamed between her bare toes. She slapped at the earth again and again, railing against the bright line of light that was clinched between her eyelids. That's where the money went, she thought, Aura's house. We were all right before I went to Paris and when I got home we were poor. I thought it was my year of school in Paris that did it, but all the time it was another one of these narrow houses. I didn't believe that on my own. Momma let me believe it. She never said she needed help. It was just there, the need. I thought a life was hard to come by and all that time we were paying for our life and another life. It would have been easier. It would have been as easy as it is now. She could have managed alone. I'd have had a different life. Nadine stood up. Her breasts swayed among the singed scraps of silk. "Everybody on this side," she screamed. "Save Aura's house. Save my baby sister's house." She ran around to Mose, caught him by the shirttail and pulled him away from the window. "To the far side," she yelled. "Save Aura's house. Mrs. Martin's house is gone."

"I can't see," Mose yelled back. "I can't see."

"Carl, you take the water hose from Mose. Mose, you hold on to this crazy dog. Squat down here in the yard and hold on to the dog."

"I will, Nadine," Mose said. "I won't let him go." He held the dog to his chest with one arm and rubbed at his own eyes with his other hand.

"Your chest is burnt, Nadine," Carl said. "You stay back. We'll wet down Aura's house. We'll save it." He took off his undershirt and threw it at her.

Nadine caught the T-shirt. She knelt down next to Mose and the cowering dog.

"I've got smoke in my eyes, Nadine," Mose said. "I'm sorry for all those things I said. I shouldn't repeat things people say."

Nadine pulled the shirt over her head, winced when it crossed her breasts. "Mose, honey," she said, "I love old things. I can't stand to see old things go by."

"Is the porch on fire now, Nadine?"

"It's gone, Mose, the whole place is gone. Poor old Mrs. Martin's tearoom is burning down. All the people who lived in that old house don't have anywhere to go now."

"I got too close to the fire, Nadine."

"I'll take care of you, honey. We're safe where we are. I'm sure a fire engine will be here soon."

"Are they saving Aura's house, Nadine?"

"They're saving it."

"What about Effie's house?"

"The fire is going straight up now, Mose. Her house is all right too."

"Why did your momma love him, Nadine?"

"I don't know, Mose."

"I wish Aura were my daughter. I wish you and Aura were my daughters, and that little baby my granddaughter, and I wish Marshall would come talk to me when he didn't understand you girls. I wish I had the memories that Howard doesn't care anything about."

"Don't cry, Mose."

"I'm not crying. There's smoke in my eyes. I've thought all this through. I feel awful on purpose. What will we do now, Nadine?"

"Mose, just hush."

"OK, Nadine."

7:53 Mose and Nadine keep looking my way even though there's a house afire next door. She has on the worst outfit I've ever seen her flaunt.

7:54 Aura holding a live baby!

"Where have you been? Somebody has taken everything. We've been robbed. Everything is gone. Why didn't you wake me? Where have you been?"

"What do you mean?" Mrs. Haygood said. "Let go of my arm."

"We have been robbed, you stupid woman. Where were you?"

"I was hiding from the storm."

"Where?"

"At Mazelle's house."

"Did you see anyone at our house?"

"No."

"Well, everything is gone."

"What do you mean 'everything'? Do you mean me?"

"My toys. What else do we have? My toys."

"You didn't hear anything?"

"I was asleep. You know I was asleep."

"Are you going to help with the fire?"

"Don't you understand? God almighty. We have nothing, nothing."

"Did you call the police?"

"The phone is out."

"Let go of my arm."

He threw her arm back at her body as if it were something separate from her. "Get your ass back to the house."

"No. I'm helping with the fire."

"I'm going for the police. I'll find you at home when I get back." Mrs. Haygood didn't answer. She watched him turn toward his car, then realize the streets were blocked by debris. "I'll run down to the intersection and flag a policeman down. Maybe the phones are working at the convenient store."

She nodded at him as he stumbled down the street, out of the firelight. I'll not see you again, she thought. That's the last I'll see of you. It seemed to her that the past had always been overwhelmingly vast, but now, in an instant, it turned small and insignificant. It was the future that loomed up large and unavoidable. She looked for Mazelle's husband. He was walking out of the smoke from between the houses. Marshall was slumped over his shoulder like a thin roll of carpet. Mazelle's husband had carried heavy things all his life, she thought, in preparation for this moment.

7:55 Mr. Haygood has left the scene. They have all moved onto my lawn to escape the smoke. My house is getting smoke damage. I hear sirens again. I would carry all my things outside if I weren't sure it would be a free-for-all.

"It's all of us now," Aura whispered to her baby. "We're included. We're not fat or skinny. We're a family. We're just right. So many odd parts have come together to make an ordinary whole. We get to talk to each other till the day we die. We don't feel too hot anymore. Look, we're getting a perfect tan in the light of the moon. You're our moon pie and we're gonna eat you up." Aura sat on the grass of Mazelle's lawn, among shingles and leaves. She tucked the baby in, held it close, rolled over and used the very tautness of her skin to propel her body up to standing. She was about to yell that the house wasn't important, for everyone to back away, when Marshall came out of the smoke folded over Mazelle's husband's shoulder. Marshall's fingertips bumped across the grass. That's not right, she thought. She called out his name as if he'd done something wrong, as if he were thinking too little of himself. She'd always tried to convince him he was worth more than he thought. Her steps were small because of the pain between her legs. She stepped down off the curb and took the straightest line to Marshall's side, which was over the top of a section of house siding in the middle of the street. Marshall was lying among her neighbors just as she had been earlier in the evening. His body seemed deflated, as if he'd given birth too. She'd heard screaming as she'd crossed the street, but it apparently wasn't coming from Marshall. He lay quietly on the ground, his mouth open, his eyes shut. Aura put the baby on his chest and began mouth-to-mouth resuscitation.

"He just collapsed in front of me," Mazelle's husband said. "I could hardly see him for the smoke." Then he allowed himself to cough.

Aura had only begun, had delivered only one gust of breath into the limp sock of his body, when Marshall blew it right back at her. It returned smelling of smoke and bone. The baby rose and fell on his heaving chest.

"I'll be goddamned," Mr. Postlethwaite said.

Aura turned to Mazelle's husband. "Thank you for carrying him out of the smoke."

"Thank goodness," Nadine said. She picked the newborn up and held it close while Aura tended to her husband.

"Lie still, Marshall," Carl said. "Your house is safe. I'll help fix it if there's any damage. We'll fix up all these old houses."

"Aura, honey," Nadine said, "I'm going to take the baby with me into Effie's house to get her out of the smoke."

Aura nodded. She put one of her hands on Marshall's neck, the other on his temple. She bent down and whispered in his ear, "We're not tired at all. We're just right."

7:59 There is finally a fire engine pulling up at the bottom of our street. Effie to the rescue. Maybe they can get all these people off of my grass. Nadine coming this way, no doubt wanting my advice.

8:00 Nadine at my door knocking.

8:01 She is still knocking.

8:02 Nadine kicking at my door with her foot!

Nadine entered Effie's shop with one long stride attached to the end of her last kick, her body wrapped in a nightgown of smoke, the baby crying. She screamed, "Come out from behind that counter, Effie. Right now."

"You always know right where I am, Nadine, honey."

"You always hide in the same place, Effie!"

"Is there something you'd like to see?"

"I'm not here to shop, Effie. Were you just going to burn down with your house? Why didn't you come outside and help us?"

"I don't know, Nadine. I called 911. The fire truck is here. It sounded like someone was trying to break into every one of my windows. I had to protect my things. I think Mazelle's husband and Mrs. Haygood are having an affair."

"I think you're right, Effie."

"You do?" Effie put her pad and pencil down on the counter and approached Nadine and the baby. "What have you got there?"

"This is Aura's new baby, Effie. I want to know what you can tell me about Aura being my sister."

"What? Wait a minute. I need to write this down." She retreated to her counter. Nadine stood in firelight, then shadow, then firelight, as firemen crossed in front of the window.

"I want to know what you know about my momma having a baby while I was in Paris thirty-five years ago."

"How should I know anything about that?"

"Because you and Howard are the only neighbors left who lived here then. You had to notice if she was pregnant. Why didn't you tell me? Why haven't you, at the very least, told me since she died?"

"How did you find out?" Effie asked.

"Howard."

"You haven't opened the safety deposit box yet?"

"What safety deposit box?"

"Can't you make that baby be quiet?"

"Effie!"

"Does Aura want all my things? Your momma put her here so she'd get my things. What my husband did doesn't pertain to me. I had no sexual part in it. My things are my things. Can I see if the baby looks like my husband?"

"Why would Aura and Marshall's baby look like your husband?"

"Because my husband is Aura's father."

"What?"

"It's all in the safety deposit box. You'll see."

"What safety deposit box?"

214 • JOE COOMER

"The one your mother left for you if I ever told you she got pregnant."

"There's no safety deposit box," Nadine said.

"Your mother's lawyers had instructions to give it to you if you ever found out about the baby."

"My mother never had a lawyer."

"You didn't know she had a baby either, Nadine," Effie said.

"Tell me what your husband had to do with all this."

"My husband and your momma made the baby."

"No, they didn't."

"Yes, they did," Effie yelled. "Why are you asking me if you think you know everything?"

"It was Howard, Effie. Howard and my mother. He's already admitted it."

"Your momma told me it was my husband. Why would she have a baby with that old Indian? My husband was a handsome man."

"Did he admit the affair too?" Nadine asked.

"I never asked him."

"For God's sake, why not?"

"I knew your momma wanted him. Every woman on the Row wanted what I had. But he stayed with me till he died. Your momma said she would take him from me if I told on her. She was pretty."

"Another woman told you she had an affair with your husband and you didn't confront him?"

"He knew that I knew."

"How?"

"I treated him bad from then on. From that day on."

"Effie, Momma just told you it was your husband so you wouldn't tell me about the baby. There's no safety deposit box. Momma didn't even have a bank account, much less a lawyer. Howard has admitted he is Aura's father. He told Mose today. You treated your husband badly for no reason. Everybody knew your husband loved you, Effie. Nobody could understand it, but they all knew. You should have confronted him."

"He would have denied it," Effie said.

"Of course he would have," Nadine said.

"If he hadn't denied it," Effie said, "I thought he would move across the street and live with you and your momma."

"Effie, you treated him bad for eighteen years? From nineteen fifty-one until the day he died? Is that why, when he was sick? I mean, is that why you refused at the last minute?"

"What's mine is mine."

"So you not only lost your husband but also your son because you were afraid to even ask if you'd been compromised?"

"My husband cheated on me."

"No, Effie. You cheated on yourself."

"If Aura is your sister, she's my stepdaughter, and that baby is my stepgrandchild."

"Neither one of them have any claim to your things, Effie. You're free and clear."

"Let me hold her."

—✦—

8:10 They are putting out the fire.

—✦—

"You are an old man and you carried a young man out of a fire," Mrs. Haygood said.

Mazelle's husband straightened up. It looked as if Marshall would be all right. "He was the lightest load I ever carried," he said. "And I only carried him out of the smoke." He looked at her. "Is everything all right?"

"We should leave now. I've seen him. While you were fighting the fire. He knows the toys are gone."

"Did he find them?"

"No. He's run up the street. I haven't seen him run in thirty years. He's trying to flag down a policeman or see if the phones are working at the convenient store."

"All right then. It's time to go. Are you ready?"

"I'm ready."

"Will you want some clothes?"

"I don't want anything. But your car is stuck. When I pulled it over the hole in the cistern it stuck in the mud."

"Can we take Mr. Haygood's car?"

"We could, but the street is blocked."

Mazelle's husband looked at the tree limbs, the section of house siding. "There's nothing that's too heavy for me to move. Why don't you take the toys from my car and put them in your car. I'll start clearing a path in the street."

"There's the fire truck. Can a fireman arrest us?" Mrs. Haygood asked.

"I don't think they'll care anything about us," he said.

"I just feel like the whole world is watching me," she said. "I've never felt like this before. I committed adultery tonight. No wonder Mr. Haygood did it for all those years. It feels so good. I was thinking we might go to New England. Roses grow so well there."

"It's a short season," Mazelle's husband warned.

"We can look at seed catalogues in the winter."

"Maybe a little south-facing greenhouse for seedlings," he added.

"It wasn't just you. I want you to know that," she said. "We're both infertile. We're both just a couple of annuals."

"If you'll get the toys, I'll clear the street."

"I'll get the toys."

"I'll clear the street."

8:11 I knew all along. Effie knew.

❧

Arthur heard the approaching footsteps (they were in the same cadence as the hoofbeats of a radio sound-effect horse) and braced himself as well as he could. Smoke had worked its way between the studs and the pavement, and he could also hear the roar of the fire. He could see through a two-inch gap beneath the siding, could see leaves flattened to the road, pebbles, a twig and then Aura's bare feet. Her toes were bunched together like ripe grapes. She took little hops as she advanced toward the siding. Her feet disappeared when she jumped up on the section of house. All the nails in Arthur's body were extracted momentarily, and then as Aura stepped farther along, were driven home again. He screamed. As Aura ran directly over him, and he took the full weight of her body, the scream he would have screamed came out as ineffectual gusts of breath. As she reached the far edge of the siding the nails were pulled and replaced once more. Arthur passed out.

When Mazelle's husband lifted the siding up on its edge, he was surprised to find Arthur plastered on the underside, hanging between two studs. He was either asleep or dead. It almost looked as if he were trying to hide.

"Arthur?" Mazelle's husband said.

Arthur woke when he felt all his blood rushing to his feet. His eye swung wildly around to Mazelle's husband.

"Are you stuck?" Mazelle's husband asked.

Arthur nodded, pivoting his head on the nail through his cheek.

"OK, I'm going to lay you back down, right side up."

"I've lost Tradio," Arthur mumbled.

"Can you move at all?"

"I don't want to."

"How many nails are you stuck on?"

"Many," Arthur said. It was such a relief to be lying on the siding, rather than beneath it.

Firemen were dragging hoses up the street toward them. Mazelle's husband turned to his neighbors. Aura sat over Marshall. Mose held the dog. Carl was up against Effie's house, his hands and face pressed between the iron bars that protected a window.

"Carl," Mazelle's husband yelled.

Carl turned as if he'd been pinched.

"I need help."

With the section of siding overturned, Carl recognized it as part of his house. The heavy cypress sheathing had been removed and replaced with thin plywood. But he didn't recognize the amorphous lump between two of the studs. Not until he reached Mazelle's husband's side did he realize it was human. "What the hell?" he asked.

"He's nailed himself to the wall," Mazelle's husband explained.

"What was he doing in my house?" Carl asked.

"Your house came to me," Arthur choked out.

Carl stepped farther out in the street in order to see the front of his home. The porch was gone. The gable surrounding his bowsprit was gone. He could see the bow of his boat quite clearly. He ran up into Verda's front yard. All four walls of his house were gone. The first and last ten feet of his roof had blown away too, and the rest had collapsed onto the cabin and deck of his sweet yacht.

"Carl," Mazelle's husband screamed.

"I'm coming," Carl yelled back. He ran to the middle of the street again. "This siding came from my house," he said. "The nails only protrude through the plywood sheathing by three-eighths of an inch or so." He squatted down next to Arthur. "Now, I can get a pair of nippers and cut the shank of each nail between your skin and the plywood, but I think that would hurt worse than just pulling yourself away from the lumber. The nails don't go into your body as deeply as you might think. If I stand on the studs on each side of your body, can you push yourself up?"

"I don't know," Arthur said. He moved his free hand up to his face.

"Do you want me to pull you away in one quick jerk?" Mazelle's husband offered.

"No, no, no," Arthur whispered, "I'll do it." He ran his flattened, splayed fingers between his cheek and the plywood, on each side of the puncture wound, and slowly worked his cheek off the shaft of the nail. There was surprisingly little blood.

"There you go," Carl said. "Just like a fish."

A fireman stood over them. "Is he all right?"

"He has nails in his body," Mazelle's husband explained, his hands on his knees.

"We've already called paramedics in for the man with smoke inhalation. It may be a while before they get here, though. Lots of calls. I've got men in that fire that I need to help."

"Go ahead, we're with him," Carl said.

Arthur pulled himself off a nail embedded in his bicep, then off another in the loose skin of his elbow. Both arms were now free. He pushed his torso up and three nails popped from his side in succession. None of them had struck a rib. He sat for a moment, breathing heavily against his fear and pain, waiting for the courage to continue. "Has anyone seen Tradio?" he asked.

"Howard took him," Carl said.

"Mose said Howard put Tradio under a bathtub," Mazelle's husband said.

They turned to Howard's front yard. Two of the old tubs were overturned.

"I'll kill that old Indian," Arthur trebled.

"It might have been the safest place for him," Carl said. "Look what happened to you."

"I've got a nail in my hip and I can't get any leverage," Arthur said. "Bend down, Carl, and take me by the waist and give me one concerted tug."

"I'm not going to be gentle with you," Carl said. "I'm really going to pull. We don't want to do it halfway."

"I'm ready."

Carl jerked.

"Ow, ow, ow, ow," Arthur stuttered.

Carl lowered Arthur's hips back down to rest on the stud. "You're just a little fellow," he said.

"That one was deep. There's one more in my ankle. I'll get it." He reached down and pried his ankle from the nail. Carl helped him up and off the siding.

The three men now stood in the beam of a car's headlights. It was Mrs. Haygood's car. As soon as Arthur was free from the siding, Mazelle's husband picked up the entire section and dragged it off the street. "Don't want anybody to get a flat," he explained. Then he walked around to the passenger side of Mrs. Haygood's car and got in. Then he got back out. "Do you need to go to the hospital, Arthur?"

"I'm sore, but I'm OK. It's Tradio I'm worried about. I think he was having a heart attack."

Mrs. Haygood's car was running, but she too got out and ran to Aura and Marshall. "We can take you to the hospital, Aura. You and Marshall."

"We'll wait on the ambulance. The firemen have already called for it," Aura said. "But thank you, anyway. Are you really gone for good, Mrs. Haygood?"

"I hope so," she said.

"We should have been a better neighbor to you," Aura said. "We knew you weren't happy."

"Things are better now," Mrs. Haygood said.

Marshall lay sprawled between them, wheezing easily in the grass. He held on to his wife's polished, bulbous ankle. Above him, beyond his wife and Mrs. Haygood, the clouds scudded away, revealing a bright moonlit firmament that provided a backdrop to the spiraling smoke and embers of the fire. He opened his mouth to let the smoke in his own body escape into the sky.

"Lift this one first," he heard someone far away say.

※

8:12 Effie knew.

8:13 Effie knew.

※

In Verda's dream all the figurines in her shop were alive, spoke in whispers and slowly, solemnly, made their way to her side. Two by two they came, Jack and Jill, George and Martha, cherub and cherub, pairs of Scottie dogs and Siamese cats, the Campbell's Soup Kids, Jimmy and Rosalynn, Oliver and Hardy, salt and pepper sets by the hundreds. They gathered around her prostrate body, took one another by the hand or paw, and with mouths pinched to ruby red circles, began to sing a throaty dirge. Before long, Verda was among them, become porcelain and paint, the dirge issuing from her own glazed lips, her old body humped and graceless above her. She looked down at her new arms of fired clay, coated with a flesh-colored slip and a clear glistening glaze. They were free of wrinkles. In her left hand was the smooth hairless paw of a sheepdog. In her right was another hand of the same clay and glaze as her own. It squeezed her fingers. She looked up and saw that it was her long-dead husband, his ashen and guilty face turned pink and blushing. The buttons on his coat were hugely oversized. And although he sang sadly, he was obviously happy to be paired with her. Glassy tears of joy bonded to her cheeks, and she sang proudly of her death, of the life she'd lived.

8:14 Then why did he act guilty? I have more pieces of Van Briggle than any other shop on the Row.

8:15 I would never move from here because my house is paid for. It would have been my fault if I'd accused him.

Tradio's rage faltered when another pain gripped his chest. Take your nitro this time, he thought. He reached into his pants pocket and found the vial there, along with some change and his truck keys. After placing the tablet under his tongue, he wondered why they'd bury him with the keys to the house and truck in his pocket. He wondered who had taken over his broadcasts. He wondered what his daughter would think when she found out he'd left the house and business to Arthur. He still couldn't understand why they'd buried him so quickly. He was in the same clothes he'd died in. He wasn't Jewish. He was a radio personality. Perhaps he'd died of some horrible communicable disease and couldn't be touched. Then why didn't they burn me? he thought. He wondered if he was buried next to Alice. He wouldn't mind that. He was comforted by it. He hoped they'd put Arthur on his other side some day, when he passed away.

By the time the wind wallowed to a vibrating hum over the end of the pipe, the dripping water also ceased. It was very quiet. The nitro was taking hold. The pain lessened. He'd had these attacks before and always come through them. The last thing he could remember was thinking Arthur had been shot. He'd run toward him and found that it was Aura on the ground, not Arthur, and she was birthing a baby. But he'd already been swooning. He'd thought he was dying. He remembered the beginning of his fall but not the impact. He'd thrown himself toward his old neighbors. I died, Tradio thought, at the same instant that baby was born. So I had to be buried whether I died or not. It was some strange computation of God.

Then, by holding his eye up to the pipe opening as if it were a telescope, he made out a single star that was eclipsed from time to time. He figured it out: they'd buried him under a tree. A tree branch or a leaf was blowing under that star every once in a while. He wondered if it cost more to get a burial plot under a tree. At least, he thought, I've got a view and some shade. It's a good thing I was never spastic about bugs the way Arthur is. It's a good thing I'm not claustrophobic. For a coffin, this one's kind of roomy. That's the prettiest star I've ever seen, and it's mine. If I'm lucky, I'm under the moon's orbit. That would light things up in here.

He smelled smoke, then watched as it grew thicker, obscuring his star. My God, they are burning the corpses. I was one of the first to go in the epidemic. Maybe everybody on the Row, everybody I ever knew, is dead. But I'm not dead. It's some kind of near-death sleeping sickness. They're making a horrible mistake. He heard voices, then yelling, then sirens. He put his mouth to the pipe and cupped his hands around it. "Down here," he yelled. "I'm alive. Down here." And then, he couldn't resist, he howled. "Booooooo," he said, rolling it up the pipe. "BOOOOOO."

8:16 People make mistakes. I don't fault people for their mistakes.

Howard woke from his nap. There was the unmistakable odor of dog shit in his nose. He'd somehow broken the dry skin on an old dog turd. He must be lying on it. The smell was thick in his nostrils, as if his sinuses were packed with excrement. I have to get out from underneath this tub, he thought. His hands had fallen asleep beneath his face. The porcelain seemed closer than it had before, more constricting. It was all he could do to shift his body enough to get his palms against the bathtub's cold surface. He pushed upward. The tub didn't move. He pushed again, straining with his entire body. The tub rose a half inch and scooted forward an inch and a half. His elbows were too close to his stomach to get any leverage. He tried flexing his arches and pushing up with his knees. Still, the tub only lurched forward a couple of inches. He cursed at it as if it were a beam that wouldn't come free from an old house. He turned, writhing, till he lay on his stomach. He felt the turd marking his body as he rolled. His breath became harder to get, the smell now in his mouth, coating his tongue. He brought his knees as far forward as they'd come, pushed against the wet earth with his palms, and the tub rose on his broad back, but he himself could rise no far-ther. Then he thought, If I could make it to the curb, I could roll it off of my back, and so he began to crawl, inching along, paus-ing to catch his breath. The offal followed him. He felt it on his kneecap, his hip, crammed in his belt. He felt it working its way through the fabric of his shirt, staining his skin. It hung from a cord around his neck and sat on his life with the weight of a cast-iron bathtub, so that he crept along like a monstrous hard-shelled bug that would never die because no one would come close enough to kill it.

8:17 One of That Old Indian's bathtubs is creeping across the grass upside down. Mose has my dog. Could be a very valuable dog. Firemen have walked all over my lawn putting out the fire. If it weren't for the smoke I could see Aura's house very well. I would not be surprised to find she set the fire to make spying on my house easier for her prying eyes. Still much scurrying about. Verda's porch is in Tradio's front yard. That will cost her plenty. Mrs. Haygood has left her car in the middle of the street with the lights left on. Very dangerous. Darker now that fire is out. Several people in a group in my front yard. Several gathered in That Old Indian's yard. Their faces very dark. Could be anyone. I have always thought his bathtubs were very vulnerable to theft. Many shadows.

The dog Himself had never been so close to people before. Confined as they'd been in the close quarters of the den, their smell was overwhelming and unmanageable. His own nose became distorted, warped. He'd been able to do no more than bury his snout in his own crotch in order not to suffocate. When they'd all left the den, he'd been able to escape, only to be chased across the street and tackled again. His own home was too hot, too bright. It was leaving the planet's surface, hurtling into the sky. He tried to leap into the air to follow it, but they held him down. And it took only moments before the porch was gone, the hole in the lattice risen, the smell of the Earth utterly changed, his own fur turned brittle and black, the stars afloat in water. It took only moments for everything in the world to smell the same. He huddled under the human's arm and scratched at his own eyes.

8:22 I have just tried to call my lawyer at his house about all of these supposed allegations made against me. Phone is still out of order. Nadine has accused my husband of not being an adulterer, a thing I would never have done. Aura, as my husband's daughter, could help me out in several ways. It is her responsibility.

8:24 They've turned over a bathtub and found a man inside. That other tub is almost out in the street now. I have never once seen my own bathtub move one inch.

❧

Arthur, Carl and Mazelle's husband jammed their fingers under the porcelain rim of the overturned bathtub, and on Arthur's "Three," rolled it over on its side. Tradio was lying there, covered in wet leaves, his mouth still in the shape required to pronounce the word *Boo.*

"Oh, Tradio," Arthur cried, and fell on top of him. "I looked everywhere for you."

"Where was I?" Tradio asked, and blinked at the mesmerizing quantity of stars now available to him.

"Howard put you under one of his bathtubs to protect you from the storm," Carl said.

"I'm not buried alive, then," Tradio said.

Arthur pushed himself off Tradio's chest and began to brush the leaves from his body. "Well, not very deep, anyway," he answered. "How's your heart?"

"I've taken a tablet. I'm better now. I thought you'd buried me, Arthur."

"Do you want to sit up?"

"No. I'll just lie here for a few minutes longer. I thought I'd been buried. I smelled the burning corpses. You didn't embalm me."

"No, Tradio. It's old Mrs. Martin's house. It's burned down. The firemen have just about put the fire out."

"I thought Effie had shot you in a fit of jealousy."

"No, no. It was Aura. She's had a little baby girl. I helped. You collapsed in the middle of my helping. There was the storm. It was a terrible storm. Howard put you under the tub so you'd be protected, only I didn't know it. As soon as the baby was safe, I came looking for you. I looked everywhere. I must have run past you a half dozen times. But now I've found you and you're all right."

"You were right to help the baby first." Tradio shushed him.

"I knew I was right, Tradio."

"I'm an old man."

"Yes, you are."

"I was happy when I thought you'd buried me under a tree."

"You're going to make me cry," Arthur said.

"When I go, Pie Bird, you'll put me next to Alice, won't you?"

"Well, of course I will. But please let's don't talk about it now."

"And then, if you want to, you can come in on my other side later. When it's your time."

"I'm going to die when you die," Arthur blubbered.

"I've made everybody sad," Tradio said.

"You've made him cry," Carl said. "How do you make somebody feel that way about you?"

Mazelle's husband bent down, putting his hands on Arthur's and Tradio's shoulders. "I'm going to leave now, if y'all don't need me," he said. "Arthur, you might think of getting your tetanus shot updated."

"I will, thank you."

For an instant, Tradio thought Mazelle's husband was making some sort of wisecrack about homosexual contact, but Arthur hadn't taken it that way at all. "What's wrong?" Tradio asked.

"My house fell on him," Carl explained. "He has some puncture wounds."

"What?" Tradio asked.

"I'm OK," Arthur said. "We'll go to the emergency room together. Don't worry. My mother always said that all our worries are wasted except for the last one. So we may as well not worry because odds are it's not the last one."

"There's a hole in your face, Arthur," Tradio said.

"I think I'm going to be able to whistle through that one. It's the one in my ankle that hurts. I think it messed with one of my tendons."

"I'm awful sorry," Carl said.

"Well, how could you know your house would fall on me?" Arthur sissed.

"I took all the good lumber out of my walls and replaced it with cheaper, lighter plywood. I just hope my walls haven't hurt or killed anyone else in Fort Worth. Every wall of my house is missing. If y'all don't need me, I think I'll go home and have a better look."

"No, you go ahead," Arthur said. "We'll be all right. The ambulance is on its way. We'll sit right here and watch these firemen."

"Is everything else OK?" Tradio asked Arthur.

"I think so. I think everyone's going to be fine. Marshall is lying on Effie's front yard, but Aura and Mose are tending to him."

"Effie's all right?"

"I think so."

"Where's Howard? I should thank him."

8:25 I don't know why Aura would want Nadine's things, as my things are so much better. Nadine says I convicted my husband without ever accusing him. At least I never put him on a pedestal without accusing him, as Nadine did her mother. It was always how wonderful Nadine's momma was at this and that, never "Nadine's momma was a sneaking slut." If my husband didn't commit adultery then why did I seduce my best friend's husband to get back at him? I did this after he was dead because I was still so mad at him.

8:29 Just because I am a few days late with my phone bill they've shut it off.

8:30 That carpenter has left the scene. Nadine has taken that baby to her house. My baby!

※

Mrs. Postlethwaite saw the bathtub moving toward the street in a series of lurching spasms. It moved away from the failing light of the dying fire like something that had been badly burned. She and Mr. Postlethwaite arrived at the tub during a period of stasis. It seemed impossible that the cast-iron bulk could ever overcome its own inertia, and so they began to doubt that they'd ever seen it move. It had been a deception of light and their smoke-filled eyes. The tub was painted a pale green on three sides, and white where it had stood close to a wall. Flakes of color curled away from the bottom of the four ball-and-claw feet, leaving bare rusty planets for the claws to grip. The tub rose suddenly, gasped, fell forward. The Postlethwaites backed away, looked around themselves for help, but everyone else was busy, hadn't seen. They moved back to the tub's side, holding their hands close to their bodies. They tried to look down through the drain. It was too dark, but they heard the heavy breathing of an animal near exhaustion. The odor of dog feces rose to their nostrils and clung there like an insect.

"Howard?" Mr. Postlethwaite speculated.

There was no answer.

"We're going to lift the tub off of you," Mrs. Postlethwaite said.

"Leave me alone," Howard bellowed. The sound came out of the tub's drain like escaping steam.

"It's too heavy for you," Mr. Postlethwaite said.

Mrs. Postlethwaite cupped her hands and yelled, "You're stuck."

"No," he answered. "Get away."

"Howard," Mrs. Postlethwaite pleaded.

"If you put your hands under here, I'll break them off."

"Let him be." Mose had let the stray dog go and walked up behind Mr. and Mrs. Postlethwaite. "Leave him under there."

"Oh, Mose," Mrs. Postlethwaite whispered.

Mr. Postlethwaite slid his fingers beneath the tub's rim. His wife joined him. Mose took two of the claw feet in his hands and pulled as the Postlethwaites lifted. The tub rose a few inches but held there, the weight too much for them. A fireman pushed between the Postlethwaites then and together they rolled the tub to its side. Howard didn't fall free. He was still lodged tightly in the tub, his palms facing outward, as if he were trying to fend off an attack. Mose walked around the tub and stood with the fireman and the Postlethwaites.

"Are you all right?" the fireman asked.

Howard didn't answer. He was still breathing heavily.

"Can you get out of there? Let me help you," the fireman said.

"No, no," Howard moaned, and by twisting his shoulders and hips came writhing and slithering out of the tub like an engorged larva. Mrs. Postlethwaite bent down and put her hand on his shoulder. He swatted at her arm, pushing her away. "I don't owe any of you anything," Howard said.

Mose dropped down to his knees. "You don't understand. You've already paid us. We just saved you. You've paid us and you can't take it back. We'll always have the gratification of saving you."

Howard stood up. He knew they could smell the dog shit that covered him. The concern on the Postlethwaites' faces made him want to retch. "How did it feel," he asked Mr. Postlethwaite, "to touch your little girl's parts?"

It was Mrs. Postlethwaite who stepped forward and hit him, hit him so hard with her open hand that he fell back over the tub. And after he'd hit the ground and begun to laugh, she started after him again, but Mr. Postlethwaite grabbed her by the waist and held her close till she stopped struggling. "That's the worst of it," he told her.

"Slimy bastard," she yelled at Howard.

"Let's go," Mr. Postlethwaite said.

"It's our family," Mrs. Postlethwaite cried.

"I know," Mr. Postlethwaite said.

"I don't want him to hurt you."

"How can he hurt me? The damage has been done. The only people who can hurt you are the people you love. And I don't love him."

They turned away. "It's me that hurts you," Mrs. Postlethwaite said.

"It's only because you don't know," he said.

"I don't want to know. I just want to go back to our home."

"I don't think I can live there anymore," he said.

8:31 I cannot keep track. They've found another one underneath a bathtub. I thought it was dead but when it stood up, Mrs. Postlethwaite slapped it, so I guess it was still alive. Looked like That Big Indian. Now he knows what it's like to be hit by Mrs. Postlethwaite as I have known since she hit me with her cane. Firemen are walking on the coals and spraying them down. Much foul smelling smoke. Smells like old Mrs. Martin's armpits. Mose let go of that dog but the dog just stayed there next to Aura and Marshall who are still mashing down my grass. When I'm not looking they all glance my way. Mazelle's husband has joined Mrs. Haygood in her car. Very bold.

"Oh, she hit him," Mrs. Haygood said. "Mrs. Postlethwaite just hit Howard."

Mazelle's husband fastened his seat belt, then looked out through the windshield. He watched Mr. and Mrs. Postlethwaite turn away. "Can you bear not knowing what that was all about?" he asked her.

"I suppose."

"I guess we should get going then," he said. He looked down at Mrs. Haygood's legs and feet. They were coated in the mud of their garden.

"The mud sucked my shoes off," she explained.

"Drive slowly," he said. "We don't want to get a flat tire now."

"Can I leave my lights on?"

"Sure."

"That way, if I see him, I can run him over."

"Those shingles there have nails in them," he warned her.

She worked her way slowly to the curb in front of Carl's house. "The storm has whipped Carl's house into a boat. He's standing under it."

"Can you bear not knowing what that's all about?"

Mrs. Haygood turned her wheel hard over to miss another section of siding and a fence post. Her headlights spotlighted Nadine, who stood on her front porch holding the baby. Mrs. Haygood had to cut the wheel hard again to squeeze between the fire truck and the corner curb.

"You're doing a good job," Mazelle's husband told her.

"Do I turn left or right?" she asked.

"You decide."

"I don't know if I can."

The revolving red lights of the fire truck lit a glistening, leaf-strewn street, seemingly abandoned. Mazelle's husband leaned toward the windshield. "It's clear this way," he said.

She held her foot to the brake, the mud drying between her toes.

"Is there something you've forgotten?" he asked her.

"No," she said. "I've just been waiting for this moment for so long, and now this is the last of the waiting."

He said, "I didn't know I'd be doing this until today."

"It's funny, in this single afternoon you've caught up with my whole life so that we've arrived at this same moment together."

"I think we should turn left."

"Left is toward Wal-Mart."

"Left is toward Vermont."

8:35 I just went out on my front porch and told Aura that my things were my things. She was plainly waiting on this decision. Nadine wouldn't even let me hold that baby and now she is flaunting it on her front porch. The red lights of that fire truck are lighting up Nadine's house as it has been for all these years. Mazelle's husband and Mrs. Haygood have made their long-standing affair public, having driven off together in front of all assembled. My husband was not so brave. History will judge him. If Aura wasn't his love child why did Nadine's momma wait till he died to move her to the Row? It is just like That Old Indian to claim a white baby. That Old Indian never acted guilty the way my husband did.

"Why are you crying, you old fool?" Howard asked.

"I'm not crying," Mose answered. "I've got smoke in my eyes. I can hardly see."

Howard's back was in the grass, his legs sprawled across the tub he'd fallen over.

"That was an evil thing you did," Mose said.

"She hit me good, didn't she? I didn't hit her back. As far as I'm concerned, we're even. That guy has been wearing what he did on his face for a dozen years."

"They're the saddest people I've ever known, and they're vulnerable, and you picked on them because they helped you when you were vulnerable."

"I told them not to help. I didn't need their help. Let's stop talking about them. I have something else to tell you." Howard rose to his feet.

"I don't want to hear any more," Mose said.

"This is the last of it."

"You can't burden me with it. I can't carry it. I told Nadine what you said. I told Aura. They know who you are. Your secrets aren't secrets anymore."

"I saved that man over there today." He pointed toward Tradio and Arthur farther up in his yard. They returned his gaze and Tradio waved weakly. Aura was watching Howard too. Marshall lifted his head from the grass. Mose put his fists in his eyes and rubbed. He sat down on the tub.

"We're listening," Mose screamed suddenly. "What's so goddamned important?"

Howard unbuttoned and removed his shirt. The stench was unbearable. He bent down and whispered in Mose's ear, "I'm not an Indian."

"He says he's not an Indian," Mose yelled out.

A fireman paused momentarily in his work. Effie opened her door a bit more. Nadine walked to the near end of her porch. Howard bolted. He held his shirt over his face as he ran into his darkened house.

━☵━

8:40 Mose and That Old Indian were clearly talking about me and my situation, as they quite openly looked in my direction several times, and then Mose started screaming at my house and That Old Indian started to run away so I screamed at him as he ran away, LIAR, LIAR, I screamed, and he covered his head.

≫✠≪

There were six inches of standing water below Carl's boat, contained by the stones of his foundation. Scraps of lumber, shavings, his measured drawings, floated beneath the hull of the sloop. The four walls of his home had been toppled, but the boat, heavy and indolent, sat solidly among the debris on its keel blocks and stands. The flag he'd hung from the bowsprit earlier that day was in shreds, but the sprit itself showed only minor scarring. The front porch and gable had disintegrated around it. Carl sloshed through the water, scanning the strakes for damage, inspecting the rudder and prop, the stern escutcheon, the eyes in the bow that now openly stared across the street. The only parts of his house still recognizable were the heavy kitchen appliances, the bathroom fixtures and the section of roof that had dropped down onto the boat's cabin when the house walls had blown away.

Looking up beyond the roof, he saw that all the leaves of the nearby trees had been replaced with forms of light, a star at the tip of each twig. The moon lay coddled in the branches like a bird's nest. He began to back away from his boat, first into his side yard, then farther out, across the sidewalk, past the fire truck and into Hemphill Street. For the first time in two years he could see the sheer of his hull, the sweet flowing lines of her raked stem and counter stern. She was as big as a house and probably heavier, but seemed as if she might take flight at any moment. Her white topsides reflected both the moon and the flashing red lights of the fire truck. He walked back to his boat, raised a ladder to the cockpit and climbed aboard. Most of the rainwater had exited through the scuppers, but a bit had fallen through the open companionway and pooled in the bilge. Carl switched on the battery-powered bilge pump and listened as the stream of water fell into the collected water of the foundation. I'll hear that sound again someday, he thought, except that it will be saltwater joining salt. The house roof perched on several stanchions and the lifelines. It wouldn't be too difficult to remove. Standing in the cockpit, he took hold of the gentle curve in the laminated tiller and scanned the horizon above the shingles. There, where the sun would come up, was Nadine. She was still wearing his shirt. Carl was suddenly cold. Funny, how small the temperate zone was, between a hot fire and a cold fall. He shivered. He went below to put on a shirt, and when he flipped on his light he realized he had the only fully functional home on the block. He lit the small propane heater, combed the smoke out of his hair, changed his wet, sooty clothes and then, closing the companionway so the cabin would warm up, went courting. He rigged a plank that crossed from the foundation to the second step on his ladder so that when they returned she wouldn't have to get wet. He did all of this knowing he would never suggest the possibility to Nadine. He backed away from the boat again, approved of the warm, oily light exiting the ports, negotiated the debris field between his home and Nadine's and arrived at her front porch as if he'd just sailed into Fort Worth from Cyprus.

Nadine stood there, a blanket over her shoulders and the baby in her arms. "I'll return your shirt if you'll wait," she said.

"I don't need it."

"No, I'll go inside and change right now."

"I don't want it back right now," Carl said. "The least you could do is wash it before you return it. I wouldn't borrow something of yours and return it dirty. How's the baby?"

"She's perfect," Nadine said. "I've been trying to see some resemblance to Momma."

Carl pulled a sleeve of Arthur's jacket back and peeked. "Little," he said.

"Precious," Nadine said, and re-covered the baby's head. Then she looked directly at Carl. "Your house is gone."

"The house isn't gone. It's become a boat. I live on my boat now."

"I can't believe we lost two of our old houses tonight. And Verda's porch ripped off. She'll be so upset when she comes home. I just saw Mrs. Haygood and Mazelle's husband drive off together. I don't think they'll be back."

"I'm leaving too, Nadine."

"But why, Carl? I wish you wouldn't say that. Don't mouth the words. Everything's slipping away. I lost my mother tonight. I thought she died years ago, but she really died tonight. I never knew who she was."

"Maybe it's not true, what Howard told Mose."

"I talked to Effie. She says it was so. I mean she's confused, but she confirmed the only important part, that Momma had another baby besides me. Aura may or may not be my sister, but I've a sister somewhere, and I'd just as soon it be Aura. So it doesn't matter."

"I don't think Aura looks anything like you. And I didn't want to say anything there in the cistern, but she doesn't look anything like Howard either."

"Why are you going away, Carl? You're a carpenter. You could rebuild your house."

"Nadine, the truth is, I'm the reason my house fell down. I took my house apart from the inside out to build my boat. There was nothing but an eggshell of a house left. That's why it blew down."

"That house belonged to all the people who lived in it before you, not just you. It belonged to Fort Worth. And now it's gone forever. It was a historic landmark, Carl."

"Now it will be a historic watermark."

"That's not funny, Carl. I've worked my whole life to make this street successful. So did my mother. If you really loved me, you'd know how important all these old things are to me."

"I'm not an antique dealer, Nadine. But it makes me upset when you question my feelings. I can certainly love you and not understand you. I don't know why you have to be surrounded by all

238 • J<small>OE</small> C<small>OOMER</small>

these old things. To me they're just used. They're other folks' castoffs. It's like you're trying to replace something you never had. You wear other people's clothes and what's more you wear another person's life. You're a new person, Nadine. Just like that baby. Just like my boat. It's made from old materials but it's new. You ought to cut up all these old dresses and make one that fits you. I've heard you talk about the quality of old things and how that's disappeared and, well, cover that baby's ears, that's bullshit. If you want to own something of quality you have to make it. You can't buy it. You can't own a painting that someone else painted. You've got to build your own life, Nadine. Don't go on living your momma's life."

"You just want to fondle me, touch my chest," Nadine shouted.

"I want to touch your toes too, and your forehead, and the backs of your hands. You won't make me be ashamed of loving you."

"You're just a fountain of wisdom tonight. You've worked everything out."

"Don't make fun of me, Nadine. I know I'm not a good speaker. But I've thought about it since the day I started working on the boat. Every day. That boat is my heart and it's all exposed now so I've got little to lose by speaking plainly to you. I need to think that you've known how I feel. I've tried to keep it a secret but I've failed. And I know you've given me little encouragement. So I've put all my love into that boat, touching it the way I'd touch you. I think of it as you. I'm leaving, though. A trailer will come soon. Down at the Gulf, I'll step the mast and bend on the sails and I'll be gone. I'll use my skills to work occasionally at different ports. But I intend to sail my way down among the islands and see beautiful things and meet people different than me. I've never done anything like that before but I'm going to take the chance that I'll like it."

"You think an awful lot of yourself."

"I do not. Look at me. I'm standing here on your porch for perhaps the five hundredth time trying to see if you might like me. I've got no pride whatsoever. You're in total control here, just as you always are."

"I've got to go. There's the ambulance. I've got to take the baby back to Aura."

"OK," Carl said. "You go ahead."

"It was unfair of you, to bring all this down on me at once."

"I'll repair all the damage to your house before I go."

8:44 I have just gone outside to inspect my house and found that all the paint has melted off my house. I stopped a fireman to ask him what he was going to do about it and he just stared at me like a cow would.

8:47 My son will use this against me, no doubt. He has already tried to have me institutionalized (see, I <u>can</u> spell that word) in a blatant attempt to get my things. He will say I had no right to treat his father the way I did when he was dying.

8:49 I forgot to mention that Marshall and Aura are still in my yard and that Tradio and his man friend are lying in the grass next door. They all think I will pop right over and satisfy their curiosities. I may have taken more of my medicine than I should have, as Saturday's section in my pill box is empty and it's not Saturday yet. The Row is in a fine mess and tomorrow our big day for sales. Now there is an ambulance at the end of our street. I cannot make out its license plate number, but will get a good description of its driver. It's possible they have been sent by my son to carry me to the state hospital. I won't unlock my door this time. Every time I go out of my house I'm sure someone is going to grab me. I don't like being afraid.

Aura watched Howard run into his house and thought, So we're not half-Indian, and the baby's not one-quarter. That was a shame, because she'd always been in favor of miscegenation. She'd even thought, for the short time that she was a half-breed, that it explained her tanning qualities. Maybe Howard was denying his Indian blood because he was ashamed of being a minority. She'd have to include him too.

"A storm sure mixes things up, doesn't it, sweetie," she told Marshall. "Are you breathing all right?"

"I'm hot inside," he coughed.

She lay down next to him and put her arm across his body.

"Where's the baby?" he asked.

"Nadine has her. She's standing on her front porch with her so the baby won't breathe any smoke."

"We'll need a bigger house now," Marshall said.

"You stop talking. Smoke's coming out of your mouth."

Aura put her fingertips on his lips and Marshall closed his eyes. "We could have a separate thermostat in every room in a new house," he mumbled.

"Shh," she said. "We were thinking about how we're a matched set now: a knife, spoon and fork. We'll have a spoon engraved with the baby's initials, and one day she'll give it to her baby, and that baby will give it to her baby and on and on till one day they'll forget where the spoon came from, whose monogram it is, and by that time we will have blended in perfectly, become part and parcel of everything around us. It makes us so happy and secure to think about it. It's been a banner day: we've had a baby and we personally have lost ten pounds, and you saved our house from burning down without dying. When we get home from the hospital we're going to make you a fresh batch of chicken wings and ourself a ham cutlet and we'll stand there in the kitchen while we eat and let the baby eat too. Won't that be nice? It makes a person awfully hungry to have a baby."

A fireman brought Marshall a small oxygen bottle attached to a clear mask. Marshall held the canister over his upper chest in the same way he'd once held a baby bottle. The oxygen was cool and sweet. It was like sucking on a fresh bone. He looked up at his wife who was smiling at him and wondered how she managed to accept all things with equanimity. She'd just had an unexpected baby, nearly lost her husband, discovered she had a half-sister, that her biological parents lived on the same street, that her mother had brought her here, that her father wasn't an Indian. How could she contain so many improbabilities and uncertainties? She's so compact, so prepared for the end of the world. And I'm worried that my body, lying here on the lawn, is impeding the firemen, that they have to go out of their way to avoid me. I'm too long and I have no other alternative.

"I'm too long," he told Aura through the mask.

"That again?" she said. "You're just right. And if it makes you feel better, we're pretty sure that from now on you'll be getting shorter. It's a miracle of aging. Look, here's an ambulance, finally. What do you think about adopting this little stray dog?"

8:55 I'm not coming out, I yelled at them through my closed window. I yelled it three times and so they decided to take Marshall instead. I've always known he was crazy. They are shining a flashlight in his eyes and are trying to put him on a hospital bed but he hangs over top and bottom. Nadine is supervising, of course. My baby! Nadine looks hideous in that outfit, a blanket over her shoulders as she plays the refugee to the hilt. Aura waddling around like a penguin and with no more brains. Won't my son be surprised when he finds out he has a sister who'll reap half the profits at Effie's funeral! Someone should watch over my things during my funeral as thieves often read the obituaries.

9:00 Mr. Haygood is dragging a policeman up the sidewalk toward his house. The policeman seems to be looking my way with much interest. He may be one I've had to my house before. Mr. Haygood might pay good money for what I know. I'd pay good money to see his face when I tell him.

"You left your front door standing wide open," the officer stated.

"Well, the hinges are torn, and there's nothing left to steal anyway," Mr. Haygood said.

They stepped inside the toy shop. The officer toggled the beam of his flashlight from empty showcase to empty showcase.

"You see, it's all gone. It's a major burglary. These toys were worth close to half a million." Mr. Haygood walked farther into the house. "Where is my goddamned wife?" He went back outside and looked across the dark street toward Effie's house. None of the shapes looked like his wife's shape. It was then that he noticed his car was gone. What the hell?

"Let's walk back down to the patrol car and I'll take a report," the officer said. "There's not enough light here."

"A report?" Mr. Haygood said listlessly. "Can't you get some detectives out here to lift some fingerprints?"

"I'll have to take a report first. Then we can see if anybody's available."

"My car's gone too," Mr. Haygood said.

"Do you think it was stolen as well?"

"No, it was here after the robbery. My wife must be in it. It would be just like her to take somebody to the hospital in it knowing that I've been robbed."

"Do you need me to help you back down the steps?"

"No, sir. I'll meet you back at your patrol car. I want to see if my next-door neighbor saw anything."

Mr. Haygood made sure the officer was a good piece down

the sidewalk before he himself turned into Mazelle's yard and climbed up to her porch. Her door was standing open as well. He stood at the threshold and called her name into the black rooms. His breath came in short, quick bursts. He stepped inside and kicked a book across the floor. He heard it skid and then fall, tumbling downward. Moving out of the doorway to allow what light there was to enter behind him, he saw Mazelle's stool was turned over, the carpet rolled back, and the hatch opened. He didn't call her name again but closed the hatch and replaced the carpet and stool. He hurried back to his home, found a weak flashlight, threw open his own hatch to the cistern and stepped awkwardly, unquietly, down. It was the water that surprised him most. He said "How?" out loud. Then he pointed the flashlight over the limestone-weighted mattress and up at the ceiling, which revealed the underbelly of Mazelle's car. She'd tried to destroy the cistern intentionally. It was clear to him now that Mazelle had stolen his toys. Who else could it have been? Who else felt that strongly about him? She couldn't stand her life with her husband any longer and had taken the only things that she knew would make him follow her. He felt a great wave of relief roll through him. He'd get his toys back now. She was just trying to scare him. She was jealous. There was really no need to make a police matter of this. It was family business. He just hoped she'd wrapped each of the toys in bubble wrap as she'd stolen them. He wasn't worried about the cast iron but some of the tin toys could be easily scratched. He'd go tell the officer it was all a big misunderstanding. He closed and covered the hatch. It might be possible to get through this without Mrs. Haygood becoming any wiser. He'd kept his little secret from her for thirty-four years, so he had little doubt of his abilities and her stupidity. There were still a few vague points: whether Mazelle's husband had seen the open hatch, how the hole in the cistern roof might be repaired, how to find Mazelle and his car and toys. It surprised him, and gave a little start to his ego, that Mazelle loved him as much as she did, enough to go to all this trouble. He was an old man, but he still had a big old thing. Damn, it was a lot of trouble. But he'd always known this day would come, the day Mazelle demanded her cistern life become her real life. He would tell the policeman that Mrs. Haygood took the toys. It was simply a case of marital dispute and it could be settled without the law. That would convince him. As he walked down the sidewalk he considered the possibility of repairing the cistern roof before Mazelle's car could be towed away. He'd need a couple sacks of Portland cement and some heavy boards for bracing. There certainly was a great deal to consider. He couldn't imagine what had set Mazelle off, to make her mad enough to try to collapse the cistern with her car. He thought he saw Mrs. Haygood among the bathtubs on Howard's lawn. But he'd get rid of this bothersome policeman first.

9:04 That one handsome fireman paused while he was rolling up his fire hose to admire the display of Lalique in my window. Perhaps his wife will return as a customer. I took a moment to tell him the Lalique would only be available at its current price through the weekend.

9:06 They are rolling Marshall away. Nadine has finally given the baby back to Aura. That Aura doesn't look anything like my husband. Nobody looks like anybody.

"Aren't you a good-looking young man," Tradio said.
    "You leave the medic to his work," Arthur told him.
    "But he's such a beautiful boy," Tradio insisted.

"That's what my momma always said," the medic said. "Now, if you'll just be quiet for a moment, I'll listen to your heart."

Nadine leaned over too, her blanket now covering her head as well as her body. "How's his heart?" she asked Arthur.

"You look like Death himself, Nadine," Tradio said. "Have you come for me?"

"Hush," Arthur said. "Did you hear that, Nadine? That was his radio voice. He's doing all right."

"All the same," the paramedic said, "I think we'd better take him along. We'll carry him with the smoke inhalation victim. Your puncture wounds should be treated as well, sir, but we can only carry the two serious cases in this ambulance. I've called in another unit. They'll be along shortly to bring you and the birth mother along."

"I can't go with Tradio?" Arthur asked.

"No, sir. We'll take the more serious cases first. If you can drive you can follow us, but that second ambulance should be along any minute. I'd advise that you wait for it. The woman with the baby says she knows you?"

"I delivered her baby," Arthur snorted. "I guess I know her as well as any gay man ever will."

"What is your sexual orientation?" Tradio asked the medic.

"Tradio!" Nadine snapped.

"Well, Arthur can always tell, but I still have to ask."

The paramedic looked up and smiled. "Me, I'm as straight as a dollar bill."

"Well," Arthur said, "you know, they're going to phase those out someday." The medic laughed. "Look at that, Tradio. You've got a straight medic who doesn't mind joking with queers."

"Stop talking like that, Arthur," Nadine hushed.

"I'm just happy not to be buried alive," Tradio said. "Even though it was kind of peaceful."

"Was that you howling?" Arthur asked.

"It may have been me. I thought there had been an epidemic and all mankind was lost."

"What?" Nadine asked.

"He's sort of delirious," Arthur said.

"I am not," Tradio said. "I'm something more. I'm satisfied. I have to be. I'm a pompous old scrap-trading fag who loved his wife for twenty-five years and lived to tell the tale to his new little Pie Bird. I never cheated on her, Nadine. And I've never cheated on you, Arthur."

"Well," Arthur said, "I'm going to drop a bathtub over you twice a day from now on."

"I apologized to Effie today, Arthur. I told you that. You were going to mow her lawn for me. I felt better after I'd apologized. It wasn't her fault she loved me. I don't think I've traded heaven for the life I've lived."

"Pompous is right," Arthur said.

"I only have a strong affection for you, Tradio," Nadine whispered.

Tradio smiled and closed his eyes. "I think I'll go to heaven. I do."

"Well, in the meantime, you're going to the hospital," the medic said. "OK, we're going to lift you up on the gurney."

"Such a pretty face."

"OK, everyone lift on three. One, two, three."

"Does my voice sound like it comes from heaven?" Tradio asked as he was being carried away.

9:07 That ambulance is backing up, beep, beep, beep, backing up the street.

9:08 That Old Indian has lit an oil lamp. He's walking through his house too fast.

9:09 They are loading Marshall and Tradio in as a strange pair.

9:10 My pencil is dull.

9:12 He is carrying another thing in his other hand. Very suspicious and quite dangerous to run through a house with a flame and what might be a pair of scissors. I know he has dirty magazines in there.

As the doors closed and the ambulance began to roll slowly down the Row, Tradio folded his hands over his heart and whispered to Marshall, "Ever been to a live radio broadcast?"

Marshall shook his head. An oxygen mask still covered his face. He'd never lain down next to a homosexual man before.

"You talk and talk and you haven't got the damnedest clue whether anybody's out there listening to you." Marshall lifted his mask a half inch and began to speak, but Tradio shushed him and said, "It's the miracle of radio."

"I was just going to say," Marshall said, "that your listeners call you back on the phone."

"That's right. But I always have to speak first. I've just realized I've been taking a leap of faith all these years."

"They tell me you won't go to bed with women lesbians," Marshall said.

"It's closer to the truth to say they wouldn't go to bed with me," Tradio answered.

"Well, then, I don't understand what all the fuss is about. They won't go to bed with me either." Then Marshall wheezed, "Tee hee."

"Tee hee," Tradio answered, "tee hee hee."

The ambulance began to turn, and everyone inside braced themselves to leave the Row.

✹

9:14 It is a gun as big as a boot. My husband told me he had guns in there. I saw the dirty magazines in his trash. I sold them to Jim Evans who takes them to the Cattle Barns and gets very good money for them. I never looked inside but one of them.

✹

Aura, Nadine, Mose and Arthur stood in the street and watched the ambulance leave. It swayed as it turned the corner, as if it were being dipped in a slow dance. They all leaned slightly to help right it.

"They'll be fine, I'm sure," Nadine offered.

Arthur favored his left leg. When he tried to stand on both feet his ankle tended to collapse. "My punctures hurt a lot more now that Tradio is gone," he said.

"If that second ambulance isn't here soon, I'll take you myself," Nadine said. "You and Aura and the baby. I'm sorry, Aura, about the way I acted. I wouldn't mind one bit if you were my sister. I don't know for sure that you are, but I wouldn't mind."

"We wouldn't try to take your momma from you, Nadine. And if she bought our house, we'll give it back to you."

"I don't want it. If Momma bought it for you, she did it with her money, not mine."

"Maybe I shouldn't have said a word," Mose said. "I let that son of a bitch make me the messenger."

"It's all right, Mose, honey."

"That's right," Aura said. "It's good for us to know."

"I thought I was all alone in the world," Nadine said.

"But we're all related," Aura said. "Do you think Howard knew we were going to have a baby today? We didn't even know."

"He knew it was going to be a bad storm," Mose said.

"What was all that about not being an Indian?" Arthur asked.

"I don't know," Mose sighed. "But he's just worn me out. I haven't thought of anything new today. I've just thought of old things that were none of my business."

"It's all new to me," Nadine said. "The past isn't at all what I expected. My own mother is a different person now than the day she died."

Arthur said, "I'm going to go over there and sit down on the curb."

"Us too," Aura said.

"I'll go check on Howard," Mose sighed.

"Tell him I'll want to speak to him later," Nadine told Mose. "Here, Aura, you and the baby take my blanket."

"Listen to that, we've got a big sister," Aura told the baby.

9:16 Back and forth, back and forth.

9:17 Here comes Mr. Haygood. He's always holding his pants like somebody is going to take them.

Howard's sign still read Open so Mose just stepped into his shop. Bells jangled. Light from the back of the house tumbled toward him.

"Howard?" Mose called out.

"I'm not here," Howard said, but Mose could hear him pacing, saw his shadow passing through the doorway.

"I've just come to tell you the girls don't mind. Aura isn't too upset. Nadine might be a different story, but she'll get over it. Your granddaughter seems healthy."

Howard stopped in the doorway between his shop and bed-room. He held the lamp in one hand, the pistol in the other. So that he wouldn't have to look at the gun, Mose used the pall of light to look around the shop. There were showcases of Indian arti-facts, boxes of doorknobs, cabinet hardware, screen door hinges and stained glass windows stacked like painters' canvases. Dozens of light fixtures hung from the ceiling, all but one of them bulb-less. Effie's been here, Mose thought. At his feet was a wooden crate filled with chrome faucets.

"I'm glad you've come," Howard said. "I'll need a witness. I'm going to commit the last of the Indian depredations in Texas. I'm going to kill myself."

"But you said you weren't an Indian," Mose said.

"That's right," Howard coughed. "I'm going to kill myself for pretending to be."

"Then it won't be a depredation. It'd just be an old white man killing himself."

"All the same."

"I'd think a person might kill himself for a lifetime spent denying his Indian heritage, I mean, if they'd pretended to be white when they were really an Indian. But pretending to be an Indian couldn't have been a step up. I remember back in the thir-ties and forties, we treated Indians real bad. Doesn't make any sense, killing yourself for a lifetime of pretending to be a minor-ity. In fact, pretending to be a minority doesn't make a whole lot of sense."

"When I was a kid," Howard said, "all the kids around me were Indians. They wouldn't let me be one of them. So when I left home I told everyone I met I was Indian. It was my way of getting back at them. Then when you tell everyone you're an Indian, they think of you as an Indian. Even your own mind thinks it. The thought leads you to different places, places where an Indian would be, places where I've been."

"But you're not an Indian."

"No. My mother was Irish. My father was something else."

"So there's no dog in your path?"

"My last name is Roberts. Old Grubbs gave me that Indian name when I left him."

"Did you sign your organ donor card? You don't want to shoot yourself in one of your transplantable organs."

"Where can I shoot myself then?"

"In your head. They wouldn't try to transplant that. But make sure you don't damage your eyes."

"I'll shoot myself in the head then," Howard said.

"Maybe you'd want to wait till the ambulance came," Mose suggested. "They could take your body straight to the hospital. Your organs would be fresh."

"The ambulance has already left."

"There's another coming for Aura. You could ride with her."

9:18 The firemen are all going home. Mrs. Martin's house is gone but for the back wall, and the kitchen door is standing wide open. Her bathtub and toilet are in plain view. I'm about as hungry as a person can be.

9:20 Mr. Haygood is standing in the street talking to Nadine, Aura and Tradio's man friend. None of them even bothered to get up off the curb when he came over. They look like hear no evil, speak no evil, smell no evil. I guess I am going to be forced to tell the truth.

"I'm afraid she's gone," Nadine told Mr. Haygood.

"But she was here, helping with the fire. I told her to go home."

"She left with Mazelle's husband," Nadine said. "They were in your car."

"It's none of our business," Arthur said.

"My toys have gone missing," Mr. Haygood stammered. "Have any of you seen my toys? Have you seen Mazelle?"

"Mr. Haygood, it's only fair to tell you, we all rode out the worst of the storm in your cistern."

"I saw Mazelle leave," Effie said. They turned to her in one choreographed sweep.

"Now, you stay out of this, Effie," Nadine warned.

"Speak no evil, Nadine," Effie countered. "I saw Mazelle run away earlier today. No doubt she discovered what you are discovering now, Mr. Haygood. Did it never occur to you that Mazelle's husband and your wife always left the Row within moments of each other? I've known about their affair for months now. It's hard to feel sorry for such a stupid man. Aura, just because you're my husband's daughter doesn't mean it's free dinners every Saturday night at Effie's."

"What?" Aura asked.

"Effie, you go back inside, right now," Nadine said.

"You're sitting on my curb," Effie said.

Nadine stood up. "Right now."

"I'm not afraid of you anymore, Nadine. And your momma's dead. You've got nothing to hold over me now. I've admitted what my husband did. And it may be that Aura has a right to some of my things but it will take a good lawyer and several years of litigation, by which time I'll already be dead. I'll win the case dead or alive."

"You're confused, Effie," Nadine said. "Aura, Momma told Effie that it was her husband that fathered her baby so she'd keep quiet about the pregnancy."

"So, no one knows who stole my toys?" Mr. Haygood screamed.

"Effie knows," Effie said. "There's only been one car leave the street tonight. How stupid can a stupid person be?"

"Effie, God knows you've been done wrong by my momma. But the only reason you've got two kidneys is your own pride. Your husband was a good, sweet man. Your boy knew that, and that's why he never forgave you after his daddy died."

"We don't understand any of this," Aura said.

Mr. Haygood turned and walked slowly back to his own house.

Nadine said, "Effie's husband died of kidney failure. Effie was all lined up to donate one of her kidneys to him, but she pulled out at the last minute. There wasn't time to find another kidney. He died. I think Effie refused him because she thought he had cheated on her. But she never even confronted him."

"Oh, Effie," Aura said. "We're so sorry."

"She believes that old Indian before me and her momma," Effie said. "I have two kidneys for a reason."

⊷⊶

9:28 My presentation of Lalique is certainly an eye catcher. Nadine is a bitch.

⊷⊶

With great effort he roused Himself from the overwhelming burden of smoke. All the people had moved away, leaving him alone in the grass. When the last of the firemen left, he stepped slowly back toward his home but couldn't find the scent. He snorted repeatedly, trying to clear his nose, but finally concluded this spot was never his home. And then he recognized something familiar, something reassuringly comforting: his own hunger. He looked over his shoulder at the people on the curb and watched the lady who threw rocks come out of her house and go to them. None of them looked his way. He was still free. He trotted along the scorched path that still, oddly, led him to the tire with water in it. He stepped into its center, bent down and lapped from the narrow opening. The water tasted of storm. He always felt his throat was vulnerable while he drank, so he hurried. The water was wet and barely controllable, but soothing. There was an old used bone near the tire that he picked up and dropped because it tasted like his tongue. He decided to make his rounds. He walked back down the path, feeling again its odd familiarity, its strange openness. Then, watching the people closely while his feet worked away from them, he made his way to the house on the corner where the man gave him meat, but while the time it took him to get there was the same, the house had moved to some other time. All he found where he used to scratch at the back door was water. He lunged across the street and leaped over the fence, and the Earth slammed up once again into his body. The small bowls on the stoop were as empty as he'd left them that morning. He looked up at the windows where the two little ones sometimes snapped at him. He waited for them. They didn't come. He jumped back over the fence, whining uneasily at the frustrating insistence of the planet's surface to chase him, and moved in a slow arc through the yards back toward what should have been his home. His nose was suddenly assaulted. He scampered. Where, where, where. Matted in the wet grass, blood and mucus and fat, raw and sweet. He bent low, hoping no one would see he'd found something, and taking it gingerly between his front teeth, carried it swinging into the darkness between two houses.

9:29 They are reproducing carnival glass so as a person cannot hardly tell the difference from the original. I myself was fooled by the new Fiesta and bought several saucers and a sugar bowl before I learned I'd been cheated. Some say there is good money to be made in selling reproductions but I say it is the world turned upside down.

9:32 I was going to say everyone's porch lights hadn't been turned on but then I remembered the electricity is still off.

9:33 Here comes another ambulance! Mose is in there with That Crazy Old Indian. It's a very nice oil lamp he's holding, perhaps a Bradley and Hubbard.

✦

"Let's go back to the mall," Mrs. Postlethwaite said.

"But why?" he asked.

"It's Friday night. Jocelyn works tonight. I like the way she handles the photos. She always smiles at us."

"It's after nine. The mall's closed. I'm tired of looking at other people's lives anyway." He sat on his stool in the shop. Mrs. Postlethwaite leaned against the doorjamb between the shop and their bedroom. She interweaved her fingers and flexed her hands like a hinge.

"Are you hungry? I could fix you something," she offered.

"I'm so hungry," he said.

"What do you want? We have soup and some sandwich meat. Or there's that leftover pork chop. You could have that."

"I want to go away," he said.

"I don't know which restaurants would be open now. I'll have to change. My clothes are smoky."

"You don't change in the bedroom anymore," Mr. Postlethwaite said.

"What?"

"You used to change your clothes out in the bedroom where I could see you. You go into the bathroom now."

She paused. "I don't remember when . . . I never even noticed. Did I change in the bedroom? I'll change wherever you want me to."

"I don't care where you change."

"Then why did you bring it up?"

"I don't know. I want to go away. Maybe we could sell the shop and buy an RV, go to all those places we've seen in the photos."

"We don't have to leave here like it's the scene of a crime."

"It's awful, what's happened here."

"No amount of driving will get us away from it."

"Do you think she'll come back and take care of us when we're old?"

"We're already old. I don't think she'll come back."

"So you really don't know where she is?"

"I only know where you are."

9:34 I will not go with the ambulance. They cannot take me away and leave my things unprotected. I have a gun too. There are more ways to kill a person than withholding a kidney. It is 9:35 for the record.

Arthur lay down on the second gurney next to Aura. Although the gurneys were the same height, her body towered over his. She held the baby on her chest while a medic listened to its heartbeat.

Nadine stood at the open door. "I'll come to the hospital first thing in the morning to see how everyone is," she said.

"We'll be all right," Aura said.

"They might even let me go tonight," Arthur said.

"Your blood pressure is very low, sir."

"Oh, it's always low," Arthur told him. "That, and I've bled a couple of pints tonight."

"Well, we can replace it."

"Just don't put any of that heterosexual blood in me," Arthur said and winked.

"Arthur," Nadine said. "Don't pay any attention to him."

"No," Arthur said, "I like my life just the way it is. Don't start confusing me now." He turned to Aura. "I want to thank you. This is probably the closest I'll ever come to being a father."

"I'm a little confused," the medic said.

"We includes you," Aura said and took Arthur's hand.

"I do feel a little groggy, now that everyone's safe," Arthur said. "We're going to the hospital now, aren't we?"

"Yes, sir."

"Tradio and I don't have any insurance. This is going to cost a fortune."

"Now, Arthur," Nadine said, "don't let that thought replace the one that everybody's going to be all right."

"I'll try, Nadine, but now that Tradio seems so happy, I feel like I have to worry all the more."

"Try not to touch your wounds, sir," the medic cautioned, and took Arthur's hand from his cheek.

"Nadine," Aura said, "don't be hard on poor old Howard. If he could have helped who he was he would have. Some people are born human and stay that way. We're all included in the we."

"Well, we're going to give him a piece of our mind," Nadine said. "Free of charge."

"Do you have to strap me in?" Arthur asked.

"Just a safety precaution, sir."

"You didn't strap Aura in," Arthur protested. The medic put his finger to his lips and shushed him. "Don't you shush me. If you can't strap Aura in, I'll go along unstrapped too."

"It's all right, Arthur. They couldn't get the strap over us. We're too . . ." Aura faltered. "We're just right. The strap is too short."

"I'm just right too," Arthur said. "My strap is too long. Would you lock the door to our house, Nadine? I know I left it unlocked."

"Of course I will. I'll lock yours too, Aura. I'll check everybody's door."

"We're going to ride in an ambulance," Aura whispered to her baby. "You're going to turn on the flashing lights, aren't you?" she asked one of the attendants.

"Sure, if you'd like," he answered.

"We want to leave the Row in style," Aura said. "We want to arrive at the hospital like we're everybody else."

9:36 They're loading up Aura and Tradio's man friend. Nadine giving the orderlies advice like she's been to medical school all her life. I guess all that lawn watering today went for naught, as we've had a pretty good rain. I am very upset that they removed my big toenails. They had nothing to replace them with and they have been tender and sore ever since. See my tablet for March 23rd, three years ago where I protested the removal of my toenails but they were taken from me anyway, owing to their being very thick and untrimmable. I had to throw away all my open-toed shoes at very great expense.

9:40 Mose is coming out of That Big Indian's house. He looks like an old man. His posture leaves much to be desired. No doubt he and That Big Indian have decided what to do about me. They are both Nadine's henchmen. Cut off the scorpion's head and he won't pinch me. Mose has paused among the bathtubs and put his hands over his ears. Strange behavior for a man already hard of hearing.

Using a set of parallel rules and working off the compass rose on the chart, Carl laid out the various legs for a cruise from Miami down through the Bahamas. The first jump, across the Gulf Stream to West End, Grand Bahama, could be a long day, depending upon the set of the tide and wind. If they were working against each other a steep chop would develop. Or so he'd read. He might be in Puerto Rico by Christmas if everything went well. He rolled the chart and placed it back in the overhead rack with the hundreds of others he'd collected through the years, long before he began work on the boat itself.

What's wrong with Nadine, he thought, was that she had no destination in mind, no plan other than tomorrow. You don't wait for your ship to come in, you build it and sail it away. He was so certain of the correctness of this philosophy that he couldn't understand why Nadine was so upset when he explained it to her. What possible advantages were there to staying at home year after year? You had to replace your life with another life every once in a while. He himself had been in the United States Army, worked on a farm, spent time as a cook, as a house carpenter, before learning the cabinet trade, before becoming a boatbuilder. And now he was going to learn the arts of a sailor.

He took down a ragged copy of Chapman's *Piloting, Seamanship, and Small Boat Handling,* its cloth corners tufted like the ears of a cat, and turned to the chapter on rope work. His bookmark was a length of quarter-inch nylon line that had seen so many knottings and unknottings that it was as supple as skin. He tied a bowline, a square knot, and then put a clove hitch around his wrist in quick succession. Then he unlaid both ends of the rope and made a short splice, much stronger than any knot. Its only drawback was it couldn't be used where it would pass over a sheave or through a block, because splicing almost doubled the thickness of the line.

If your compass was out of order you could follow birds back to land in the evening. In a storm it might be possible to jury-rig a jib to act as a trysail. If you run low on fresh water, collect rainwater in an impermeable awning. A temporary rudder may be assembled from bunk boards, pulleys and line. In heavy weather it is often advisable to heave-to rather than attempt to "make time." The captain's responsibilities are first and foremost the health and safety of his crew. In the event that abandoning ship becomes imperative the time for preparation will be long past. For the first time in his life, Carl had the feeling that he could not go alone. He was ashamed and bitter for a moment but this quickly passed. He'd never been a man to reproach himself for how he felt. It would have been like his left hand quarreling with his right. He needed both hands free to shape the world.

He thought about making himself a cup of tea, thought this would be a way to start over, but on the way to the galley he stopped at the small locker containing his ensign and dress flags. Among them was his personal burgee that he'd been saving for the day he stepped the mast. On a field of white, bracketed with red stars, was the blue wave of Nadine's name. The burgee was triangular and so the letters became smaller as they approached the tip of the flag, as if they were being funneled into the neck of a bottle. Or, as if they were trying to squeeze out of one. He'd built his own ship in a bottle, and the storm had broken it, so that the boat wasn't a miracle anymore. It was only a chip of wood that would float until it sank. He was a fool to think that a product of his hands would sway something as strong and even-tempered as Nadine's heart. A fool to think her happiness depended upon his, simply because his depended upon hers. He knew that in the morning there would be hundreds of people on the street looking up at his boat and asking how, asking why. It would be easy to explain that he'd destroyed an old house to build a new boat, harder to admit he'd done so to save himself from an unrequited love. He'd destroyed his house so he couldn't live there longing for the rest of his life, built a boat so he'd have a means of escape. Carl climbed up and out of the companionway, crawled onto the peak of the collapsed roof and knotted his burgee to an old copper lightning rod that was twisted like the tusk of a narwhal.

9:43 Ambulance is pulling away. That leaves just Nadine and Mose out front. I am much put out concerning the condition of my house and who will pay to make it right. This is my retirement home and must last the rest of my life, short as it may be if my neighbors get their way. My gun is much heavier than my pencil.

9:45 Mose and Nadine are having a conference in Howard's yard. No doubt they think the coast is clear, having depopulated the street as they have and the phones out of order. She is giving him a hug no doubt to seal the deal. Shameful, as she is thirty years younger than him and is <u>not</u> wearing a bra. My husband put the bullets in this gun so I know they are loaded correctly. I am putting all this down as evidence. There are three of them but I have six bullets, and I will not hide where I always have.

"Did you hear a gunshot?" Mose asked, and took his hands down from his ears.

"No," Nadine said.

"I didn't either."

"Why?"

"Howard was going to shoot himself. I left him alone so he could do it before the ambulance left. But it's gone now and I didn't hear a gunshot. So I'm guessing he decided against it."

Both sets of their knees buckled at once and they fell to the grass. The gunshot rang loudly in their ears.

"Oh, Jesus, Mose, he's shot himself."

"He's late. Now we'll have to call another ambulance to save his donated parts."

"Mose, I can't believe you left him alone," Nadine said. "Come on."

"Well, he didn't want me to shoot him. He wanted to shoot himself."

Nadine dropped her blanket on the porch and opened the front door. Howard was crouched behind his counter, pointing the gun at her.

"Are you all right?" she asked.

"Put that gun down," Mose ordered.

"Who's shooting at me?" Howard asked.

"You shot yourself, you damn fool," Mose said.

"No, I didn't. I'm not shot." He stood up and held his arms out. The lamp cast his shadow against the wall. He looked at Nadine. "I thought maybe you'd come to kill me."

"Why would I kill you? That was between you and my mother. I don't think much of you but I've got no desire to kill you."

"Pitiful, pitiful," Mose said.

"Next door then," Howard said.

"Carl?" Mose asked. "Does Carl keep guns?"

"Oh, Jesus," Nadine whispered.

"No," Howard said. "That crazy old white woman. Maybe she's trying to kill me."

"It could have come from Effie's. Let's go, Mose," Nadine ordered.

Mose stepped across the shop first and snatched the gun from Howard. "Now, do you want me to shoot you?"

"Yes."

"Well, Howard, I'm one man who won't do that." Mose slammed the door behind him.

They approached Effie's house slowly, looking for the telltale eye in the slats of her closed venetian blinds. Nadine knocked. "Effie, are you all right in there?" Mose stood at Nadine's hip, the gun at his side.

"Go away," Effie cried.

"Are you all right, Effie? We heard a gunshot. Come open this door, right now."

"You're going to kill me."

"Now, Effie, you know that's not true. We would have killed you a long time ago if we'd really wanted to."

"That big Indian has a gun," Effie said.

"I've got it now, Effie," Mose hollered. "It's here with me."

"I didn't think you'd be the triggerman, Mose, honey," Effie yelled.

"I'm not no triggerman, Effie. Here, I'll put it down. I just took it from Howard so he wouldn't kill himself."

"Effie, open this door right now."

"I will, Nadine. Please don't yell at me. I've shot my dishes."

Effie unlocked her door and stepped back. A flashlight lay on the floor, illuminating broken pottery and a pistol.

"What in the world, Effie?" Nadine asked.

"My husband's gun went off and shot through a whole set of Autumn Leaf. The teapot is shot and the creamer and eight dinner plates. The pepper shaker has been blown to bits. I dropped my husband's gun and it went off. It's very heavy, Nadine. I could have sold that set of dishes two weeks ago if the woman had remembered her checkbook."

"What were you doing with the gun, Effie?" Nadine asked.

"It was so dark, Nadine. I'm an old woman all by myself. I know everyone wants my things."

"Effie, I'm going to take your gun, all right?"

"Yes, Nadine. Everyone wants my things."

"Now, we're going to leave. You lock your door behind us and put yourself to bed. The lights will come on in a little while, and I'll come check on you in the morning."

"I miss my husband, Nadine."

"I know you do, Effie. You get some sleep."

"My house has melted."

"It's just paint, Effie."

➼✦

9:55 Nadine has just visited and advised me to go to sleep. That's the last thing they told that cowboy actor before they jumped him with a rope. It doesn't cost a person anything to be suspicious. They have taken my husband's gun. Now all I have left for protection is my pencil and tablet. I'll go to sleep when I want to. Fort Worth is where the west begins. I write with a white pencil. My tablets will tell the truth long after I'm gone. Nadine is practically indecipherable. A regular Charlie Chan, as I cannot make up my mind as to her intentions. Vigilance pays for itself. Put pennies in a bank and they multiply. If I pack that broken Autumn Leaf in a box and mail it to my sister insured I ought to make a bare minimum of profit. That Big Indian has turned off his oil lamp. I am constipated with phone calls because my phone is out of order. It's hard to run a business without a phone. My ears are still ringing with the loudness of that bullet, which went very close to my undefended head. It was very loud for such an old bullet. I will be sweeping Autumn Leaf out the door for a week. Mose very handsome in the dark. He did not take advantage of the opportunity to kill an old lady as many men would have done. He and Nadine are now making the rounds. I'm so tired of people talking about Effie. I took a picture of them at Aura's house, of which I now have a better view. I think they noticed the flash. Possible it won't come out, making it very hard to prove the conspiracy. I am the center of their little world. Well, I guess it's nice to know you're needed. If it weren't for me and my things this street would die of boredom. Long ago and many times I told my husband it would come to this. And he would always say, Come to what? Then he would say my name.

Mose shoved the barrels of both pistols into his pants at his stomach. He was surprised at how uncomfortable this was. He and Nadine walked through Aura's darkened rooms to the back door and locked it.

"I'm always undone by these old houses, Mose. All of them just alike. Seems like I forget that between visits. I walk into your house or Aura's or one of the others and I feel like someone's thrown out all my things and brought in new things. I feel like my old life's been done away with, that maybe I'm gone too. Do you ever feel that way, Mose?"

"You're full of wist, Nadine. You're a wistful person."

"I don't know if these old houses will stand another storm. We lost two out of twelve today, Mose. Old Mrs. Martin's house completely gone and Carl's warped into a boat."

They stepped back onto Aura's porch and locked the front door. The latch clicked to like a knuckle popping.

"They're just houses, Nadine," Mose said. "Let's go check on the Postlethwaites. Howard brought up that evilness again when they helped him out of that tub. Mr. Postlethwaite looked as if someone had shot him. If Mrs. Postlethwaite hadn't slapped Howard, I would have."

"She hit him?"

"It was a beautiful thing."

"What's got into that old man today, Mose, that he would tell so many old hurts and meannesses?"

"Nostalgia," Mose said. "He's had a life of bile and vomit and it's so thick around him he's begun to slip on it."

"Do you think his mind is going?"

"I think he's had an awful lonely life. But it was all his own making. The way he tells it, your momma would have taken him in. He says it was him who refused her."

"If that's the case it must have been some kind of sickness, Mose. She must have been addicted to him. She was a fool not to love you. I'll say that here and now."

They climbed up the Postlethwaites' steps and knocked.

When Mrs. Postlethwaite opened the door, the flame of the candle in her hand tried to pull away as if it were on a leash.

"We just wanted to check in on everybody, Mrs. Postlethwaite," Nadine said. "Are y'all OK?"

"I wish the electricity would come back on," she said. "I'd like to turn the TV on. But we're all right, Nadine. I know everyone says TV is bad but it's a comfort to us. It takes his mind off of things."

"How is Mr. Postlethwaite?" Nadine asked.

"He wants to go away. I can't get him off the idea. He wants to sell everything and buy a motor home."

Mose crossed his arms and rested his hands on the butts of the pistols.

"Is there looting, Mose?" Mrs. Postlethwaite asked.

"Oh, no," he said, and took his palms off the guns. But then his hands were lost. No other place but the handles of the pistols seemed comfortable. "I'm real sorry about what Howard said."

Mrs. Postlethwaite brought the door close to her face. "All that Mr. Postlethwaite said today in the cistern: it's not true."

"That's all your family business," Nadine said. "I've always known Mr. Postlethwaite to be a good neighbor and a stand-up antique dealer. I hope y'all don't sell out. The street would miss you both."

"Maybe you could just rent a motor home," Mose suggested. "Then you could try it out before you sold out."

"I don't know," Mrs. Postlethwaite said. "We're so old, Mose. I worry when we drive from here to the mall. He doesn't see well at night. It's our problem. Did Aura and the baby get off to the hospital?"

"Yes, and Marshall and Arthur and Tradio too," Nadine said. "I think we've all survived another day. We're going to check on Mr. Haygood now. Things will look better in the morning, Mrs. Postlethwaite. You get a good night's rest."

"Thank you for coming to see us," Mrs. Postlethwaite said.

Mose waited on the porch till he heard the deadbolt latch. As they walked toward the street, he told Nadine, "I have a confession too, Nadine. I've rented a space in that new antique mall."

"Oh, Mose!"

"It's just seventy-five dollars a month, and they're going to let me put a sign in my booth saying I repair clocks and radios. I'd only need to sell one or two clocks a month to pay my rent, and then there'd be all that advertising to bring people here to the Row."

"But leaving your things there unattended, Mose."

"They've got locked showcases if I want to rent those, and dealers walk the aisles."

"You have to work there too?"

"Just one day a month. They've got so many dealers signed up that there are five or six working on any given day. It's like a cooperative. I thought I might meet some other dealers on my workday."

"I just can't believe you'd give up the Row to go to a mall, Mose. I can't believe you'd let somebody else sell your things."

"It's just one day a month, Nadine. I'm closed on Sundays as it is. I was thinking I could work at the antique mall on a Sunday."

"I'll bet they want a percentage of your sales."

"Just the monthly rent."

"To change your whole way of doing business, Mose. Someone's pooted on paradise."

"It's only a three-month contract. If I don't sell a single radio I'll only lose two hundred and twenty-five dollars and three of my Sundays. It's just an experiment."

"Two hundred and twenty-five dollars would buy you a lot of advertising for your shop here."

"Nadine, I'm just as ignorant of the future as I have been of the past. I stuck by your momma and what did that get me? And I'm stubborn enough to stick by you. I'll never leave this street. I'm too old and I've come too far to admit I was wrong. I can't believe that your momma was a fool. Not loving me doesn't make her a fool. And I don't think it makes me a fool either. That's just where we were. Now you stop worrying about my loyalty. I'm just trying to make a living."

"Mose, I can't believe you're speaking to me like this."

"Well, Nadine, I don't mean much harm. One of us has to make some plans. You act like the street won't exist if it changes one bit from the way it was the day your momma died. The street isn't your momma, Nadine. She's dead. It don't hurt nobody more than it hurts me to say that."

"Just stick a couple of pistols in your pants and you know everything, Mose."

"Now, Nadine, I'm still your elder, your momma's old friend."

"I'm going to check on Mr. Haygood. You can come along if you like."

Mr. Haygood's door hung open. Mose and Nadine walked just inside the shop and called out his name. They both started when he rose out of the darkness that was the floor, stepping quietly up the cistern stairs.

"Mr. Haygood," Nadine said softly.

"She's gone and she's taken all my toys," he told them. "At first I thought it was Mazelle, but it was Mrs. Haygood. Only she knew where my showcase keys were. She did it while I was asleep. What do you want?"

"We've come to make sure you're all right, Mr. Haygood," Nadine said.

"How long have you known?" he asked her.

"Known what?"

"About me and Mazelle. I guess the whole neighborhood knew. But how did my wife find out?"

"Mr. Haygood," Mose said, "it's none of our business. We didn't know anything. It was all between you folks and Howard. He asked me to get involved but I refused him."

"Howard told?"

"I don't know how Mazelle's husband and your wife come to find out. I didn't tell them. I didn't want to get involved. But they knew about the cistern because they invited us down there when the storm came. I don't think Howard would have asked me to start taking up the blackmail payments if he'd already told your wife. I guess they found out on their own, your wife and Mazelle's husband."

"All the same, Howard told you? Today?" Mr. Haygood asked.

"Yes, he did. Was it the truth, Mr. Haygood? It's none of my business, but have you been carrying on with Mazelle for thirty years in that cistern?"

"It seems like it's only been a few weeks," he said. "You can take me off that newspaper ad, Nadine. I've got nothing left to sell."

"Are you all right, Mr. Haygood?" she asked. "Your shoes are wet."

"There is something owed to me, but I'll get it back. And I guess you two have finally gotten your noses about as deep into my ass as you've always wanted. Neither one of you have any more reason to step on my property. I'll mow my goddamn grass when I please."

"Come on, Mose," Nadine said. "I can see he's his same old self."

"Wait a minute, Mose. Why did Howard want you to take up blackmailing me?"

"He thinks he's going to pass away soon. He wanted to give me something."

Mr. Haygood stood in his doorway, squinting down at Mose in the front yard. "You've never known what it's like to have a woman, Mose. Don't think you're better than me."

"I'll try not to think of you at all, Mr. Haygood."

"You old son of a bitch," Nadine cursed at Mr. Haygood. Then she turned, took Mose in her arms and kissed him firmly on the mouth. She let one hand fall out of his hair, dropped it along his back and squeezed his slack rear. Mose pulled away then and Nadine looked up at Mr. Haygood. "He's having one that's twenty-five years younger than he is. How's that? Come on, Mose." She took him by the arm and dragged him toward Mazelle's house. Mr. Haygood's door slammed behind them and then fell off the house.

10:10 Nadine kissing Mose in Mr. Haygood's front yard and I could not get my camera rewound fast enough. She has taken all the available men for herself. Mose staggering along behind her like a wounded duck. Now they are going into Mazelle's empty house to perform other acts of perversion. When Nadine is wearing white pants she shouldn't mistake them for her napkin.

10:13 Every once in a while I have to put my hand on my side to make sure my kidney is still there, then I remember it's not possible to steal a person's kidney without their being aware of it.

"I swear it's like being in another life, Mose, walking through these rooms, or like I never lived at all."

They locked Mazelle's back door, then felt their way back through the many books, their fingers counting spines.

"You shouldn't have done that, Nadine. I felt like I was kissing my own daughter."

"Well, I couldn't have him saying things about you."

"Be careful. Don't fall in that damned hole."

"Did Howard really say they've been at it for thirty years?"

"Yes. At fifteen dollars a month, that's about six thousand dollars."

"What?"

"He's been blackmailing Mazelle and Mr. Haygood for the thirty years at fifteen dollars a month."

"Fifteen dollars?"

"Well, it was quite a bit thirty years ago."

"You'd have thought with inflation Howard would have increased his prices."

"I guess he figured the value of the merchandise was depreciating over the years."

"Mose, that's awful. All that time Mazelle's husband and Mrs. Haygood working that garden and their spouses six feet under sowing their own oats."

"Well, the soil's given out now," Mose said. He pulled the front door to, but had to lift it up on the sill. The wind had broken the upper hinge. He pushed in on the door twice to make sure the lock held securely.

"I saw Mazelle's husband and Mrs. Haygood leaving. I don't think they'll be back, do you?"

"Not with the toys, at any rate. The way Mazelle looked when she left doesn't make me think she'll be back anytime soon either. She looked like a person who'd forgotten how to run but was still in a hurry, all skips and hops and tumbles."

"I guess she didn't want to face all those people she'd deceived."

"No," Mose said.

"Momma didn't either."

"No, she just left us here to look at each other and wonder why."

"Do you think she was relieved when she died, Mose? She didn't have to lie to me anymore."

"What a thing to say about your momma, Nadine. I imagine dying took her by surprise like it does most people. And when it does I think you're mostly just surprised, because you've never known anything else but being alive. Maybe at the end of a long illness you feel some relief. You're so vain, Nadine honey, to think she was thinking about you when she was dying. You always think about yourself through her. I know she encouraged that. I catch myself doing it sometimes because I loved her too. But we need to start thinking about Nadine and Mose now."

"My cup is just brimming with ignorance, Mose. I don't know what to think, where to go."

"Take it one step at a time. Let's go lock Tradio's doors. Then we'll check Verda's. If you're brimming with ignorance maybe you're about to spill over into some knowledge."

"That doesn't make any sense, Mose. My mother was a fool not to love you. I'll say it again."

"You know, Nadine, somehow, to me, that doesn't make her any less lovable. I suppose Carl feels the same way about you."

Nadine pushed open Tradio's front door and they began to make their way through the closely stacked furniture, through a maze of odors: varnish and wax and oil.

"All this old furniture smells like old people," Nadine said.

"I never thought of myself as smelling like a bureau," Mose answered.

"Well, you do. We all smell like old wood and what's left of furniture polish once the liquid part has evaporated. It's not so bad. It's better than smelling like old clothes, like dust and mold and mouse droppings."

"Maybe that's an idea for an invention," Mose said. "We could bottle cologne and call it 'Mahogany Wardrobe' or 'Old Sideboard' or 'Cherry Hoosier.'"

"Or 'Nightstand,'" Nadine said.

" 'Nightstand,'" Mose said.

The back door was ajar. Nadine closed and locked it. The old linoleum of the kitchen floor crackled under their feet and reflected the moon.

" 'Moon Over Linoleum,'" Nadine said.

" 'Moon Over Linoleum.'"

"Isn't it funny," Nadine said, "how we all put our kitchen tables in the same place."

"Not much room for it anywhere else."

"But we all sit here every morning and evening and the light comes in the window the same way, and the stove is warm at our backs, and the walls hold pictures at the same distance. It's just so familiar and comforting. I think I understand Aura now when she says 'we.' Arthur sure keeps a clean house. Have you ever seen his Pie Bird collection? It's just here in the bedroom. Well, it's hard to see now, but there are dozens of them there in that case, holding their little beaks open to the sky, wanting to be fed."

"It gives me the image of people putting worms into their pies," Mose said.

"I've never told Arthur, because he loves them so, but to me a Pie Bird is a symbol of unfulfilled desires, always wanting, never getting."

"Maybe Arthur's never told you they mean the same thing to him, and that's why he collects them. You know, maybe he's trying to ease their troubles by bringing them all together so they won't feel so hungry."

"Mose, my mother was a fool."

"It makes me feel better when you say that, Nadine. Please don't say it ever again. I'm proud to say I loved your momma. Even now, when I don't hold any delusions of her loving me. I mean, I don't believe it was wasted effort on my part."

"When you loved Momma, it wasn't just for her being a woman, for sex?"

"Oh no, Nadine. I don't think so. I wanted all of her, body and temper."

"But wouldn't you have preferred that she'd loved you too?"

"Well, of course, Nadine. It broke my heart. But at least I know I did my part."

"I won't talk about it anymore, Mose."

They locked Tradio's front door. As they stood on the porch another camera flash erupted from Effie's house across the street.

For an instant the neighborhood was split off from both the future and the past.

"It must cost her a fortune to develop all that film," Mose said.

"I don't think she even puts film in the camera. It's just the flash going off."

They climbed slowly up Verda's porch steps and Mose turned the knob till he felt the firm resistance of the bolt. Above them, the attic was broached by a triangular hole where the porch roof had been torn away. They could see boxes, a tricycle, the end of a crib, an old vacuum cleaner.

"She hasn't been home all day," Mose said.

"This will be hard on her. But Verda always makes her way. She's probably gone to spend the night with her daughter."

"What are you going to do, Nadine?" Mose asked.

"I think I only lost a few shingles, Mose. Carl said he'd repair my house."

They walked through the grass to the base of Mose's porch steps and stopped there, looking at the boat across the street.

"I mean," Mose said, "are you going away too?"

She took his hand. "If I went away, Mose, someday I'd come back and you wouldn't be here. I don't know if I could bear that."

"Isn't that the strangest thing," he said. "I hardly believe it but I know it's true. How did I get to be an old man? But if you're lucky, Nadine, you'll come back someday and you won't be here either."

10:22 Mose and Nadine have ransacked Mazelle's and Tradio's. I can tell Mose's pockets are bulging. He'll never get away with it, as I have ample photographic evidence. Luckily, Verda's door was locked, even though she has nothing worth stealing.

10:23 That stray dog has just peed on my juniper.

"Who was that?" Mr. Postlethwaite asked.

"It was Mose and Nadine," Mrs. Postlethwaite said. "They just dropped by to see how we were."

"They pity me," he said.

"You pity yourself," she said.

"If we could get some distance between ourselves and here. If we could find her."

"She doesn't matter to me anymore. Only you matter to me. I believe you. I have complete faith in you."

"Somehow, that's not enough."

"It's all I have. It has to be enough. It's enough for God."

10:24 Mose and Nadine have gone inside their houses, counting their booty no doubt. The things I have seen. It's starting to cloud up, starting to rain again. We had only a brief respite. Mrs. Martin's house steaming in places. But otherwise the street quieted by water. I think I will sleep in my clothes again, just in case. It seems safe enough to count down my drawer for the day's sales. The street quite lonely.

For all the things he did not know, he never once thought of Himself as ignorant. Everything he didn't understand was simply noise. Something in his nose made him lift his leg, and the only struggle was to retain enough urine to satisfy the ensuing aroma, the next bush. There was a small tree and a hydrant at the corner that regularly required his attention, that smelled of vagrancy and encroachment, of imminent collapse. He wet them both, the nails of his hind foot gingerly scraping against bark and rust. He barked once, without opening his mouth, and his jowls flapped. There was a warning sound far away. The hair on his spine rose in a wave of uncertainty, and he turned back up into the street. Even though it was beginning to rain again, the Earth felt as springy as ever, almost jubilant. He leaped up over the stream of water coursing along the curb and the ground leapt after him. But with his stomach full he felt equal to the work of being followed. He peed on Mazelle's crepe myrtle, on a Japanese viburnum at the Haygoods', and dribbled his last on a Texas mountain laurel beneath Aura's outdoor spigot. This brought him round to the path that led to his home, which had fallen into the sky. He sat on the path, the hair of his hind legs touching the ashen grass. The anxiety of his missing home made him yawn. When his mouth closed there was the taste of food on his tongue, carried there by the rain. It lay on his tongue like an arrow pointing back across the street. An old man was there, sitting on the top step of his porch, eating.

Mose had walked through his own house and found it inundated with water. All his windows had been open during the storm. His rain alarms had failed for lack of electricity. He made himself a sandwich, then sat on the gray paint, the cracked board, the top step, of his porch, watching his shoes darken. The pain in his eyes was beginning to ease. You survived her momma dying, he thought, you'll survive Nadine leaving too. He lifted his heel, dropped it back down, lifted his toe. The bean sandwich on his plate was cold and dry, the plate on his knees solid. What if, he wondered, I put some button sensors on the bottoms of my shoes, buttons at the toe and heel and on each side, and when you stepped on them they played a musical note, a button for each note? If you were a good dancer you could play songs. It'd be a far sight more interesting than tap shoes. He'd begun a list of parts he'd need when the dog, sitting a few feet out into his yard, yawned at him. Mose lifted the sandwich off the plate, and he and the dog had the simultaneous thought, which was only and distinctly: give it to the dog. Mose tore off a corner of his sandwich, making sure there were some beans between the bread, and pitched it to the dog. Mose saw it fall through the sky of his neighborhood, and here their two minds diverged, for the dog watched the Earth rush upward to catch the bit of food, bringing him happily along for the ride. They finished the sandwich together, and Mose set the plate on the porch. "We're members of the clean plate club, aren't we, boy?"

The dog looked over his shoulder. He wasn't used to being talked to but was beginning to learn the language. Mose took the plate back inside and brought out a frozen soup bone. He threw it out into the yard, where it glistened in the rain. The dog picked it up, dropped it, picked it up, backed up a few steps, turned toward the old Martin house, moved sideways, then finally dropped the bone between his forepaws and began to lick it where it lay. Mose stepped down, heel, toe, heel, toe, do, re, mi, fa, turned and walked slowly back toward his house. Then, with one sure chord, he kicked a hole in the lattice beneath his porch. He decided not to look back at the dog, decided to find his own bed, to find sleep, to invent a dream made up of all the spare parts of his own past that were without meaning.

10:27 The silence in my phone sounds very deep, as if someone is there listening. I have said hello many times but they will not answer. The repairman was very angry the last time I boiled my phone to kill all the bugs, but did not charge me as he had a spare phone to give to old ladies. But what am I to do if this phone has become infected too? I do not know how to fix electronics but to boil them. I am not one of these people who slams things down to repair them.

10:32 I find that I have had zero sales today but my drawer counts down as even. Saturdays are always better.

10:33 More cars are passing down on Hemphill Street now. I do not even have to look outside to know this as their headlights zoom over my bedroom ceiling and down the walls without my permission. I am often afraid these lights are going to break something.

Since the phone and electricity were still off, Nadine was surprised to find there was water pressure. She decided there was a whole world of cause and effect out there of which she had no inkling. She pulled Carl's T-shirt over her head and slipped out of the tattered nightgown, to find herself naked in a mirror that worked only intermittently with the passing of cars. Her face was blackened and there were dark creases across her stomach and where her thighs joined her torso. Her whole body seemed to have been drawn in charcoal, an art student's rendering, a two-minute study by an unsure hand, her pubic hair delineated by four quick strokes, her kneecaps and breasts smudged with a wet thumb. Between cars she stepped into the shower. The smell of Mrs. Martin's burning house flamed again, and the shampoo fell between Nadine's feet in charred clumps. Her body hadn't felt familiar in twenty years. Her skin was as wayward as a dress in the wind, and it was all she could do to hold it down, to stave off indecency and embarrassment. She worked the bar of soap over her body as if it were a lint brush. At last she found herself leaning against the wall of the shower to wash her feet, and remembered that as a young woman she'd stood in this same shower like a stork, examining the whorls on the bottoms of her toes. It seemed a long way to travel simply to lose your balance.

Her bedroom, the placement of the furniture, the order of the socks in her drawer, were unfamiliar, as if her things were arranged in someone else's home, as if she'd been burned out and was now a guest. The kitchen was lit by a pair of pilot lights on the stove top, burning blue and white. She stood in the middle of the room till she could hear the murmuring of the flames and then above this the distant dripping of water off her eaves. How could she not have known that boat had been abuilding? She looked down at her feet and found there were shoes on them, saw also the bright yellow slicker cinched at her waist. And so she locked her door and crossed the street, smoothing her hair over her head and clipping it in back. The light rain pecked at her coat and fell across her face as if she'd never left the shower. Carl's front door was lying in his yard. Nadine stood on it and looked up. She saw the pennant flapping loosely in the wind. She moved around the hull as if it might fall on her, continually tripping over debris because she couldn't avert her gaze from the boat. Light held as a solid in the portholes. She stepped along the gangplank, and knowing there was no door, knocked on the cypress hull. It felt as solid as a standing tree. The water below her was dimpled by the rain and reflected her own vibrating body darkly. She knocked again. She said Carl's name the way she might if she were alone in a vast field. He poked his head out over the coaming and said her name back to her. It seemed so unearthly she clutched the ladder.

"I didn't know if you'd be at home," she said.

"Looking down at you this way," he said, "makes it seem like you're under water."

"Well, I'm going to be if you don't invite me up."

"You've worn a skirt," he said. "On a boat it's best to wear shorts or slacks."

"Carl, these are my clothes. This is what I've got on right this minute. Will they do or not?"

"Of course, of course, I just meant—"

"I'll come up these first two steps and then you give me your hand."

"OK, Nadine."

"Do I have to call you captain?"

"No, Nadine."

"That would make it harder."

He took her by the hand and led her down the half-dozen steps of the companionway to the cabin sole.

"I've never been on a boat before," she said, "except for a canal boat on the Seine. But it was tied to the shore. It was much larger than this."

"You can sit on this bunk, Nadine."

"These old oil lamps are very nice. I like the light from a lamp. There's no glare to it. And they provide heat too. It's very cozy, Carl. I can see you've applied your trade to all this woodwork."

"I've hoped you'd like it, Nadine. I know you like a change of clothes. I've built these lockers here." He rose and opened them. "There's lots of storage there."

"You're the most presumptuous person I've ever met."

"I know, Nadine."

"You have framed our relationship so that my only options are to deny it completely or capitulate."

"Capitulate? Allowing me to love you is capitulating?"

"You built this boat without telling me. It's your ultimatum. It was you saying I only had two years to make up my mind."

"I'll set a match to it if that's what it takes for you to accept me."

"Stop saying things like that."

"I know you see my way of doing things as a series of mistakes, but I wish you could be me for a while and see them as the only way I know how."

"It's so warm in here."

"I'll open—"

"No, I'm all right. It feels good."

"If you came," he said, "you'd still be inside one of these old houses. I know it's not shaped the same, but it's the same wood, the same walls. I thought that might make you more comfortable. The trim around the door to the head and around these bunks is the very same that leads from room to room in your house. Those latches came from my kitchen cabinets. This beaded ceiling might have come from the very same tree as your porch ceiling. And I'm from here, Nadine. You could talk to me about the old neighborhood. I know how you like to reminisce. As we go from port to port you could look forward to letters from Mose and Aura and everyone else. Maybe they'd want to come visit us."

"I couldn't sell my house, Carl."

He sat on his hands so they wouldn't be caught in the draft of her words and flutter away.

"I've got too much in it to let somebody else live there, at least until I die," she said.

"You could keep it," he said. "Maybe we could come back here for a few months every year, during hurricane season."

"It's so warm in here. Don't let me fall asleep," she said.

"Do you want a pillow?"

"I'd feel like I was abandoning them all: Mose, and Aura, Mrs. Postlethwaite. Who'd watch out for Effie?"

"I don't need you to take care of me, Nadine. I just want you to. If it's any help, I have Mose's blessing. He's for us. And Aura has Marshall. And Effie is the world's problem, not yours. I'm the only person on this street who can't replace you."

Nadine sank back into the cushion, let her temple rest against the bulkhead. "It's not that I'm afraid," she said.

"In Martinique," Carl said softly, "that's an island in the Caribbean, they speak French, just like in Paris."

"It's been so long since I've spoken French, Carl. When I came back home, Momma said she'd missed me so."

"She won't miss you now, Nadine."

"Well, I miss her. If I fall asleep, you'll wake me up. I still have some of the clothes I wore in Paris. They smell like mothballs."

"We can pin them to the halyards and let the wind blow through them."

Carl sat still for a moment, then he reached up and turned down the lamp. He sat there on his bunk for five, ten, fifteen minutes, watching her sleep. His hands were numb beneath his thighs. When he heard her breathe deeply for the first time, the wood around him seemed suddenly to expand, to become replete with oxygen. He got up slowly and stepped up into the cockpit. He didn't want anybody to disturb her in the morning, policemen or gawkers, and so he slid the ladder softly away from the hull and let it slip into the water, where it floated slowly away and bumped lightly against the rocks of the foundation.

10:39 I put some more of my husband's hair tonic on his pillow. It only lasts about a week.

10:43 I thought I heard a door slam but I got up and looked and saw nothing.

10:57 The lights have come back on. Like to have scared me out of my wits. I had to go through the house turning off lights and the TV. There are a thousand electric bells going off over at Mose's house. Phone is still very dull. I shouldn't be charged for this period of service. The Postlethwaites' porch light is on.

Mr. Haygood walked up and down the few stairs to the cistern as if he were winding a clockwork mechanism. When he finally left his house he couldn't lock the door, but even this reminded him that he had nothing. Even though the house was paid for there would be property taxes in January, and now all this storm damage. The water bill alone was close to fifteen dollars a month, not to mention the sewer rates, the electric bill, the telephone. The government didn't take into account the finances of an old person. Too much was demanded for too little opportunity. This house was a poor resource. He'd never had a child but was forced to pay taxes to schools. If this wasn't inherently unfair, a seventy-five-year-old man paying school taxes, then he didn't know what unfair was. They'd miss him then. There were places with better opportunity and by God he'd walk there if he had to. But before he left there was something that was rightfully his. He didn't knock on Howard's door, he didn't pound on it, he walked right in, and the door slammed against a stack of fireplace mantels.

"I've come for my money, Howard," he yelled.

Every light in Howard's house came on at once. Mr. Haygood blinked and when he opened his eyes, Howard stood in front of him, naked to the waist.

"What money?" Howard asked. Then he banked his head like a dog and smiled and said, "Old Mose knows it's raining."

Mr. Haygood stepped to one side. "My money. The blackmail money. You told." He nearly tripped over the leg of one of the fireplace mantels but caught himself on a glass showcase full of artifacts, and quickly jumped behind it. Howard was now between him and the door. The hatchet, a stone biface hafted to a stick with a leather thong, extended from Howard's loose arm to the floor.

"All that money was spent long ago," Howard said. "I wasn't a savings bank for you to come someday and make a withdrawal. You got a good silence in return for that money, thirty years of silence. It was a good buy."

"They've taken everything," Mr. Haygood said. "If you'd given me some warning, I could have protected myself." There were arrowheads and hand axes on the top shelf of the showcase. Mr. Haygood chose a six-inch obsidian knife.

"I found that knife in a grave in the hills above Rancho de Taos," Howard said. "It was probably made a couple thousand miles from there. I'll bury it with you if you want me to. And then that knife will have made it another five hundred or so miles from where it was made. It's something the scientists study: how things get to their last resting place."

"There's money that's mine. I don't care about Mazelle's share. She's gone too. I'm not responsible for her."

"Reconsider," Howard said, and he reached over and turned off the lights in his shop. "You got to sleep with two women for thirty years. Whatever you've lost should have been worth it."

"You think I'm somebody to be played with. You backed out on our agreement. I was faithful in my payments. I don't want it all. I put a payment in your mailbox two days ago. A month's payment in advance like always. You owe me that money back."

"You're kidding," Howard said slowly.

"I'm as serious as this knife. I want the seven-fifty back and I'll be on my way."

Howard let the ax head rest on the floor, let the handle fall soundlessly against the door behind his leg. "Those payments weren't made in advance. You were paying for the previous month's silence. I don't owe you anything. In fact, you still owe me for the first two days of this month."

"You think I'm afraid of that ax, that I'm afraid of the dark."

"You're a paleface. You'll always be afraid of me. You're losing heart? How about this: it took you thirty years to find out that neither one of those women wanted you."

Howard felt the blade against his neck for an instant and fell through the doorway, down his steps and into the yard. Then Mr. Haygood was on top of him and they were rolling. As much as he wanted to, Howard couldn't help holding out his hands, a reflex against the slashing. At one point he even pushed Mr. Haygood off of him and ran out into the middle of the street. Between breaths he told himself this was only instinct and that he could overcome it. They fought in the street without yells or curses, conserving their strength for the fight itself. Howard slapped Mr. Haygood to make him madder, to blur his vision.

Then the blade plunged into Howard's kidney and tripped across his bicep. He found himself squeezing the air from Mr. Haygood's lungs, and so he relaxed a bit, and felt the obsidian score his collarbone and slice into the taut tendons and muscles of his straining neck and then he was able to let go of Mr. Haygood completely and smell the rainwater pooling in the asphalt, and able then to rest, while he listened to Mr. Haygood's fading footfalls mimic the beating of his heart.

➵✦➴

11:07 Mose's bells have finally stopped. I had to put a pillow over my head. My bedside clock and my watch say different times and I have no way of knowing which is true. This makes me feel very anxious ridden, not knowing what time it is.

11:10 I thought I heard something but the street is very quiet. That car still parked in front of Nadine's.

11:17 How often I hear things that my neighbors don't hear and how unconcerned they are when I tell them of shrieks and cries in the night. If it weren't for my lawyer and my tablets this would all go unrecorded.

11:31 All the writing I did in the dark and with my flashlight is almost unreadable. It brought me to tears but I think I can correct it all if I can only remember.

➵✦➴

Verda was sitting up before she realized she was awake. Dideebiteya and Yeseedid sat up with her, slid off her body to the floor and yawned at each other. I feel much better, she thought, and put two fingers between the blinds to look outside. Raining still, and the neighborhood a perfect scene of chaos. Two men fought in the street, their bodies stumbling and spinning as if they were falling out of the clouds. Then, through the rain, she beheld a vision of Noah's Ark, just as it was pictured in her Bible, a great wooden hull with the roof of a chicken barn. She pushed herself up from the floor with both palms, then stooped back down and picked up both dogs, placing one under each arm. "This is our chance," she told them, and opened her door, let it swing wide. She walked slowly onto her porch and was surprised when the rain touched her. She wasn't expecting it for another few steps. Her porch roof was gone. It lay in Tradio's front yard. That's right, she remembered. That's right, I don't need it anymore. She saw Howard collapse, and Mr. Haygood pause, then run away. She whispered to her babies, "They're caught up in the end of the world. They can't help it." She walked past Howard's body, crossed the street, held the dogs tightly. "Two by two," she told them. The gangway was a test, but she passed it. The dogs whined and she cooed to them, said, "I'm sorry, my sweet babies, but you'll have to stay here on Earth and multiply. You can't come with me. Momma's going to heaven." And that said, she summed up all her remaining strength and tossed first Dideebiteya and then Yeseedid high up over the Ark's side and heard them drop into the cockpit with nothing more than muffled thumps. Then she inched to the edge of the gangway and jumped into the standing water, but it was only calf deep. She sloshed her way to the boat and sat down in the water, spit out her third eye and leaned against the heavy oak rudder. She found herself surrounded by fragrant shavings, curled and floating around her, and here Verda ended her long day of dying, her heart bumping one last time over a small sandbar, her mind wandering along for a few moments more with a thought of the tiny porcelain hands of God, so slender, so fragile, so tiny.

➵✦

11:44 I miss that old moon peeking in my window.

11:48 Something.

The dog Himself, the bone in his mouth, stood at the corner of the street. He lowered his head slightly to the rain. There was something on the wind that made the Earth spin slowly beneath his feet, and he took a step to balance Himself, then had to take another. He set off in the direction he last saw his mother go.

11:59 Noises.